TALK ACROSS WATER

TALK

MERRILL GILFILLAN

ACROSS

STORIES SELECTED AND NEW

WATER

FLOOD EDITIONS

PUBLISHED BY FLOOD EDITIONS

WWW.FLOODEDITIONS.COM

ISBN 978-0-9981695-7-6

COVER ILLUSTRATION: KARL BODMER, *VIEW OF THE*

BEAR PAW MOUNTAINS FROM FORT MCKENZIE, 1833,

WATERCOLOR, JOSLYN ART MUSEUM, OMAHA, NEBRASKA,

GIFT OF THE ENRON ART FOUNDATION, 1986.49.209

DESIGN AND COMPOSITION BY QUEMADURA

PRINTED ON ACID-FREE, RECYCLED PAPER

IN THE UNITED STATES OF AMERICA

NOTA BENE

Most of these stories took shape during the latter twentieth century, a period when I was regularly exploring the topography of the American Great Plains (especially the "Indian country" of Montana, Wyoming, and the Dakotas) and beginning, with hesitant steps, to engage that landscape as the rich, if airy, theater for human action and culture that it is and has been for a humbling number of centuries. Having made a certain peace-of-understanding with the vast reaches of the domain, I slowly sensed that the landscape itself, the high, honeycombed visibility of the grasslands, was rendering, offering up at its own sweet pace, the human tales—above all, those of the deep-rooted native peoples—afoot within its wind-cut spaces.

I wrote the stories at an age when I wrote only what I wanted to write in just the way I wanted to write it. Reading through them now, I am most struck by, and happiest with, the warm-blooded actual-size intimacy of the original details—certain looks on certain faces, hearsay overheard, light laughter from the shade of a tree—the pedigreed details that both ignited the stories and, with luck, anchor them now.

TALK ACROSS WATER

ALL HEART

They always took the back way into Rapid City, if the weather allowed, so that Kabere could see the Indians. Magbar drove her new car and her three brothers always found the same seats: Kaleab beside her—he was nearest her in age—and Asmelash behind her, lost in adolescent squint-thought, with Kabere at the right rear window, his quick eyes snapping it all in like a cat at cream.

They drove east from Flicker a few miles and then cut north on the dirt road, along the best of the Flicker River Valley with its pale bluffs and cedar frettings. Then they were into the Indian country, and Kabere grew more intensely silent and leaned closer to the window and watched each Indian home intently and carefully considered each of those evocative, two-track, white gumbo roads disappearing lazily over the short-grass hills.

They were children of a late, prominent Ethiopian family. Their father had been a quiet well-read man, the governor of a remote Ethiopian province when the political williwaw blew. Then all the children fled to America and eventually, through a network of benefactors and friends, west to the prairie town of Flicker, where they began their American studies at the small red-brick college on the hill. They lived together in a rented house with Magbar smiling at the helm. She was twenty-five, bright, gracious, and long-betrothed, all her pecan-tinted skin, to an Ethiopian boy named Neaman, who was finishing his university education in New York.

The first Flicker winter was lonely despite their neat and able English. Every two weeks they drove the one hundred miles to Rapid City for shopping, for daily things they could have found in Flicker, but especially for whole, fresh spices at the big food store: spices, especially, for *watt*.

Magbar could easily have laid in enough seasoning for six months, but that was not the idea. The Saturday trip was the thing, the outing through the new landscape, the larger city with its stir and its circling traffic. And then, back home in the early darkness, the steaming trencher of *watt*, the spicy ground-beef dish they had known forever, that made the house smell right and the dreams apricot-colored and breezy.

The boy Kabere, seventeen, had been taken with the western Indians since childhood, taken in the antipodal daydream way that old-world boy children have been taken for a century and a half in London, Paris, Dusseldorf, Dublin, and certain sectors of Addis Ababa. At the age of nine he spent long windowside afternoons gazing at picture books full of free-flowing, war-bonneted men and idyllic tipi villages pitched along sumptuous valleys. He gathered cast-off feathers from city streets, tying them carefully to a tall, peeled willow wand leaning in a corner of his room, and struck alert aquiline poses as he crested hills in the neighborhood park.

Kabere and the youngest brother, Asmelash, were the last to arrive in Flicker. During his first months there, as spring crept in, Kabere took regular, shy drives in the area, carefully visiting the small museums and historic points within a twenty-five-mile radius of his home. He would stop some days as he walked the streets of Flicker and look up at the clouds and think: "These are the sort of clouds the wild Indians lived under, saw from their ponies."

One June day as Kabere was leaving town with his little camera, he

ALL HEART

saw a broken old man on a single crutch thumbing a ride at the city limits: a Sioux man, the boy said. He stopped and backed up and the man crawled in and said a short hello.

As he drove, Kabere sneaked glimpses of his silent rider: his dark, weathered face, a nose like a windfall pear, large hands that looked as though they had been run over and over and over again. The man had a fast and acrid odor to him. He breathed slowly and deeply as though he were sound asleep and very wise, with his splayed hands interlocked on the bandaged crutch handle.

Three miles from town, the man pointed at a group of house trailers and said, "I get out here." Kabere pulled off the highway at the gravel entrance beside a fleet of mailboxes. The old man leaned in before he shut the door, his dewlap swaying, to thank the boy thoroughly for the ride. That night in bed Kabere told Asmelash in a low voice that he had met an Indian.

A week later Kabere saw the old man standing on a downtown corner. When the boy had run his errand and returned the man was still there, standing heavily with a carton of cigarettes tucked under one arm. Kabere slowed, then timidly approached and said hello.

The old man slowly shifted his eyes to take in the boy's face.

"I gave you a ride last week, out east from town," Kabere said softly.

"Yes."

"Do you live in those trailer houses?" Kabere asked.

"I live in number seven, way in back."

"Perhaps I will visit you one day, if that is alright."

The old man looked at the boy's face again. "Sure, that's alright."

Two days later, a Saturday when the car was available, Kabere drove to the trailer park late in the afternoon. He had his camera in his pocket. He drove slowly among the dozen ramshackle trailers until he spotted number seven. He knocked at the ramshackle door. No reply. He got back in the car to wait.

By the next trailer a car and a pickup truck were parked. They were

ALL HEART

full of luggage and household goods. Both carried Missouri license plates. Now and then a man came out to carry something inside. Behind the trailer a young boy sat rocking trancelike in a chain swing and wailing like a howler monkey.

Kabere sat there almost an hour. Cars and trucks came and went noisily. All the trailer people were blond and fat. An Ethiopian boy had never seen so many fat people in all his life. He wondered if they would be fat even if they were starved, if they would stay fat on the outside and starve up in the center. Kabere from his car could hear kitchen crashings and toilet flushings. He smelled cooking food. The vague sounds of either people copulating or maybe a puppy locked in a bathroom. The day began to dim.

Then a pickup stopped by the mailboxes and Kabere saw the old man climb from the passenger side, lean in to thank the driver, and come limping down the gravel lane.

Kabere got out and hailed him as he neared the trailer. The old man looked and waved the boy inside. Kabere stood just inside the door while the man took off his coat and hat and leaned his crutch in a corner and replaced it with a cane. The man smelled of liquor. The trailer smelled like the man. From a paper bag he slid a can of corned beef hash and a can of cheap sardines and a bottle of muscatel.

"What are you up to?" he asked the boy.

"I wanted to come and visit you," Kabere said. Then, after a moment: "I am interested in the Indians."

"Hunh," the old man grunted as he emptied an ashtray into the garbage sack. "Hunh. Sometimes the Indians treat me right and sometimes they don't." He talked through a fog as he fiddled with his cigarettes and fumbled to light lamps.

"It's hard to say about that . . . They don't go for me much. I've been up here thirty-five years and I've had good and bad from the Indians. I don't know. I was born in Nogales, Mexico. Came up here in 1951. I still speak pretty good Spanish, too."

ALL HEART

Kabere looked away from the old man and caught his own reflection in a window glass. He watched it for a short moment, tall and thin like a crooked stick.

The old man had settled onto a ratty sofa and had opened the muscatel. After a pull he told Kabere the patchwork tale of a professional football career. He had been pretty good. He smoked and drank and stretched the story out. Quarterback with the Green Bay Packers after the war. Made pretty good money. Never quite broke beyond second string.

"Vanceneas is my name. Vanceneas—that's a Spanish name. I'm in the football books."

Kabere left the trailer after a half hour and climbed into his sister's car. There were lights on in nearly all the trailers now, harsh, strident lights, and scattered music. He drove slowly west toward town. The latter sunset was sending shafts of unearthly orange up from behind the pine ridge.

The boy was disappointed, but not cowed. He had made a small mistake his first time, that's all. A small, dignified mistake. No one would ever know about it. The Mexican himself didn't even know about it. And there would be *watt* tonight.

ALL HEART

ON SLEEP CREEK

Saturday mornings just after daybreak in the Flicker River country, on one of the faint gravel roads threading the gumbo hills and the buttes, a dilapidated green and yellow school bus crawls at a walker's pace before a halfhearted cloud of blond dust. Being the largest, clumsiest thing by far to travel these byways, its oversized, gaudy stripes are recognized from miles away by local rural people, who have known it for years and call it "the Caterpillar."

The bus is driven by an elderly man, tall and stout, wearing thick spectacles and a black cowboy hat. His wife sits behind him in the single remaining passenger seat. The rest of the vehicle is stowed with odds and ends spilling from cardboard boxes and hanging from the sidewalls. There is a portable hanger-rack of dresses, a dolly full of winter coats, a wooden bin on skate wheels crammed with toys, and a bit of everything littered about the floor.

Each Saturday the old trader and his crusty wife drive their load of secondhand goods up into Indian country to set up in some public place. There, in a parking lot or a wide spot in the road, they deploy their wares in the sunshine and sell and trade for half a day, then load up and move to another village. It is a desultory, pre-burgher commerce old as dice. One week they show up on White Clay Creek at the edge of a box-elder grove and later down at Slim Buttes. The next week they rattle into Red Shirt, almost under the shadow of the Black Hills, and then into Oglala for the afternoon, where the rack of dresses rocks brightly in the wind. Another Saturday they start before daylight and make the long drive to Potato Creek and Lost Dog and the staggeringly vast Eagle Nest Butte country, and crawl and grind around that top-of-the-world terrain for a long day.

It is pleasant to see them moving along far off across the hills, plying their low-gear trade. They are remnants, perhaps the final descendants of the wandering peddlers, the reddlemen and the liniment hawkers and the itinerant scissor-sharpeners of yore. The old bus moves at a sane pace through sane country, all the lofty plain from Beaver Creek to the Badlands: the miles of sinewy grassland; ranges of huge columnar cottonwoods lining the streams (the cottonwoods are crucial, always and actively there, like whiskey in the Irish stories); and above, presiding, the dark, pine-netted hills and fragrant ridges with their chalky, wind-gnawed cliffs that shine for many miles. Indian land: unharassed, knowing land, rarely gashed or uprooted. And in the simplest of transactions it seems to reciprocate: as a theater for human life and drama, it cradles, resonates, consoles . . .

*

In the old days the green and yellow bus often visited a fellow (though considerably more anchored) specimen of the tradework, a root-hog outpost on the northern edge of the Sioux lands. That was where the bus trader drank a cup of coffee and swapped a box of hairnets for a coil of heavy-gauge wire, then spat on the ground and turned the Caterpillar back toward Flicker.

The trading post was a jerry-rigged place built of rough slab lumber. It stood on the flats on the east side of Sleep Creek a few miles above its juncture with the Cheyenne River. The place still functions today in a diluted afterthought sort of way. Rusty gasoline pumps stand in front and old pale tumbleweeds pile high on the west wall. A weathered sign above the door reads "Sleep Creek Merchandise" and a

ON SLEEP CREEK

smaller much-abused handmade one on the porch railing reads "Used Cow Parts" and shimmies nervously in the steady Sleep Creek wind.

The white-bearded man who runs the place today lives in the two dark rooms in the rear of the building. During summer months, when there is still a certain amount of tourist traffic on the Sleep Creek road, he opens the store regularly, selling ice and beer and candy and the occasional souvenir: a pretty mule-deer antler or a fossil from the Badlands. Badger hides and dusty snakeskins hang on the walls. The old man leans heavily on the thick glass case and recites oft-rehearsed wild-west talk for touring easterners, the perpetual cold sore on his lower lip filling periodically, well-like, with thin blood to overflowing, when he daubs it with a gory handkerchief.

The other half-dozen homes in the one-time village, some of them sizeable frame houses, are empty and broken. The tiny post office is boarded up, the slab-lumber saloon locked and full of spiders. But in the years following the Second World War, Sleep Creek was doing well on the tourist trade. Its level, handsome valley was a natural approach to the Black Hills in those days, before the superhighways. A daily train went through. Things happened there.

On a good day back then, the owner, a man named Frankie, would have his hands full. He had a hired boy to pump the gasoline while he himself handled the steady flow of tourists, on the one hand, and vicinity Sioux on the other. To the former he sold many pounds of refreshments and groceries, keepsakes and trinket beadwork. To the Sioux he provided kitchen utensils, lunch pails, lamps, Jell-O molds, Czechoslovakian seed beads, dog collars, dolls, dinner plates, tweezers, antelope hooves, plastic wreaths, children's sunglasses, penny ashtrays, deer tails, cascades of rubber ivy, salt-and-pepper sets, car jacks, napkin holders, and fry pans. He lived alone in a nice house off behind the store and found his fun in Rapid City to the north.

But first and foremost, Frankie was a snake-and-bone man, and proud of it. Those were the cargoes that distinguished him from ordi-

ON SLEEP CREEK

nary merchants like the Caterpillar man. Frankie was a plump, unambitious, mercantile man with flighty brown eyes that tended toward warmth and good humor, then shied away, jumped to skyline. They gave him an unfastened quality that was heightened by his habit of continuously hoisting his blue jeans and fiddling with his belt. He came across one day as a good, odd man and the next as mercurial and possibly mean.

He was proud of the oddball slot of his main commodities, the snakes and the bones. He collected two or three hundred rattlesnakes a summer, hunting the den sites and the prairie-dog towns with a buddy or two, and sold them to the Reptile Gardens up in Rapid City. He loved taking a visitor into the backyard building he called his "bone shed" and rummaging through the man-high tangle of old elk and deer antlers, fossilized buffalo skulls, longhorn racks, piles of antelope horns and steer femurs. Tourists took them home to hang above their doorways or to set out in the petunia patch. Frankie would whistle and mutter as he bent and tugged in the pile. "I must have a thousand dollars worth of elk in here, my friend."

And more than that he loved escorting tourist families into the snake room, a catchall compartment just off the main store. There he would lead them to a heavy table supporting three large fish tanks full of seething, pent-up rattlers and an occasional prime bullsnake. Frankie would stand nonchalantly to one side while the family uneasily admired his stock and asked him the same daily questions. To a pretty woman he would say with a twitching straight face, "There's a nice little bullsnake right there. Reach in and pick him up. Go on."

All summer long he did that. Showed the bones, showed the snakes and rapped on the tank to make them churn and sizzle. Stood, hitching his trousers, behind the counter with a loaded double-barreled twenty-gauge beneath it. Late mornings, the train rocked up the valley beyond the highway and Frankie bent his head an inch or two to watch it go by. And toward noon, as he was dusting off and bagging a coyote hide

ON SLEEP CREEK

or a painted-up calf pelvis for a tourist, he saw the Slows come striding into town, right on time: four lank middle-aged men approaching down the railroad tracks in stiff single file, in the halting rhythm of tie-walkers. Opposite the store they left the tracks and marched, without breaking figure, across the highway and into the little town.

For three decades a woman rancher some miles downstream recruited and hired these men and boys; befriended, housed, and fed them in exchange for ranch work. She began the practice shortly after being widowed, bringing a pair of slow-learning brothers from a nearby shattered family and getting them through high school and even into the army. She did it out of Christian sentiment and practical need. She was straight with and good to them, and to the half-dozens who followed over the years, an ever-changing kaleidoscopic group of four or five at most, men of varying age and mentality from all over the upper plains. They came for a year or two, or five, and then left for who knows where, and were replaced. They had a part of the big well-kept ranch house to themselves. She fed them well and left them alone.

One summer late in life Anna knew she had a winning combination: four men who had been with her a long time. They were dependable and got along well and she had come to enjoy them like family. So one fey September she made her will, leaving the ranch with guardian provisions to the foursome, or whoever among them would stay with it. It was a beautiful spread at the junctions of Sleep Creek and the Cheyenne: The spruce white and green house surrounded by a flock of white and green outbuildings and a pair of barns, all situated on a pleasant flat on the leeside of the valley. Her white-faced cattle roamed up the creek and down and over into the wide Cheyenne bottoms.

And before too long her "slow boys," as she called them, owned the place and did just fine. Each had his own shaving mirror on the kitchen wall. They had four radios stationed in far corners of the house. They showed up in Sleep Creek village several times a week, tall and gaunt the four of them, stalking through in their faded overalls on various

ON SLEEP CREEK

errands, always in the stately single file with a body-length between them, cowboy-hatted, poker-faced wanderers stepped down from a haywire Grecian urn. Everyone called them the Slows as a sort of surname. The four men bought chewing gum or cigarettes or groceries and stood quietly in front of the store watching the traffic pass by. The first of each month they visited their benefactress's grave on the edge of town—a heartfelt, rent-like day.

Niels was the best known of the foursome, the most social and the strongest of the group. He wore a wide leather belt on the outside of his overalls, with a heavy bucking-horse buckle. The woman had found him at a mission in Rapid City; he came originally from the Moreau River country up around Maurine. He worked hard and was even enterprising. For some years after his arrival in Sleep Creek he had been a prolific, matter-of-fact rattlesnake catcher, appearing regularly at Frankie's door just after sundown, deeply sunburnt, with a lidded plastic bucket that, if you hushed and leaned over it, emitted a low and steady, sand-gritty sound.

After the woman died, Niels frequented the store more than ever, standing to one side quietly. Other than "Hello, Niels. How's Niels today?" people paid him no mind.

One Friday night eight months after the old woman was buried, Niels walked into the store with a burlap sack. He had found a big snake near the barn that day. Frankie was having a little party. He was sitting at the coffee counter with three floozies from Rapid City and his friend Jake, a skinny man from down the road with inexpensive watery eyes. It was a hot night. They were drinking highballs, hard at it for the weekend.

Frankie came over to meet Niels and took the sack back into the snake room. Niels stood blinking, staring at the dressed-up women in the bright light: brash red lipstick and cool white teeth. Frankie came out and paid Niels for the snake and looked quizzically at the big man's blinking face. Then Niels left and walked off down the dark tracks,

ON SLEEP CREEK

past the haystacks and the warping stock chutes and across the trestle bridge toward home.

The next day about noon when Niels appeared across the road, Frankie whistled into the back of the store and one of the floozies hurried out. She peeked from the window on tiptoe, then threw a thin sweater over her shoulders and left the store. She hailed Niels as he cut across the highway. He stood stone still and watched her soberly as she talked, rocking from one high-heeled foot to the other. Cajolery in the cool Saturday air.

And then, just like that, the two walked off. She took him to an abandoned, half-finished house with a ratty sofa and beer trash in it a hundred yards from the road. Frankie and Jake and one of the girls were already there, hidden stocking-footed and smirking in a closet with their peepholes prepared.

*

It was months before Frankie's occasional rough-hewn insinuations penetrated Niels's quotidian and a nasty glimmering took hold in his mind. It fluttered and guttered, and one day it was all clear as flint.

The revelation was stark but its chemistry was complex for Niels. Once he knew what had happened, he thought about it a good part of his days and weeks, mulled on it at work in the barn and while greasing his clodhoppers and over the favorite supper he cooked for the Slows, a huge mound of mashed rutabagas with fried eggs on top.

It was an intrusion of consequence, he knew that. A year after the woman had taken him to the sofa, he thought of her occasionally and simply. It was a love, the only way he knew what lurked behind that word: a simple, barnyard love. He had *loved* her, his love was once and for all upon her, regardless if she never entered his life again. It was his only private height. Now it was contaminated by the new thing, the shifty leer through fat prairie-dog cheeks. A flushed resentment focused and grew to a pinpoint hatred.

ON SLEEP CREEK

Niels never hinted that he had figured things out. The subject even dropped from Frankie's attention over the next half year. Niels continued to visit the store, and stood longer, even more quietly, off to one side, waiting instinctively for more light, further instructions.

He was there one early August day when the Kentuckians came. A lean dark-haired man and his wife and tongue-tied twelve-year-old boy. They were headed for Wyoming to fish and were going up to Mt. Rushmore to see "the faces." Frankie took them in back to see the snake tanks. When they returned the Kentuckian drank a cup of coffee and talked Appalachian snake talk; told about the religious snake handlers moaning and lowing; and how the poor mountain folks and wageless striking coal miners turned to timber rattlers for table meat; how in bad-blood time a sack of snakes might be dumped in an enemy's parked car just to let him know he's thought of.

And three days later, Sunday morning, Niels put in a long day poking around his old haunts with his grimy lidded bucket and his forked pole of ash. He chose only strong, good-sized snakes. He worked steadily the following days, going out each morning and evening when he could spare an hour to hunt the dens and wander sharp-eyed through the big prairie-dog town down by the river.

Friday night Niels ate an early supper with his ranchmen—pork chops and rutabagas and fried eggs and applesauce. Then he left the house. He sat in the near-dark of the small barn. One by one he fished out his best big snakes from the bucket and held them down with his feet and cut off their rattles with his Barlow knife, then dropped them back in. Then he put the lid on and took up the bucket and struck out surely across the stubble field to the tracks.

He walked slowly along the old cinder bed of the railway, thinking about the thing he wanted to do. When he stopped to rest he heard the angry sandpapery stirring in the bucket. He would walk to the edge of town and wait for darkness in the fencerow trees behind Frankie's place.

ON SLEEP CREEK

As he moved along the tracks, thinking all about the thing, he spied a dead pronghorn kid crumpled in the ditch below, thrown there by a thundering truck. Niels stopped and looked and then clambered down the embankment. He stood and gazed at the creature for long seconds while redwings sang around him in the late sun. It was a runt of a critter with giant foggy eyes. It was sad and pretty as a puppy. It lay there numb and finished off with all its bones pulverized like glass in a sack and its tiny tongue lolling out.

This would be better, Niels thought. He bent a little to see the body in the apricot light. Yes, this would be a better thing than snakes in the truck. He set down his bucket and hoisted the dead kid over his shoulder. He carried it to town and into the brushy grove and waited still as a stump under a cottonwood until it was full dark and nobody moved in the half-lit yards and houses. Then he took it quietly across the lot to Frankie's, stood for a moment, and carefully set it up on the porch at the top of the steps—fixed it up facing the door just the way he wanted it, like a spread-eagle voodoo mantis or knock-kneed kamikaze angel, and slipped back into the dark of the trees.

ON SLEEP CREEK

A PHOTO OF GENERAL MILES

Three or four times a summer I would pack my knapsack good and full and hike off up Deer Creek for a long day. Up the stream about two miles one leaves the ponderosa hills and gullies and steps forth onto a little-suspected plateau, high and open and powerfully rolling and lush enough with its tiny headwater streams to have the comfortable feel of a northern meadow.

I would hike for an hour across this secretive steppe without seeing a human being, seeing little but the meadow birds flushing up from the tall grass and an occasional edgy horse herd. There was a single minimal dirt road crossing the plateau from east to west. It hooked and sliced and led past a rocky jumble of deteriorating cliff known locally as an old buffalo jump site. A regional entrepreneur took a busload of Japanese tourists there once, but when the first of many rattlesnakes sounded from the scree the visitors stampeded back to the bus and refused to get out until they were back in Billings.

A few minutes beyond this place I arrived at my knoll, from which I could see the Rosebud Mountains to the south and west. I set up my sawed-off easel and lashed down my pad against the jaunty wind and painted or sketched—on clear days the Big Horns were visible still farther south—and ate my lunch of bread and cheese and olives. When I tired of painting the far mountains or the cloud-shadowed swells of the plains below I turned to the plants at my elbow and drew the wild roses or the lovely bunches of delicate June grass with their sharp, plaintive upthrust as of nestlings in a nest.

Then I would pack up my things and give myself a once-over for ticks and walk down over the hill to see Ruben Bear. I happened across his house two summers ago on a day with the easel. It was a small old house, but firm and well-patined. It was the only home I knew of on the whole vast plateau.

Ruben was in his sixties, sturdy and quiet, with a quick and nimble grin. He lived there with his wife and often a handful of visiting grandchildren. He still took plenty of deer for the table and his wife put by plenty of cherries and plums. By the end of August there were festoons of sliced, strung squash drying from the porch rafters.

That first day we talked a little in the yard and I showed them my sketches and soon we were drinking coffee around their table. Out the kitchen window I could see, perched on a low rise immediately above the house, a rickety metal folding chair, sitting there alone amid the patchy sagebrush.

As I was saying goodbye in the yard I noticed it again—standing out against the sky—and said, "That's a good spot somebody has up there."

"Yes," Ruben said. "That's my spot. I go up there with my drum sometimes at night. To sing. Just to entertain myself."

I hadn't seen the photograph that time. That was the next visit, maybe three weeks later. It was a small photograph in an ornate wooden frame, sitting on a chest of drawers. The print was creased and splotchy and showed three Indian men with carbines and a white-haired soldier squinting in a hard sun.

"That one is my grandfather," Ruben said, pointing at one of the long-haired men in calico shirts and moccasins. "He was a scout for General Miles. That picture was taken at Fort Keogh, up on the Yellowstone River."

Ruben and I became friends, in a widely spaced way. I stopped when I could. I would halloo as I entered the yard, or, more likely, Ruben

A PHOTO OF GENERAL MILES

would have heard me coming and, tapping an old contrary vein of wit, burst out the door looking in the opposite direction, scratching his head and saying in a rhetorical stage whisper, "I could swear I heard somebody drive in." They were tonic visits, those hours spent sorting beans or scrubbing melons from the garden with a near-content man of good ear and good eye who when the night was right climbed the little hill to the rickety chair to sing with the stars.

Some days, I saw that the photograph was not in its usual place. Other times it was there, front and center. One afternoon when it was missing I alluded to it as obliquely as I could and Ruben went to the chest and lifted it from a drawer.

He brought it over and sat down and told me about it in one gentle, well-tempered stanza. His family had always been proud of the picture—his grandfather was widely known as a good man, a good father, and a good fighter. Then some years ago when things stirred up on many of the reservations, and Indian peoples began to stand forth more publicly for their ways, some young people began to talk about the grandfathers in the fighting days. They began asking questions and reading the history books and finding out about those days.

Some of them read about those among their people who had helped the white soldiers in their later campaigns, scouted for them against Chief Joseph or the holdout Sioux, located the tired hostile camps and led the soldiers to them.

Those names and those stories spread quickly among the younger generation. The elders had of course known all those stories forever; they knew the grandfathers scouted to avoid the staked-down dry-rot life at the fort. But people began to look at the other people and think of what their grandfathers did in the fighting days. People talked and said things and others heard them. It was a difficult time for many families when the good, sleeping past came back bitter and wild-eyed.

So when Ruben looked out his door in those days and saw an unfamiliar car coming down to his house, he would sometimes walk over

A PHOTO OF GENERAL MILES

and put the photo in the drawer with the good tablecloth. Just to avoid some things, some little troubles. He didn't like the thought of people talking about his family in town.

But eventually Ruben himself began to think about the thing. He went back and forth with it, and still did. He summoned those old days and tried to see them, tried to see what that scouting for the white soldiers amounted to a hundred years later—was it such a good thing after all? Some days he thought no, and the picture went into the drawer. Other days he looked again with his good glasses on and said, "Father of my father," and set it on the table beside a chewed-up prayer book and a tumbler of spoons.

From then on, I always stole a glance around the room when I got there, to see how the issue stood that week, to gauge how the ancestral karma ran. It was a detail among many, but I knew it fed the star songs and I simply made a point to notice it as I noticed the direction of the wind through the web of things and the light and lay of the Rosebud range on my way back over the hill.

A PHOTO OF GENERAL MILES

VICTROLA-MAN

A beautiful girl knelt beside Milk River in the summer of 1930. Beautiful enough that, even though she was simply filling a bucket of water, there were boys watching through the low willows nearby.

It was a large gathering on Milk River just below Harlem, a summerfair camp that stretched a good way along the south bank, from the river up through the open cottonwoods and onto the broad valley floor. It was only mid-Friday, but the place was filling up fast with wagons and horses and wall tents and a few white tipis. Families were erecting shade arbors at their campsites and thatching them with fresh-cut boughs that smelled strong of the river bottom. People laughed and called and there was the constant sound of stakes being driven. Motorists driving down Milk Valley saw the bright sprawl of the camp a far way off and knew it was a happy one, white and shimmering and wind-pestered like sailboats on a sea.

The girl carried her water bucket back to camp, slowly and cautiously, with her free arm out from her body for balance. Her thin dress snapped in the breeze and her long hair blew over her face. Her parents were arranging the wood stove in their shiny wall tent, fitting the smoke pipe up through the hole in the roof. Her grandmother was patiently carrying small things from the wagon to the tent. They had arrived that morning after a three-day trip from the Fort Peck reservation and they had a good place to camp. They had seen other families along the way bound for the fair, saw them short-camped on the railroad right-of-way, sleeping under the wagons, cooking and waving at the passersby. There were people on Milk River from all over the north—from Rocky Boy and Crow and North Dakota; from the Blackfeet reservation and even some tall, stout Bloods down from Canada with their big rawhide drums.

The girl fetched her grandmother a tin cup of water and then the two of them set about making coffee. The grandmother in the faded calico dress she had washed two hundred times, her head wrapped in a huge kerchief, exhorted in gruff little notes and the girl responded in her shy thirteen-year-old whisper. The old woman had all but lost anything like an appearance—she was worn and erased by water and wind—while the girl had only recently found hers, a clear-stamped beauty long known on the continent: a narrow oval face with a strong wide mouth like a bird and one dark eye slightly larger than the other, its brow set in a subtle perpetual arch that suggested both mild surprise and inborn sophistication with its faint shadow of sadness. The girl had always spent most of her hours with the grandmother—they were close as sisters—and the old woman knew well the girl's footstep among many by night. Their coffee was always good, with plenty of sugar.

By late afternoon the drums were sounding from the dance arbor and the high, driving voices of the singers carried over the camp on the lazy wind. Women hurried to and from the river for water and smoke rose from many cookstoves. It was part of the time and part of the people that everyone cooked the same supper: the salt pork and dried corn soup that was, essentially, *food*, then, up there.

There were specialties available down around the arbor, of course, because it was a fair and people worked hard to find something a little extra during those hard times—things to eat and things to look at. A woman sat on a blanket selling Juneberry soup, and on the other side a woman from Lodgegrass had a kettle of tripe stew she sold by the dipperful.

VICTROLA-MAN

There was a circular midway around the dance arena. By sunset there were people offering beadwork and featherwork for the grass dance costumes and an old woman selling toys made of chokecherry wood and pairs of buckskin dolls. Soon an old magic man hobbled out of the darkness and spread his blanket on the ground where the firelight from the arbor just reached him. He knew the old-time snake magic and sat there all evening handling his rattlesnakes, passing them over his neck and under his arms and out through his sleeves, with a broad toothless grin on his face. Down the line another magician set up, a big man with sagging breasts and belly and the skipping Alberta accent of the Bloods. A great annual favorite of the fairgoers, he sat heavy as a hill in the flickering firelight, transforming pieces of broom straw into blue-tip matches and changing handfuls of river sand into fine white sugar with a swirl and twitch of his silk kerchief and a few key words. There was a family selling old-time pemmican and an aged man and his boy selling miniature bull boats twelve inches across and painted buckskin tipis three feet high—things of the last generation, things once living full-scale in the world and now playthings shrunken up small with time-distance.

The fairgoers circled the arbor continuously, dappled with dust and firelight, strolling, watching for friends, and stopping to see the dancers inside the arbor. Until well after midnight the midway was full of the drumming and long shadows and laughter and many dogs underfoot.

Saturday morning the camp awakened leisurely, in fits and starts, with people stirring in and out of the trees along the river, then quieting again. The air was soft and cool and still on the ear after many hours of the drums. The girl and her grandmother had made a big pot of coffee and sat together while the mother was frying bacon. Now and then a car would start or a band of children tear by, off to swim in the river.

Of a sudden the wind rose from over the long narrow camp, and it carried music, a far-off soft song and a light drum. It swelled and ebbed

VICTROLA-MAN

as the wind wavered, but the grandmother caught it like a deer and her eyes grew sharp and at last she stood up from her wooden chair to listen, but right there the wind settled and a wagonload of people clattered by and the song was gone, sank back where it came from.

The old woman returned to her seat. "That was an otter song," she said to the girl. "A very old song. I haven't heard that song since I was a girl. That was one of my favorites." She lowered her head over her coffee cup. The girl watched and reached across to stroke her shoulder through the shiny fringed shawl.

"Nobody sings those real songs anymore," the grandmother muttered. "Nobody knows the words anymore."

The girl stroked the old woman like a cat as they sat quietly. If the grandmother had had the hair, the girl would have brushed and braided it for her. The wind came up again, and fell, and rose again, and the people ducked and covered their faces from the dust, but there was no music on it now. Then breakfast was ready and the store bread with jelly was passed around.

Saturday afternoon the crowd began to thicken. Latecomers pulled in on their wagons and unhitched their teams and local people arrived for a long evening. People were dressed up a little more for the Saturday night: women in nice plaid dresses and men with white shirts and their best Stetsons and neckerchiefs. The old ones wore good beaded moccasins and dress-up shawls and full skirts brushing the ground. There were striped blanket-coats as the day cooled, and mail-order coats from Chicago. The drums began again and dust was in the air.

The Assiniboine girl was dressed and ready to tour the midway with her cousin, an older girl with her hair bobbed at the ears. They wore their fanciest white dresses and white stockings and good black shoes. As they left the camp the girl's mother gave them each twenty-five cents for a treat.

The two girls walked arm in arm around the arbor. The dust swirled gray-gold in the last sunlight and the girls kept hankies at their noses.

VICTROLA-MAN

It was a big, noisy crowd that night. There were gangs of wild young boys careening through and families walking around together en masse causing traffic jams when they stopped to visit. There were automobiles from Havre and Malta with white people in zoot suits and straw hats leaning against them with their hands in their pockets.

It was a surging, jostling crowd and the young girl shrank from it in spite of the holiday excitement. Soon there was a group of boys following the two cousins through the crowd, brash boys with tight white shirts and work boots and flashing eyes. They trailed the girls like dogs and whispered loudly at them and snickered and cringed.

The girls had been around the arbor four times very slowly. The young girl had had enough. It was too loud, too harsh; nothing looked good to her, not the pemmican or even the candy in the big jars. She would come back later when the dancing was going strong and settling people down with watching it.

The girls cut away from the midway, out into the camp, and stopped to get their bearings. As they walked toward their own tents they heard, during a lull in the big drums, a man singing off to their right. It was a quiet, tendrilled song and the young girl recognized the voice. It was the man who sang the otter song that morning.

Then they saw him, sitting on a stool before his wall tent, singing, with a kerosene lamp and a woman on the ground beside him. The young girl tugged her cousin's sleeve and whispered in her ear a long moment. They walked softly over to the man and stopped at a proper distance until his song was finished. Then the older girl asked the man if he sang the otter song earlier in the day. The man looked down at his hand drum and nodded, and the girl looked over her shoulder at her young cousin.

The Assiniboine girl stepped up and shyly asked the man if he would sing it again for somebody, sometime. The old man said yes, that was what he did at the fair; he was singing the old songs that nobody knew anymore. Sometimes people liked to hear those songs or

VICTROLA—MAN

wanted to hear them to help something turn out right. Sometimes they gave him something to sing for them.

The young girl asked him how much it would cost to hear the otter song and the man shook his head: "Anything you want," he said.

Back at their camp, the young girl brought the grandmother's blanket from the tent and put it over the old woman's shoulders and told her to come on. The woman was up without asking and the two were soon off, huddled together arm in arm.

"I have something for you," the girl whispered, and the woman said, "Oh," and pulled her blanket closer over her shoulders.

They found the old singer's camp and the girl called softly and waited before the tent. They could see old people moving around inside against a lantern's light. Soon the man came out and looked at the two women and grunted. The girl said they wished to hear the otter song and then the old lady said "Oooh" very softly.

There was singing from the arbor, so the old man—he was like a Victrola-man—he motioned them to follow and led the way off behind his tent to a bullberry patch and they stepped behind it and put it between them and the midway.

They stood there, the three of them, in a little triangle. The man was saying a few low preparatory words. A boy appeared with a wooden stool and the old woman sat down on it. Then the man began to sing, just loud enough to hear above the buzzing camp noise and the arbor drums. It was the otter song all right.

The grandmother lowered her head and pulled her blanket up around her neck. The girl felt the little cold bumps along her arms and legs. She knew right then that the song had something important to do with the boy-packs and the river-cool and biting flies in the sun. With her twenty-five cents clutched in one hand, she reached out with the other to take hold of a bullberry branch and she fiddled with it aimlessly while she listened and looked down into the bushes at nothing solid in the world.

VICTROLA-MAN

SWORN BEFORE CRANES

At first glance, nothing in the valley appears animate, unless you count the few snowflakes hedging from a glaring white sky as animate, or the ice-edged low-water creeks knifing their crooked ways. Even the frozen dirt roads, snow-white against the pale grasslands, show no tracks or signs of passage.

But when the eye adjusts it sees at last a thin trail of smoke from a wooden house hidden in streamside trees. Then a dark northern hawk shakes itself on a cottonwood limb and from a solitary trailer guyed to a distant knoll a hunched old woman in a black overcoat and calico babushka walks slowly to the hand pump in her yard. That iron and that water will be cold today.

Along the worn highway moves a car from the south. A large, shining American car. Inside it sit two young men absentmindedly listening to the radio. By their cropped hair and antennaless look and skinny black ties, they are Mormons, in search of prey. A man standing by that highway would hear the car coming for a long way, and then hear it going for a long, long way.

At the end of one of the frozen-rut roads, in a home beside a woody trickle of a stream, coffee is boiling for the Keeps Guns. It is a home with all the necessities and arm's reach of a good camp; a smart, durable camp with a multigeneration feel to it.

Two boys are mending a homemade basketball goal near the house.

The summer shade-arbor's pine-bough roof is sere-red and drooping. The outhouse is a patchwork of mixed planks and sheet metal, standing at the edge of the creek's box elders. Near the main house stand an empty eighty-year-old log home, a deer-butchering gantry, and a couple of sheds, tipi poles leaning against one of them. Then, the good deep well, engineless cars filled with rough overflow storage, a brown horse and a colt, laundry frozen on the line, a big pile of firewood.

The father of the family is drinking coffee, idly watching the boys hammer down a flap in the backboard. They work with gloves on from the hood of a car. Dogs loiter about the yard. A grandmother sits near the warm stove. A grandchild crawls in the kitchen, rolling an onion along as it goes. The mother sits at the table packing gifts to be mailed to their other boy in prison over in the Falls. She fits in candy and cigarettes and a braid of sweet grass and ties it up good and tight.

It will be Christmas in four or five days and they are meatless, but they don't dwell on it. They know it but don't dwell on it, because they know in the same way that things will set up in their own good time, or not set up, which is a setup just as well.

*

One night summer before last, up in the Montana Blackfeet country, two boys were driving south on the Choteau highway. They were drinking and getting drunk. The boy driving was a Blackfeet boy, the other was a white boy from Arkansas. They got into an argument over something, probably money, and the white boy reached up and turned on the dome light and pulled out a pistol and shot the Blackfeet boy as he was driving down the road. Shot him dead and grabbed the wheel and pulled off the highway and dumped the body out into the ditch, took his money and cigarettes and Tony Lama boots and drove on. Twenty minutes later a patrol car stopped him for speeding. It was a woman cop. The boy shot her too when she walked up to the car window. At the trial all his family and his girlfriend were up from Arkan-

SWORN BEFORE CRANES

sas, sitting there stiffly in the stands. They were there to support the boy. They ate at the same hamburger place every night. The girlfriend was arrested for trying to slip the boy a knife in jail.

The same week, down in Miles City, some young Cheyennes were drinking in a bar, getting drunk. These were people who had moved up to Miles to live for a while. They were talking to a white boy, a half-silly boy with a gimpy leg. He was drunk too. They all talked loud and laughed loud and watched on the bias to see if the white boy was laughing as loud as themselves. When the place closed up they all decided to go somewhere together. They got in one of the Cheyennes' car and drove out the Baker road, drinking. The Cheyennes started talking Cheyenne. They stopped at a little park ten miles out of town and stopped laughing and began working the white boy for money. They beat him up bad and stabbed him and he died up under the pines on a pocky concrete picnic table. They caught those kids two days later down in Sheridan, Wyoming.

But the deal that the Keeps Gun boy was in on happened over toward Yankton, South Dakota. It happened a few days after the Miles City incident, in one of those ugly little South Dakota towns conceived when a locomotive stopped for water and a handful of Europeans materialized to sell things to one another.

There was a bully in this little town, a white man about forty years old. He could hardly write his name. For twenty years his family had bullied the Sioux people around this town. Stared at them through slitty eyes. Insulted them so they could hear it. Slurped and slapped at the pretty Sioux girls. Beat up men and spit on their boots, and in winter drove by so they splashed slush on Indians walking along the road.

This one man was the worst of the bunch. Everybody knew about him. The police were afraid to cross him. He was a bully of the sort you heard about in the old Indian stories, old old stories of the half-human bully-monsters who killed people for laughs and took all the good

SWORN BEFORE CRANES

meat for themselves. People used to know what to do in those situations.

The Keeps Gun boy was over visiting people in this town. He was over for two or three weeks. One afternoon the bully was drinking hard. Then he began driving down through the Indian part of town, yelling at people, insulting them, scaring the children off the streets. The Keeps Gun boy was right there, helping his friend work on his pickup truck.

When the bully drove off, the friend said, "Come on," and they got in a car and drove downtown to the police station and asked them to keep the bully out of the Indian housing before things got bad. Then they went back home.

A policeman pulled the bully over downtown and told him on the q.t. that an Indian had filed a complaint about him and advised him to go home and sleep it off. And then he told the bully which Indian had come to the station.

Just after dark, the Keeps Gun boy and his friend had the truck running and drove downtown to buy some beer. Keeps Gun sat in the truck while the older one went across the street into the liquor store. When the Sioux boy was coming out of the store, Keeps Gun heard someone yelling and looked around and saw the bully coming out from a parking lot with another white man.

The bully came at the Indian and grabbed him by the arm and knocked the Old Milwaukee to the ground. Then the other white man tried to hold the boy's arms from behind and in a minute the whole thing blew. Two Sioux boys came running down the street with a hoe handle and they were all swinging and kicking. Keeps Gun jumped out and grabbed a length of two-by-four from the truck bed and ran into the fight.

Some of the other men had clubs as well, but a prosecution expert, and then the jury with tight thin lips, said it was the Keeps Gun boy

SWORN BEFORE CRANES

who caught the bully at the base of the skull with his two-by-four and killed him.

It was nothing like the magical acrobatic antibully finesse of a thousand years earlier in this territory, but the monster was dead and stinking there in the parking-lot lights.

*

So now they had packed him up some cigarettes and sweet grass and sent it to him in prison over in the Falls. It is two days before Christmas. There will be relatives coming from Antelope and Spring Creek. The grandmother and the mother begin thinking a little more about meat. They haul the big sack of potatoes out from the side room and look them over to see that they are all good. They get out the big boxes of dried corn and check to see if mice have gotten to them and set them out on the kitchen counter. They think about the meat but don't mention it aloud.

Late in the day the two boys are sitting at the table in the house. The women are folding laundry and the father is drinking coffee, looking out at the hills. Then the older boy says, "Let's go," and the two of them get up and put on their coats and retrieve a rifle from the corner and say, "We'll be back later," and leave the house.

They drive in the pickup out to the highway and south a mile, where they turn off to pick up another boy. It is just getting dark. The three drive for half an hour, west on a state highway, then north on a minor paved road, a little-traveled, houseless road that rolls and bucks through the anonymous leased grazing lands toward the rough country of the Cuny Table.

It is full dark now and the work is simple and has been done before. On an open, lightless stretch of the highway they see cattle near the fence. They cut the radio and pull over and check both ways on the road for car lights and put the flashlight on a gaping Hereford and shoot it

SWORN BEFORE CRANES

with the .30-30 from the cab. Two of the boys jump out of the truck and over the fence while the third drives off and up the long climb to the table where he will pull off the highway and wait.

The two boys in the field cut the Hereford's throat and roll her on her back. They set the flashlight on the ground and work with large hardware butcher knives honed on a flat file. They work quickly, watching for cars on the highway. When lights come down the hill from the table, they shut off the flashlight and crouch, ready to run. After the car passes they are back at it. *Wheep, wheep*, a knife whipping on the file. They take just the four legs of the cow, severing the shoulder and hip joints with a hatchet. They drag the quarters over to the fence and under the barbed wire.

They wait low in the dark ditch until the driver comes back down the hill and swerves over to the fence side of the road. They haul the four drumsticks up to the berm and heave them into the truck bed and throw a tarp over them and drive away.

*

On Christmas Day the soup was made and bubbling on the Keeps Gun stove for whoever might want it. It was good old-fashioned soup with dried corn and salt pork and beef in it. There was an inch of day-old snow on the yard where the dogs shivered and wandered from car tire to car tire to sniff the new arrivals: cars and trucks from Spring Creek and Antelope. Magpies sat on the Keeps Gun house watching everything that moved or was about to move.

Inside, the solstitial social heart was beating. The television was on at one end of the room and the radio at the other. The various generations gravitated to their own kind. Children laughed and chased. Three grandmothers sat together in a corner, so old and leaflike and primary that they communicated by the positions of their hands in their quiet laps.

SWORN BEFORE CRANES

Midafternoon, a Catholic priest stopped by the home with Christmas greetings and a sack of oranges. He was learning to speak Lakota and always told funny stories about his recent linguistic trials and errors. He was a jovial man who wore white sneakers the year round. He sat at the table with the mother and father and ate a bowl of the hot soup—*wahanpi, wahanpi,* he practiced as he ate.

The Catholic priest drove off and before long an Episcopal preacher drove in. There was candy for the children. It was remarkably like the Catholic father's visit. The Episcopal was a good-natured man with pink cheeks and pink furry ears. He ate a bowl of the soup and smiled and then the quick receding footsteps—*quack, quack, quack*—on the cold driveway snow just as the day was fading and the dogs were creeping under the porch to their rag beds.

An hour later, the jovial priest was still making his rounds. At the moment he was driving on the dark straightaway past the very pasture where the cow was butchered, driving through the quizzical, caged-bird silence of jovial people alone.

And that night there were those saying that rocks and stones are the oldest things on earth. But there were others who might be saying that that quartered beef lying eyes open in that starry, rumpled Christmas field—that frozen, sleighless, life-biding fuselage—is the oldest thing on earth.

SWORN BEFORE CRANES

FULL HERON

First, this mild September day—we were afield sketching the big half-yellow White River cottonwoods—there was the red car. We had been following it at a hundred-yard distance for several miles through the Dakota backcountry. Then suddenly on a long empty straightaway its taillights flashed and it swerved to a sharp stop just off the highway. The driver, a Sioux boy, jumped from the car and tore across the road and off into the grassland. Immediately a second boy leaped from the shotgun seat and roared around the car and took off in hot pursuit. They were both sprinting the unmistakable no-joke sprint of the getaway and the chase. Away they went, high adrenaline over the low prairie hills, leaving the car askew with one door open and the dust cloud slowly rising. They were still at it, three hundred yards from the highway, when last we looked back over our shoulders from a rise.

Later in the morning we drew our way down Wounded Knee Creek and then headed slowly into Sharps for coffee. As we passed a remote cluster of homes near the road I glanced over and there, abruptly, near the corner of an aqua house, was a man of maybe fifty years standing on one leg—a classic, out-of-the-blue *full heron*.

He wore nothing but plaid boxer-style swimming trunks (they were no doubt setting up for a sweat lodge) and was standing—free-standing—idly in the warm sun while younger men moved here and there about the yard. His left foot rested just above his right knee; his right hand was cocked on the right hip and the left hand lay naturally on the hiked left thigh. Utterly relaxed, easy as a leaf in that vestigial stance, he seemed to rise from an alternate, other-postured world.

I remember an old photo of a native Australian standing that way, leaning on his spear. And I remember faintly a thin boy from grade-school days who stood like that for long sessions on the grass beside the village swimming pool, with his skinny arms wrapped—several times it seemed—about his neck and upper shoulders, his chlorine-riled eyes blinking. But that was thirty-five years ago; and this was a full-grown late-twentieth-century man.

It was only noon and it had already been a full-blown September outing, heavy on the buckshee. The green and maize crayons were worn to nubs and flocks of piñon jays cried above the pine hills. And the two micro-curious, sky-lit sightings—ha, I thought, a double yolk of a day. And that made me think of the Blackduck brothers.

Wilson and William Blackduck, twins, up in the Tongue River country. I knew them obliquely, ten years ago. Observed them, more than knew them, but we had some good talks on occasion.

They were men in their seventh decade, nearly identical twins of great beauty and refinement. Six-foot full bloods of slender build with small braids from fine heads of hair, the braids joined across the chest at clavicle level by a single strand of colored yarn. They too had a memorable way of standing, an exemplary, brotherly way, at a certain gentle, well-calculated angle to one another. Large silk scarves knotted at the throat and roomy old sports jackets and good felt Stetsons. They were so handsome and reflective and fine-minded that for them to simply be there in front of the grocery in town or at a community gathering, standing there gracefully and even-footed with Stetsons in hand, gazing quietly off, was enough; an accepted duty, a benevolence, and enough.

They had grown up during the hardest of reservation times, stood through famine and Caucasian glower and toxic bureaucracy, and

FULL HERON

swam daily in the Tongue. As a young man, one of them (I forget which) had "done things." He discovered at sixteen that he had certain gifts and one time he used them to good effect: When a cousin was involved in a legal scrape, the Blackduck boy sat down alone on the night before the hearing and concentrated hard on the matter. Next day at the courthouse a key piece of evidence had vanished from the file.

The brothers went to the army, together, for the second war and were prisoners in a Japanese camp for most of a year, together. They were held at a supply depot where all day long they carried boxes of sundry explosives for transshipping, while the Japanese guards laughed and prodded and cautioned them not to stumble and fall. Evenings, the guards would sidle in to smoke and ask them why the Indians even bothered to fight for the white Americans, a question the Blackduck brothers pondered, briefly, looking at the ground.

After the war, back on Tongue River, they resumed their even lives. They ran a few cattle and ponies and raised children and weighed their people's ways and smoothed them best they could for the second half of the roaring century. By the time I knew them and watched them they had been standing some thirty years since the war, reassuring, sensible, calm as horses.

Then William died, late one summer. Wilson sat alone all night and by morning had decided what to do. He walked to town and told the old man running the trading post that he wanted to sell the family bundle, then walked back home.

The trader made a phone call and that afternoon two men in suits drove into Wilson's yard. The two strangers were excited, but they acted cool as cucumbers and loitered an extra minute beside their car, jingling the change in their pockets, mock-yawning and stretching and mock-watching the magpies jumping in the pines.

The Blackduck medicine bundle had been in the family for three generations. It was well kept and even famous. A hawk-skin headdress, an ochered crane wing, a miniature lariat and hobble, a rawhide sil-

FULL HERON

houette of a stallion, various paints and herbal specialties and spherical stones, all in a rouged rawhide pouch worn smooth as driftwood. Wilson got a good price for it from the strangers, enough for the two ample family grave plots he wanted and for a good gray headstone with "Blackduck" in small clean capital letters. He even had enough left over for a quick trip to Oklahoma in the fall.

I made a small pencil drawing of Wilson one day, with his hat in his hand. I saw him several times before he died. He was virtually alone by then, with a deaf and sickly wife and his children gone to Billings. He occasionally mentioned the sale of his bundle. He considered it a desperate but heroically timed deed and spoke of it with relief and fatalistic gratitude, gazing out the window with that look that was enough all by itself.

One day as we sat there he chuckled and stirred and said, "But I still have some things like that, too." And he reached under the bed to pull out an eighteen-inch wooden box and placed it on his knees. Chuckling, he opened it and showed me his new arsenal against ill fortune: an array of Catholic-saint medals; a rabbit's foot on a chain; a plastic shamrock; a peyote button in a glass box; a J.F.K. dollar; a buffalo tooth; a splintered four-inch piece of palm leaf from a Palm Sunday service; a venerable turkey wishbone . . .

*

The Blackduck brothers. The little drawing of Wilson, I realize each time I see it, is sadly incomplete and single-yoked: Wilson alone, standing in that memorable way. I have been often tempted to take it down from the wall and open it up and add the other figure, work him in there at that delicate, mirror-image angle, but it would be working from sketchy, one-legged memory, and so far I haven't had the nerve.

FULL HERON

SILENT HERDER

Summer evenings when the light softens and the air sets, you will see boys materialize from various points of the little village and walk heavily to the playground of the knoll-top school. Two, three, four of an evening, they straggle in and take, each, privately, to one of the playground swings with a discreet distance between them and slowly begin to swing. They are lovesick Arapaho boys, sixteen and eighteen years old, and their swinging as the night falls is pensive and stop-gap. Their long black hair flows and buckles with their arcs. They gaze off at the tail end of sunflare behind the Wind River mountains or at the dusty river course, August-salty, to the east, below. They will swing in rhythmic silence through the sunset and well into the dark before they wander off in various directions and finally home.

Tonight a dog trots from behind the school building and crosses the thin gravel of the schoolyard, casts a quick accustomed eye at the faint *chee* of the swing sets. It is the black-and-white panda-faced bitch from the east end of town going home after a day of foraging. Behind her trots her longtime friend, a brown guppy-jawed powwow dog with thinning hair and prominent sunburnt teats like a Berkshire sow. They had been out along the Little Wind River and up one of its feeder creeks and back past a rural soda-pop store where they whiffed at scattered candy wrappers and watched a spry old whippet–Saint Bernard cross pull over big trash drums and rustle through the contents on the ground. Now, with her usual timing, the panda dog would get home just as the lights in the family house come on and the supper scraps are cool on the counter.

*

Twelve miles away in a roughhouse motel in the lee of the foothills, a young man was dressing and watching the darkness come on. On the desk a feeble lamplight fell on the remains of a quick meal: wads of hamburger foil and a cottage-cheese carton and a bag of green-onion potato chips.

The man was dressing and his girlfriend sat curled on the bed simple as a rabbit, watching him while the haywire television flickered and bucked in the corner. Her blond hair was up in curlers. The man was skinny and strong and bore a birthmark the size of a fifty-cent piece on his right rear shoulder, a brownish-green birthmark frilled around the edges like a lichen. He pulled on a long-sleeved black work shirt out at the elbows and spattered with red paint.

"You be there—that's the main thing."

"I'll be there."

"Just be there, no matter what. Either way I'll get there, so you just sit tight and wait."

"I'll be there," said the girl.

The man tied a dark blue bandana around his head and put on black canvas running shoes and tied them good and tight. He wore a commando sheath knife on his belt and hung a short lanyard around his neck with a tiny black flashlight on the end. He flashed the light twice to check it and finger-brushed his little yellow mustache in the mirror. Then he picked up a small haversack, looked into it a moment, and said he was ready.

They drove through the dark ranch country and onto the reservation. They knew where to go and what to do, best they could figure; they had given it a flyby that morning. The girl drove to the little town

SILENT HERDER

where the lovesick boys were still swinging and dropped her man at one shadowy corner where a dirt road cut off from the highway. The man said, "Just be there." He quietly closed the door and slipped into the dusty elms along the ditch.

He followed a brushy row of poplars across a long vacant lot, past a rambling dark brick mission building. He stopped every few minutes to catch his breath and listen. He skirted a squat, boarded-up river-stone building and followed the edge of its brushy yard until it abutted on the big open sun-dance grounds. A single arc light burned from its pole on the school knoll off to his left. Around the edges of the half-mile-square sun-dance grounds scattered houselights twinkled.

He rested there a moment in the ratty lilac hedge at the school boundary, then set off, walking quickly, across the dark open field. In a few minutes he could make out the sun lodge in the center of the grounds, its cottonwood pole structure and the bright offering cloths tied to its high rafters. A minute later he was inside it, kneeling behind a log strut to rest and listen through the dense dark.

He breathed hard with excitement and looked up at the tall center pole of the lodge, straining to see what was up there at the top. Eagle feathers, he hoped, lots of them, tied there among the religious offer-ings at the sun-dance ten days ago—prime tail feathers he could turn in Denver or Albuquerque for twenty-five dollars apiece. He tightened the pack and swiped his mustache and crept over to the center pole. He looked up along it and nudged it a little and made ready to shinny up.

He was up there, hanging like a monkey high on the cottonwood pole, twisting and leaning, trying to see around him, with his arms and legs aching and burning with the scrape and strain, when the panda bitch at her home just east of the grounds knocked a water bucket off the steps and the man inside walked over to his screen door and looked out and saw a quick flash of light from the sun-dance lodge. He knew immediately what it meant—any of the three thousand Arap-

SILENT HERDER

ahos would have known—and hurried across the room to call the tribal police.

The man on the sun pole sensed it a few minutes later, then saw the cars hurrying out from town. *Screw.* He slid down the pole and dropped to the ground and beat it out from the lodge and across the field. Just in case, he pulled out the feathers he had cut and threw them aside as he ran. He dodged brush piles and the debris of old campsites and hopped the fence into a pasture and away. Looking back as he ran he could see the police had cut their headlights and were trying to come in on the sly, but he was way ahead of them.

He found the girl right where she was supposed to be, waiting in the pitch black, and they scrammed back to the motel. The man opened a beer and washed his scratched-up forearms. Then he began to worry and fidget and after half an hour they threw their things into the trunk and drove up into the mountains and slept in the car. They were safe, they figured—nobody had seen a thing, not the man or the girl or the car. The owner of the panda-faced dog had wiped out the stew pot with a crust of bread and tossed it out the door to the dog after the excitement was over.

The couple drove away before daylight, headed north. Two hours later they cut east and climbed into the Big Horns where they paused at the edge of a fragrant meadow to stretch and the girl set her slightly blurred eye-catching beauty in the sun for a minute before the day grew hot.

Then they dropped down the mountains and curled into Sheridan where the man had a cousin. They found the little house on a tattered edge of town and the three of them sat in the backyard all afternoon drinking beer. They talked about going up to Cavalier County, North Dakota, to see an uncle and maybe find a week or two of late-summer work. It would be something to do. The cousin strolled casually over to urinate behind a shed. He wasn't wearing anything but blue jeans.

SILENT HERDER

As he walked back toward the chairs he paused at a three-foot cedar and lifted his leg to it dog-style, grinning at the man and the girl.

They slept late the next day and left Sheridan at midafternoon. They had a small bag of groceries and a pint of peppermint schnapps. They drove north into Montana and struck the Yellowstone valley and followed it northeast in the last of the lingering daylight. The two men smoked Wolf Brothers crooks and listened to the thin night radio while the girl dozed on a pile of bedding in the back seat.

The cousin shifted and pulled one bootless foot up and under him and broke a long silence, grinning suddenly over at the man behind the wheel.

"Remember when we used to drive over to Ten Sleep every Sunday and watch the Girl Scout busses unload for the camp?"

The driver glanced at him sharply and threw a quick flashlight of a look into the back seat.

"Cheap thrills of youth," the cousin said, looking again out the dark window.

Somewhere north of Glendive that night the man spotted a lonesome grain elevator standing by railroad tracks and pulled off the highway, in behind the building. He spread a blanket bed across the front seat. The girl slept on in the back and the cousin made a bedroll under the rear of the car on the cheesy old blacktop of the granary lot.

*

The girl awoke at a distant sound. Then again: *pank*. It was just daylight, the first leak of sun showed on the high white elevator walls. She rolled and dozed again. *Pank*. Now she knew what it was—the pellet gun—and even, in a split second, where she was. Her man was awake, slung low in the front seat, shooting pigeons from the window when they settled around the elevator to feed on runaway grain.

Pank—and a flurry of flapping wings. Then the girl dozed, drifted gratefully into the headless and footless horizontal world. She was

SILENT HERDER

warm and happy. She had a brief dream with her hometown in it—O Walla Walla—a snatch of fearless willowware dream with people sashaying in the street.

Pank. She opened her eyes and heard the cousin stir under the car. She had forgotten all about him. She knew they had donuts in the rear-window bay and would soon find gas-station coffee. Later they would stop to broil pigeon breasts on the rusty hibachi in the trunk. They would have them on bread with bright yellow mustard and a cut-rate dented can of hominy. She was happy. She had been happy for six months, but this was the happiest she had ever been, so far.

SILENT HERDER

F. O. B. FLICKER

A boy walked through town, cutting along the swayback dirt alleys. Some days he took the alleys to avoid the townspeople on the streets; sometimes he took the streets to avoid the snarling backyard dogs in the alley—a half-breed boy. Either way, it was the end of July and the town was full of dusty hollyhocks and late-afternoon pools of shade and young flickers cried all day from their nest holes.

He walked along until he saw the circus poster on a telephone pole. He had forgotten all about that. He read the poster, then cut three blocks over to where the circus was just setting up on a vacant lot at the edge of town.

It was a small outfit for sure—half a dozen stubby house trailers and two large trucks with Texas and Florida license plates. The boy walked shyly around the doings. The people he saw looked foreign and distant. Even though busy at their work they seemed angry and unhappy. A lone man smoking a cigarette behind the big animal truck glanced at the boy when he turned the corner, but never acknowledged him—just looked off over his head.

The boy walked completely around the edge of the camp and then sat down on a slope fifty yards away. He watched a circus woman staking out a pony and a fancy horse. A baby elephant stood near a truck, eating from a pan on the ground. The best thing he saw was three men driving the stakes for the large tent, the way they got their sledges going in rapid-fire order on the same stake—*clink-clink-clink, clink-clink-clink*—as fast as they could go.

Next morning the boy walked back to the circus grounds and sat on the same slope. By now the big tent was up and people were moving about getting things ready for the mid-day performance. The woman was saddling the fancy horse. She got on and warmed up the horse for its dance routine: sideways, backwards, round and round in a rocking, pretty-boy canter. None of the circus people seemed excited; they had done all this five hundred times across Nebraska, and Kansas, all the way from Texas. A juggler was strolling around tossing colored balls in the air.

Then the boy saw Crow coming across the field. He watched him coming across, his long braids bouncing, and knew his friend had seen him sitting there. "Hé."

"Hé."

"You going to the circus?"

"No."

"You doing anything now?"

"No."

"Come on then. I want to show you something."

"Show me what?"

"Something you've never seen before."

They walked off. Crow's step was quicker than usual, the boy noticed that. They walked three blocks and cut in through the bushy backyard of an old house. Crow led the way, in through the back door and across the yellow kitchen.

In the next room, Crow's cousin, Hill, was sitting at a cluttered table. There were lots of beer cans. Hill was just sitting there bleary-eyed and smoking. He looked up at the boys. Hé.

On the mattress against a wall, a large blond woman was lying,

F. O. B. FLICKER

asleep. She was naked. A corner of bedsheet hid her loins. The rest of her body was uncovered, in the sprawl of deepest sleep. After a moment, there was the smell of wine rising from her deep, slow breath.

Crow whispered to the boy. "She works at the circus."

Hill looked over at them. "Florida." He smoked and his gaze fell back to the ashtray.

The boy looked at the unconscious woman—her large splay breasts, the mottled pink and white thighs, the shaved armpits. He took a short step toward her, out of politeness to Crow, and looked again at the breasts and full belly, then stepped back by the table.

Another boy came quietly in the door with a friend. They sidled into the room, glancing quickly at Crow and Hill, then gaped at the sleeping woman. Hill looked at them after a while, then got up heavily. He walked quietly over to the woman and crouched by her feet. He reached out a finger and gently tickled the sole of one foot. The woman hardly stirred, but on some convoluted reflex cue her loins pumped half-heartedly three or four times, far removed, ventriloquial, ghostly.

No one said a word. Hill sat down heavily without a look. Crow and the boy sat across from him and made baloney sandwiches on the cluttered table and ate them. Now and then another schoolboy would materialize and tiptoe into the room and peek at the mattress.

Then there were four old men, wrinkled and thin. They arrived in a group—the boys heard the four car doors slam softly out front—and walked in very slowly, very formally and respectfully.

They removed their Stetsons and walked in a silent line past the mattress. In the dull gloaming light of the room, it was like a line of well-wishers filing reverently by a casket. And that is what the boy remembered for many long years: the eerie decorum, the slight shuffle of feet and clothing and a trace of guarded, proprietous public breathing above the heavy, oblivious, shore-like breaths of the girl.

F. O. B. FLICKER

EUREKA

We were taking the ranch folks into town for Saturday night dinner at the old hotel. The five of us gathered at the loose-jawed gate in the fence separating the house and its big cottonwoods, the hired man's trailer, and the bunkhouse—the domestic ground—from the wide-open range.

We got in the rancher's car and eased across a cattle guard in the just-dark onto the two-rut ranch road. One of the dogs slinked out of the headlights trailing three feet of duck entrails—they had found the place in the hay meadow where we cleaned the birds that afternoon.

It was a slow six miles down the sandhill valley to the state highway. All of us had been outside a good part of the October day at our various pastimes and we were all similarly tired and hungry and vaguely happy in the towering American emptiness.

The car's headlights bounced and cast above the elemental road, illuminating the soapweed, an occasional jackrabbit. Earl drove carefully at ten miles an hour, working the changeable road, swerving to avoid soft spots and high centers. The car swayed steadily and restfully and brought forth easy, restful talk of past work and like seasons.

At one point in the fence line the rancher told us about a heifer on the adjoining spread that he sometimes saw near here, a long-legged white Chianina heifer that looked more like a horse than a cow. She was a jumper. Earl saw her take the fence one day effortlessly, from a dead stand, right along in here. His wife had seen her too one evening. We all talked about that for a while, just before we got to the highway. She was the embodiment of the simple extraordinary the long blue day had stirred us to expect.

Then we climbed up onto the paved highway and zoomed south for the remaining twenty miles into town and the talk changed. We were rushing now; the talk was more brittle. Earl told us about his two favorite greyhounds—fast brindle dogs—finding a bucket of coyote poison mixed with antifreeze in the barn last winter. They died tangled up together on the trailer stoop.

We all had steaks at the old hotel, big raw-boned steaks sprawling over entire plates. We ate quickly. The horseradish went round and round, and then we left with our toothpicks tilting and zoomed off on the highway over the hills.

When we passed the entrance to a big ranch in one of the broad lake valleys—there were two pickups there with their running lights on, talking head to tail, like horses in fly time—Earl jerked a thumb that way and told me a story about the late owner, a tough, land-rich woman who had lived several miles back in under mansard roofs and walked among the first and only topiary in the sandhills. She died a few years ago of sour-mash whiskey.

She was widowed early and lived most of the time on a big spread just south of the Badlands, up in South Dakota. She was managing just fine, kept all the ranches going. Then one day her teenage son didn't come home from school. This was 1957. Everyone looked for that boy. They had sheriffs and detectives and airplanes and bloodhounds, but they couldn't find a trace of him.

After almost a year she was done in. Then someone told her, why don't you ask some of the Indians, see if they might help you. The woman drove over to Rosebud and found a medicine man there and asked him if he could do her any good finding the boy, dead or alive.

EUREKA

The old man was afraid to try it, they say—you must be careful about finding lost persons, because sometimes the things in charge will demand another person to replace the found one. It is a delicate, Archimedean operation. He turned her down, but told her about another man over on Pine Ridge, over around Kyle.

So a few days later she drove over to Kyle and asked around for George Thunder and finally found him living on Medicine Root Creek some ten miles out of town.

This old man was a very traditional man. He knew all the old ways. He dressed in the old way, wore a cowboy hat and neckerchief and a six-shooter in a holster. A proud man with the look and loft of one whose grandfather had frozen to death in 1910 and whose distaff grandmother had starved to death along this very creek in the winter of 1921. A traditional man with ancient manners who clasped your hand each time you met: if you encountered him on a street a quarter hour after shaking hands with him outside the post office, you would shake hands again—a single, soft shake—and feel the better for it.

This man sat down and listened to the story and the stack of things behind it, and the timbre and tone of the woman's voice and the magpie chatter down by the creek, and finally agreed to try and help the woman find her boy. Dead or alive. He looked at the ground and told her, come down here next week. Bring along a couple of your good horses, and I will try to find out something.

So she did.

Meanwhile, word spread that George was going to put on a *yuwipi* to try and help the woman. Groups of relatives began straggling into his place and setting up camp near his little cabin. Soon there were several white wall tents standing and half a dozen old cars, with good wood smoke coming up from the stoves in the tents and people eating and visiting around. This might be something to see if George could find that boy through his medicine powers.

EUREKA

And then, on the right day, the woman and one of her brothers and some of their family drove in two spanking pickups with a horse trailer behind, with all kinds of food and presents for George and his kin. The woman stopped her pickup and asked this and that question of this and that person and finally knew where to park and they all got out of the trucks and waited.

As evening came on a ragged circle of people formed at a discreet distance around the lodge where George would conduct his *yuwipi* ceremony. George had been taking the sweat baths all week, getting ready. Now he came over to the woman and shook hands and looked for a long time at the two horses she had tied beside her trailer. Then he pointed at the big black one and said, tie that horse outside the *yuwipi* lodge.

Then, when it was full dark, he began. The woman and her family sat in chairs thirty yards from the lodge. The woman was chewing lots of Blackjack gum. The horse was tethered right in close by the lodge. When the songs started suddenly within, the horse jumped a little and strained on its rope, but not for long.

The woman watched, chewing her gum with a stop and start rhythm. After the first singing there was low talk from within the pitch-dark lodge, then more singing and drumming. Then George's helper lit a kerosene lantern and began to tie him: fingers and hands bound together with sinew strips; feet and legs together. Then he wrapped him in a big blanket and tied the blanket tight around his neck with a hide rope and wrapped him all the way down to his feet with the blanket and the rope. He was bundled up like a cocoon.

The helper lay him down carefully, blew out the lantern, and then the singers began again, loud and high. Now they were calling in the spirits from the night to help George find out about the boy. There were many songs and the sound of gourd rattles and muffled voices. The black horse stood at attention, ears up. The woman sat in her lawn chair and stared hard at the dark lodge and the nighthawks swooped by.

EUREKA

Two hours later the singing stopped and the lantern was lit and there was George, sitting calm and disheveled beside the folded blanket with all the sinew cords and the hide rope coiled neatly on top. It was all finished and soon the women came out from the wall tents with kettles of food and everyone ate.

Finally George sat with the woman and her brother and after a while told them what to do. They should drive back to her ranch, get up before daybreak and, just at dawn, they should turn the black horse loose. George would drive over to the ranch later in the morning. At high noon they would start out and trail the horse and see what developed. See what the horse had learned from the *yuwipi*.

The Thunder party arrived at the ranch at eleven the next morning, ate at her table. At noon they got in their pickup with one of the woman's nephews and started off on the black horse's trail.

They followed that horse thirty miles due north, up past Kadoka. Then the tracks cut west for a few miles and eventually dropped into some rough country with a stream running through it. When the party drove up to the lip overlooking those breaks, they stopped and got out. Down below they saw the black horse grazing near a grove of trees.

George and the others watched the horse silently for a moment. Then George turned to the nephew and said, "I think you better go and call the sheriff now."

George never took a dime for doing that *yuwipi*. The woman moved down here to this ranch a short time after. They found the boy's body right down in that grove where the horse was grazing.

Earl shifted to a higher-pitched, end-of-cycle chronicler's tone older than Sennacherib: "That was nineteen hundred and fifty-eight."

Then, at a landmark it would take weeks to master, he slowed and found the gate and crept back onto the sand road and into the slow sway and we all changed our positions slightly for the terrain and its roll. Autumn grasses rustled and swiped at the underside of the car.

EUREKA

We were quiet and sleepy by now; our toothpicks hung idle in our hands.

I was thinking lazy thoughts about the "Black Houdini" I had seen once on the sidewalk of New Orleans, an affable Jamaican man who "escaped" from a strapped-up cardboard refrigerator box eight or ten times a day for the tourists' coins—when there she was at the edge of the lights, the white heifer: cool and collected, she stared big-eyed for a split second, then she was up, birdlike, owllike, over the fence and gone.

EUREKA

BONESTEEL

The Bonesteel School occupies ten level acres of lower South Dakota, its half-dozen brick and stone buildings set among tall elms and proper oaks. Some passersthrough, driving down these 1930 streets, believe the tight-lipped Bonesteel name might be of Indian origin; in truth its Elizabethan echoes derive from an early immigrant family that paused, then drifted on to California. But the hundred girls in their dormitory and the hundred boys sleeping in theirs are Indians, full bloods to be sure. Poncas from Oklahoma, Crows from Montana, Arapahoes from Wyoming—they all sleep on this September morning. Their breathing is light, almost guarded. A girl coughs once from her bunk. In the boys' dormitory, light snoring comes from a large northern-Minnesota sixteen-year-old. In the predawn darkness, a slender Lakota boy's eyes roll gently in dream: a grandfather with a cane in an open, sage-ruffled field, watching a herd of spotted dream horses swirl knowingly around him.

The harsh bell and the brash ceiling lights smashed on at the same instant, a double-blast of reveille that made the boys recoil beneath their blankets. Some groaned and muttered as they rolled to sit upright on their bunks and rub their eyes before the dorm sergeant opened the door and shouted out what they already knew: it was six o'clock and time to get a move on.

When the boys had dressed and brushed their hair they filed down the stairways and into the long mess hall, where they formed two age-grouped lines on each side of the room and stood at semi-attention while the supervisor made his rounds inspecting their uniforms of denim pants and gray woolen jackets over white muslin shirts, checking with eager eyes for missing buttons or manure-caked shoes. When another bell rang out, they found their tables and sat down to hear the morning prayer. At a third, they began to eat their breakfast of thin gruel and weak bacon.

Leland Elk and Emerson Crane always sat together at their platoon table. They were from the same Lakota reservation in upper South Dakota, and although Leland at fourteen was two years older than the other boy, had known each other well enough up there to be solid friends in the Bonesteel world. The group at the table were talking baseball, the current pennant races at the end of the season, as they sipped their sweet coffee from heavy mugs. The supervisor ambled up beside the Lakota pals and gave them a puckish smile as he rested his hands on their shoulders. "You fellows are speaking English aren't you? That's good, that's good. Leland, you know you've got extra shoe-shine detail for talking Indian last week. You don't need to get into any more of that kind of trouble." The boys stopped chewing and stared at their plates until the man shuffled on to the next table, tinkling his many keys in his trouser pocket.

When the dismissal bell clanged, the students hurried off to their appointed duties, the hundred girls leaving their distaff side of the hall through one door, the hundred black-haired boys through another. Elk and Crane walked together down the steps from the porch and out across the square parade ground in the center of the school property, a perfectly square lawn with a flag pole in the middle and large oaks anchoring its corners. This is where the various drill teams performed their tricks on occasional Sunday afternoons, followed by a concert

BONESTEEL

from the school brass band. The lawn was bordered on its four sides by two dormitories, a small brick building of administrative offices, and the main three-story classroom building. The boys angled across the parade ground and out the far corner to the workshop area set slightly beyond the main quadrangle. As they entered the door they could see the ball diamond beckoning fifty yards away to their left.

In the sprawling workshop were sections devoted to teaching the boys trades, everything from harness-making to auto-engine repair, from the business side of agriculture to wagon-wheel construction and basic carpentry. Some of the boys studied accounting, over in the classroom building with the long-skirted girls. But Emerson and Leland worked in the carpentry section every morning for four hours, where they were instructed in the art of making stairways, building and sanding the dozens of wooden flights and loading them onto trucks for delivery to up-going houses in Sioux Falls or Omaha. The only thing they liked was the good smell of the newly cut wood.

"I wish I could send one of these to my grandfather so he could use it to get down to the riverbank," Leland whispered as they planed an edge. But he had a greater notion in his head.

"I want to do it now, Emerson. I want to get out of here right now. I can't take it anymore."

"I don't know," the twelve-year-old answered. "How would we ever get all the way to Standing Rock anyway?"

"We can catch some rides. We can walk some of the time. Sleep somewhere. We can get up there in a couple of days, I know we can."

"What are the teachers going to do? Maybe they'll chase after us. Maybe they'll call the sheriff."

"We can hide out when we have to," Leland answered. "We can hide in the trees along the roads. I want to do it now, tonight. I can't take this place anymore. I want to get home before it snows. Are you ready to do it?"

BONESTEEL

"I guess I am, if we don't get caught by the sheriff and put in jail."

"We'll lay low from the sheriff and the big boss. Listen now—we need to take some bread and soda crackers, some of that yellow cheese. Anything we can get from the supper table tonight. We'll see if Ella Wildcat can get us some extra rolls tonight when she brings our food to the table."

When the bell blurted in the mess hall, the boys left their places along the wall and made their ways to the same table, same chairs, and waited quietly for the servers. Leland and Emerson gazed at a slightly older, curry-combed boy at the end of the table who was sporting a fine red silk shirt. Leland interpreted for his friend:

"He's from Oklahoma. All those Osage boys have lots of money from the oil wells."

"I'd be afraid to ever wear a shirt like that. I'd get it all tore up the first time."

"You gotta walk sideways so you don't knock into things. You know those silk shirts are made out of worm threads. That's why they're so shiny."

The server brought in salvers of boiled beef and cornmeal mush and a dish of applesauce. One of the supervisors strolled along. "Don't put your knife in your mouth, Horace. This is Bonesteel School, not woolly Wyoming."

When Emerson and Leland walked back to the dormitory, the older boy whispered: "Just put a few things in your laundry bag. Take your jacket. I'm going to poke you to wake you up in the middle of the night. Don't holler when I do it."

About three o'clock in the morning, Leland nudged Emerson and crouched beside him while the boy slipped out of the blankets and pulled on his clothes. They tiptoed with their canvas bags across the

BONESTEEL

bunkroom and down a back stairway and out a little-used door. They followed the deeper shadows across the lawn, hurried behind the long workshop building and crossed the ball diamond.

"Stay off the infield, don't make any footprints on the dirt."

Emerson was awake enough by now to lift his left hand, which bore his fielder's glove, and mime catching a lazy line drive. On the far side of the moony diamond they crept into the trees lining a small creek and made their way off into the night, following the stream cover north to the edge of the town. After half an hour, they stopped in a dense cove of brush and saplings not far from the main highway, and lay down under their jackets to wait for daybreak.

Leland Elk woke up not long after sunrise. He reached over with a twig to poke Emerson gently in the ribs. They sat together quietly in the cove, rubbing their eyes and eating apples.

"I think we should only take a ride with a truck."

"What kind of a truck?" Emerson whispered.

"Any kind. That way we know it's not a school boss or a policeman."

So they readied their gear and crept out to the edge of the creek-bottom trees to a vantage where they could watch the oncoming traffic approach. Cars puttered by as the morning lightened. Finally, Leland saw a truck come lurching around the far bend. He nudged Emerson from a sleepy September reverie and when the truck drew nearer they stepped out from the trees and moved to the berm of the highway. It was a feed truck with a picture of a Jersey calf on the side, and it slowed down, then pulled to a stop just past the boys.

Leland warned his friend as they hurried to the truck: "Don't tell him anything. Just say we're going somewhere for a funeral."

The driver was drinking steaming coffee from a thick pint milk bottle as the boys climbed in. He wore a wide grin on his bristly ruddy face.

BONESTEEL

"I'm going over to Woonsocket, if that will help you out."
Leland tried to speak in a normal voice.

"Is that in South Dakota?"

"It sure is. It's about a hundred miles over there, I'd say."

"Okay."

The boys settled back in the dusty cab seats. They tried to look not-quite-awake and avoid conversation, but when the question came, Leland fielded it smoothly.

"We've got to get up north to go to a funeral."

The driver nodded and soon gave up on small talk out of a kind of drowsy sympathy. He turned on the radio and listened to the farm and market news, and they rolled along in silence for an hour.

Leland sat up when he saw a big bridge looming ahead and a railroad trestle beside it, and lots of trees stretching out in both directions. He was trying to think of a map.

"Where are we now?" he asked the trucker.

"We're just crossing the mighty Missouri."

"The Missouri River?" Leland groaned softly and nudged Emerson with an elbow.

They looked out all the windows, up and down the wide lazy stream and the thick timber along it. A few gulls sailed overhead and loafed on the sandbars. Leland made another barely audible groan.

"I think we better get out here. I think we better stop here for a while."

"Whatever you say, boys." The driver slowed when he got across the bridge and pulled over at the weedy grounds of an abandoned gas station.

"Are you gonna go fishing?"

"No—I just forgot something." The boys thanked him shyly and piled out of the cab.

Emerson looked at his friend.

"How come we got out here?"

BONESTEEL

"We're going the wrong way! We need to go back west and then go north. This part of the Missouri River is in the other direction."

It was a blow. They were both tired after a sleepless night.

"We better get down in the trees before somebody sees us."

They walked down behind the hulk of the gas station and into the riverside brush. They found a spot where they could see the stream eddying by, and sat down to rest.

"I'm going to eat some crackers," Emerson said. They sat there for a while and the river and the warm morning calmed them.

"I'm going to call you Woonsocket, Emerson. That's your name now. That sounds like an Indian name." Emerson moaned a light moan of dread.

They napped for half an hour to the cries of the river gulls. Then they discovered a water snake dozing on the bank and teased it with a long stick until it slipped angrily back into the water and coiled away.

"Maybe we should stay here tonight and start again in the morning. This is a good place to lay low. They won't look for us over here, this is the wrong way."

They threw stones in the river, trying to hit an old cottonwood snag jutting above the flow, then, just as the afternoon was weakening, decided to move farther away from the road to camp for the night. They walked gently downstream through the thickets and chokecherry stands, carrying their little sacks of socks and provisions, Emerson wearing his worn splay-fingered ball glove on his left hand.

When they broke headfirst through a hedge of cherry bushes and straightened up, they were met with a growl and a grunt from two tramps sitting in a trash-speckled clearing. One with a wild black beard turned and rose to one knee; the white-haired one snarled and stared, reaching out for his knotty cudgel.

The boys bolted in unison, circled sharply to their left around the cherry thicket and ran back the way they came, leaping and dodging like deer. When they returned to the bridge, Leland decided to cross

BONESTEEL

back to the west side of the river, and they dog-trotted across the span just as darkness was falling.

"It's better on the west side of the river anyway. There are more Indians on this side, all the way up north."

They dropped down the bridge abutment and scurried into a grove fifty yards from the highway.

"We better not make a fire. Those tramps might come after us."

So they sat in the dark and ate the hunk of yellow cheese Leland had in his sack. They could hear the Missouri gurgling a few feet away.

"How long will it take us to get to Standing Rock when we go the right way?" Emerson asked.

"I don't know. Maybe two days if we get some good rides. One day if someone was going all the way right up there."

Emerson listened to the river slapping.

"Maybe we could make a boat. Sail all the way to Standing Rock."

"We can't make a boat. The river's running in the wrong direction. If we went that way we'd probably end up in Washington or China or some place you never heard of."

"What are those tramps doing? Do they live over there all the time?"

"I guess they don't live anywhere. They just walk around. And hide from everybody . . . When we get home, I want to go fishing with my grandfather. He goes fishing all the time. He never eats any, but he likes to catch them and look at them, and sit by the river . . . I think I want to let my hair grow long again, too."

"What's that noise?"

"Some kind of a helldiver."

"What's a helldiver?"

"Some kind of a bird that lives in the water."

Emerson lay back on the ground.

"I guess we're going to just sleep here without any blankets again."

"Maybe you can stay awake all night, Woonsocket. Your name used

BONESTEEL

to be Crane—cranes are always standing up and looking all around. Maybe you could stand over there all night and watch for those tramps. Stand on one leg like a crane."

In the morning the boys sat eating the last of their yellow cheese, looking at the river. They agreed to wade in for a short splash in the cool water. They found a patch of wild plums along the bank, just ripe, and stopped to eat a handful as their hair dried in the sun. Emerson put on his ball glove and moved ten yards across a clearing and Leland lobbed him a good soft plum now and then.

Back at the highway, they waited discreetly in the edge of the trees, watching the spotty traffic come by. At last they saw a truck lumbering over the bridge and stepped forth to hold out their thumbs.

This was a flatbed truck loaded with pine boards. The driver looked so much like the one from the preceding day that Leland glanced at him twice. But this man's face was closely shaven, with a sharp razor cut on the chin line. He had tufts of white hair curling out of his ears and drank his coffee from a rusty tin cup. There was fiddle music on the radio and nobody said much as they drove west on Highway 18.

After thirty minutes Leland suddenly realized they would soon be passing back through Bonesteel and communicated that fact to Emerson with a soft telepathic nudge when the heavy-set town appeared on the horizon. As they approached the limits of the village, Leland mimicked a yawn, sliding down low in the seat, and Emerson did the same, turning his face away from the window and feigning sleep.

They rode with the man another hour, till they reached the intersection of Route 183, the big highway that would take them north toward Standing Rock country. They were back in Indian land now, and they soon got a short lift with a couple of Rosebud boys, and then another with a gasoline truck headed for Pierre. The driver was a friendly sort, and when he reached the little town of Presho he stopped

BONESTEEL

at a drive-in diner and bought the boys hamburgers and lemonade. They liked the man, and as they ate at a picnic table, Emerson asked him if he knew how the St. Louis Browns did yesterday. It was the first time in his twelve years he had posed a question to a white man.

"They lost again. They haven't been worth a hoot since Sisler left. The Cardinals are the team now. They'll take the pennant for sure."

They continued north in the rumbling fuel truck, on into the great expanse of the northern plains with the prairie grasses flickering in the wind. The truck was bound for a delivery in Fort Pierre, so the boys asked to be dropped off at the first good place on the edge of town, right at the bridge over what the driver said was the Bad River. They were far from Bonesteel now, but they took no chances, and slipped immediately down to river's edge and into the trees. Leland watched for traffic, but there was next to none on this highway heading off into the Dakota high-and-lonesome.

They loitered for a full hour, hoping a westbound truck would pass. The streamside willows above them were just fading to a lemony yellow. One of the old box elders had a festoon of orange bittersweet berries hanging from it. Emerson poked at it with a stick—

"Can we eat those things?"

Leland had a plan. He was sizing up a small farmhouse on a dirt road a half mile upstream. He told Emerson they should wait till just before dark and sneak down there to see if there was something to eat around the place. He thought he could make out a garden behind the house with old sweet-corn stalks still standing. And a short while later they had stowed their gear in a private cherry patch and were crouched behind a fence near the back end of the farm lot. They waited till the light faded a candlepower more, then dodged through the rickety fence wires and ran across to an old barn, then crept up to the garden plot. They strained their eyes to see what was left in the rows.

"There's nothing in here to eat," Emerson whispered.

BONESTEEL

"Wait—these are potatoes right here. We have to dig some up."

"How do you know there are potatoes down there?"

"I know what the plants look like. My grandfather used to dig potatoes on farms for money. I went with him sometimes."

Leland dug below the stems with his bare hands and unearthed four potatoes the size of baseballs and handed them to Emerson. He was crawling toward another hill when a dog began to bark up near the house.

"Let's go!"

They sprinted back behind the barn and off across the dusky field toward the river. The dog was coming after them, barking ferociously, as they hurdled the fence and hurried off into the darkening timber. Minutes later, they stopped to listen. The dog was quiet, must have returned to the house, and the boys went back to their campsite and built a small, low fire in the bottom of a pit and set their potatoes in around the edges.

Emerson had cut his leg on the barbed-wire fence. He washed off the wound with river water as they waited for the spuds to roast.

"Maybe we're not really camping along Bad River."

"Maybe it's the Not So Bad River," Leland offered.

"Why are white people's dogs so mean? Indian dogs aren't like that."

"He wasn't that mean or he would have chased us all the way back here and put us up a tree."

"Why are they like that?"

"They're mean because they think they own everything."

They sat eating their small potatoes like apples. A lazy late cricket chirped nearby.

"I wish I had some salt."

"I wish I had a Lucky Strike. I think I'm going to start smoking when we get up there," Leland mused. "I want to go up to Canada with my grandfather when we get home. He goes up there every fall, to the Stoney reserve. Sometimes they shoot an elk. That's real good meat. Maybe you can go with us, Woonsocket. They have lots of pretty girls up there, too . . ."

"Gritty purls, gritty purls . . ." A train whistle keened and drawled from across the road to the east.

"You better stay awake all night again. Stand on one leg, make sure that Bad River doesn't try anything."

From your armchair you will need to rise in the mind's eye a good ways until those rivers and streams—the Bad among them—take their form and their theater as the early sun strikes them, come clear, moving eastward across the rolling Dakota grasslands to close in their own sweet time on the upper Missouri, the elegant, spidery ladder of them, the balletic lightness of the mandala from up here, hundreds of miles within view, autumn russets and golds showing the way: White River, Good River and Bad, the Moreau and the Grand to the near north, and their capillaries from the higher ground, Willow Creek, Plum and Cherry, Broken Neck and Stranger creeks, Rock and Oak, buteos and swallows in the coiling air, all moving in ocher-crimson September consensus to join, at their leisure, the big Missouri.

"*Woonsocket!* Come on! The sun's up!"

The boys washed their faces in the Bad River shallows as a kingfisher watched from a cottonwood limb.

"One of my old great grandfathers was named Kingfisher."

"Why?"

"I don't know. Maybe he liked to jump in the water."

Then they moved closer to the highway to wait for a vehicle.

"We could be home tonight if we got a good ride."

But traffic was nil. They played a quarter hour of stickball with an ash switch and bits of gravel.

BONESTEEL

"There's nobody driving on this road."

Finally they flagged down a southbound bakery truck, and happily bought four plump jelly-filled donuts.

"I wish he was going up north. We could ride in that truck all day and eat donuts."

"We're going too slow," Leland said. A swayback freight train was rolling along the tracks beyond the highway. "Maybe we should try to catch a ride on a train going that way."

They watched the big rusty cars sashay and creak a hundred yards away.

"Where do they go?" Emerson wondered.

"They're going north. Maybe up to Bismarck. Or Canada . . . We'd have to watch out the door to see when we got to Standing Rock. We'd have to jump off while it's moving."

So they walked over and crossed the highway and climbed up and over the rails and sat in a sumac grove to wait for another train. Emerson lay down in the sun and almost fell asleep.

"I hope that wasn't the only train for the whole week . . ."

But an hour later they heard a train whistle to the south. Leland roused his friend and they tied up their canvas bags tightly at the necks.

"We're going to have to run fast to get even with the train before we grab onto it. Throw your bag up onto a shelf and then get a hold of the handles on the door."

They could see the locomotive now, easing into sight and straightening out. It blew its whistle again, and Emerson thought of the warm potatoes he was eating last night by the fire. The boys crouched low behind a bush as the engine rumbled by, waited another moment, then Leland started up—

"Come on! Follow me now! *Hoka!*"

They took off after an empty boxcar. It wasn't a howling-fast train,

BONESTEEL

but it was faster than it looked. Emerson had to push himself to keep up. He saw Leland toss his bag into the open boxcar door and reach up to grasp the handle. Leland jumped, got one leg up on the car. Emerson saw him twist and yell, and then drop with his arms flailing in and under the hard raw noise of the train. Emerson fell to his knees, and saw, and screamed the first real scream of his life.

A farm woman in her backyard between the highway and the tracks heard him. She hollered for her husband and they hurried up the railway grade to see what the matter was. The woman in her apron stayed with Emerson as he knelt on his torn knees in the right-of-way gravel, while her husband ran back to the little yellow house to call the sheriff.

The ambulance took Leland to the hospital even though everyone knew he was lifeless. The farm woman volunteered to accompany Emerson to the sheriff's office while the current of events was unbraided. She fixed the boy warm tea and a ham sandwich in the hotplate commissary, as he sat in near shock staring at the floor, slowly telling the tale as a deputy took it down.

When official word from the hospital came back, Bonesteel School was telephoned. The superintendent was out of town; his flustered secretary took the call and then the details.

"Give me the names once more. Which is the last name?"

Emerson heard the deputy in the adjoining room.

"Elk and Crane. Elk: e-l-k. And Crane: c-r-a-n-e. Emerson and Leland . . . We will keep them here and proceed with the arrangements. You will notify the families . . . ?"

The secretary at Bonesteel checked the student registry and called Western Union to send a wire to the Standing Rock agency office. Elk and Crane. Please notify parents. Mortuary in possession of decedent. Plans pending. Need clearance for release. Leland, Emerson. Crane and Elk . . .

BONESTEEL

An hour later, the agent and his subaltern drove in their green coupe out the highway a dozen miles, then back a rutted dirt road to the Crane family home with dogs sleeping around it, and then on east, over near the river, to the Elk residence at the edge of a tiny stream called Clubfoot Creek, and, as magpies squalled outside the windows, they delivered the terrible news.

The following afternoon a small crowd gathered at the Standing Rock train depot. Wagons and horses were hitched at the edge of the parking lot. The elders of the Crane and Elk families stood in front—parents, grandparents, uncles and aunts—the men standing formally erect in black suit coats and black vests over their linen shirts with kerchiefs knotted at their necks, the older ones with slight braids hanging down from their Stetsons. Some of the women wore shawls or blankets over long dark dresses. Behind these granite-faced people, friends and farther relations stood in stiff unison, somber and intent. They were awaiting the train from the south bearing the casket. Just to one side, the reservation agent waited with his subaltern, hats in hands.

Finally the engine appeared, huffing slowly and drifting into the little station yard, as the people shifted their weight from one foot to the other. In a few moments a door opened and the conductor stepped down and stood to the side. Then three men eased the wooden casket out the door and paused on the platform. A few seconds after, a matron for the railway company came down the steps, leading her thin charge, Emerson, his eyes lowered, by the hand.

A sharp clap of a cry went up from the crowd, a single muffled groan like a sudden roar from a distant stadium. The agent was trying to button his tweed suit jacket, turned to his aide: "What is it?!"

"Good God. It's the wrong boy. We took the wrong boy for dead!"

The crowd stiffened and stirred. A woman keened, hands covered mouths as the meaning, the butcher-knife twist of it, came clear.

BONESTEEL

Emerson's parents hurried to embrace him. Leland's family sank together in disbelief. The agent walked over to them with his hand on his heart and his mouth hanging open.

Now it's the day after. Two wagons with their sleepy teams and an old Ford are waiting in front of the Elk home on the left bank of Clubfoot Creek. Emerson Crane, speechless, and his parents are there with the numbstruck family, and a local minister has come by to offer a long, clay-footed prayer. The family sits in dejection in the scantily furnished house. Cold food wastes on the table.

When the Crane people leave and climb into their wagon and the minister drives off in his dusty car, the grandfather, the old man of Leland's occasional dreams, retrieves his diamond-willow cane from a corner and leaves the house. He walks with a no-hurry, slightly gimpy gait, out across the backyard in heavy felt house slippers to the creekside, then follows the stream down to the edge of the grassy bluffs overlooking the big Missouri. He hobbles along the bluffs a hundred yards, two hundred yards, to the rusty shell of a pickup truck. It was abandoned there, just over the lip of the knoll, with its engine charred and an empty whiskey bottle on the floor, by unknowns ten years before, and soon settled deep into the local soil. Chokecherry saplings sprout up through the shattered rear window.

The grandfather raps on the sprung door with his cane to alert any napping snakes, climbs stiffly into the driver's seat and slowly shifts himself into a bearable position, leans back with a low moan and removes his misshapen straw Stetson. He has come to this place before and sat in the seat once or twice when he needed to, but not for a long time. It was like a cockpit for a certain kind of day.

There is an old Lakota word hiding somewhere, hiding in the trees and nodding grasses, that the man tries to recall for a moment—a long, bumpy word that holds both all-the-trouble-in-the-world and all-the-fine-spring-days twirling together and dancing like a pretty dust devil

BONESTEEL

across the prairie. But the word won't come. Not yet. He lights a crooked Lucky Strike and looks off to wait with tears on his face, off across the wide Missouri bottoms and the rolling uplands to the east, with their yellowing willows and raw-orange skunk brush on the slopes. A few horses graze and doze. A large dark bird, an eagle or a vulture, soars above the river, tilts, tacks, catches a friendly thermal and rides away.

BONESTEEL

THE NOMAD FLUTE

The fan belt broke at so gifted a place it would have been heartless to complain. The ash trees in the coulee heads were pulsing golden and when I pushed my car off onto the shoulder and climbed to a knoll near the fence line, I could see the processional bottomland trees of the Missouri River not so far ahead. I hoped there would be a phone there at the crossing because I hadn't passed a ranch house for many miles to the south.

I locked up and began to walk the dirt road toward the river. It was a bright end-of-October afternoon and the slight steady descent to the great Missouri was a pleasure in itself—better to walk it than drive it, after all. In half an hour I had topped the last of the river-edge hills and looked down on the Missouri itself, low-water but eminently respectable as she eased through the sagebrush flats.

Below, where the road struck her, I saw a ferry outfit, and beyond, on the far shore, a ranch house and buildings where the ferry keepers no doubt lived. A thrifty little spread with cattle grazing on the uplands and turkeys creeping through the river brush. Ferry operators would have to have a telephone, I thought as I started down the hill.

The ferry was a simple board-bottomed flatbed with a good-sized outboard engine built into it, the whole thing buttoned to a thick cable stretched across the flow between two pole-and-concrete bastions. The craft was just lowering its snout to meet the gravel bank and set down a large Jeep full of hunters and a pinto setter. When they were on their way I spoke to the helmsman and he said to come on over to the house and I could call up to Havre.

We ferried across in a cloud of engine fume, a ride of maybe one full minute. The ferry tender was a tall ruddy man, quiet and easy; when he lifted his Stetson to wipe his brow I saw the sharp line across his forehead where the sun-red broke off. The interior of the house was well-cool and still and, one felt immediately, under sure choreographic control. The woman of the house was there, waiting. She too was tall, but far from ruddy. Large and handsome, she struck me as someone I had seen in some semipublic place, and I thought of a photo on an album of piano music or a book jacket—she had that sort of carriage and posable poise.

They were both calm and cordial. I placed a call to Havre for the auto-parts store and soon learned I couldn't get the proper fan belt until, most likely, Monday; it had to come in from Great Falls and then be driven down to the ferry. The couple seemed pleased to offer their accommodations for the weekend. They stood there shoulder to shoulder, smiling. This was Friday afternoon. There was no real alternative, so I resigned myself to a close view of the upper Missouri for a couple of days.

The man called out the back door and soon a boy of ten strolled in, a serious dusty lad with a straw cowboy hat in hand and a red sun-line of his own across his brow. He shook hands with me and took me outside and across the road to a long three-part garage where he cranked up an old Chevy pickup. He sat on a tattered chair cushion in order to see over the dash. His father ferried us across and we drove back to my car. The boy was amiable, but oddly businesslike. He exuded preoccupation with some important, perplexing problem that kept him scowling mildly at the skyline even while we made small conversation.

We towed my little Japanese station wagon slowly back to the landing and parked it off to one side. The boy looked over the car as though

THE NOMAD FLUTE

he were studying a stud horse for soft spots, and he seemed to find it a bit weak through the withers. I grabbed my suitcase and a pair of good books and carried them over to the house, made two phone calls and went back to my bedroom. I had spent the preceding two nights in the back of my car and was ready for an hour's nap.

When I rejoined my hosts there was, I thought, a bustle in the air that was almost festive, that didn't feel quite everyday for the tone and drape of the house and its many basking violets. The woman was busy in the kitchen but she took a moment to show me the large wandering house. It was all very simple and down-to-earth, but directed in a delicate way that was admirable and cozy. She then sent me off with the boy to see his arrowhead collection. His room seemed sober and bare for a young lad. A neat row of boots and shoes along one wall; a .22 rifle leaning in a corner; a red leather Bible on the bedstand. With the trace of knit in his brow, he showed me a pair of rusty muleshoes he found at a nineteenth-century trail ford up the river.

I stepped out into the yard to smoke and check out the setup of the ranch. The north-south road—the only real road crossing the river for forty miles in either direction—ran between the house and most of the ranch buildings. On the far side of it I saw a large barn and then a smaller one with a pair of sheds at its side and then the long garage. To the left of the barns in a small fenced-off area stood a cottage-like dwelling with its windows open and pale curtains blowing in the breeze.

On the near side of the road behind the house lay a sizable garden and several beds of cutting flowers hamstrung and singed by a recent frost. On the north side stood another white shed and the entrance to a fruit cellar and great piles of friendly ranch junk waiting on call. At the far end of the truck patch was a chicken coop and then fruit trees in staggered rows that stood out sharply against the dense rusty-green of the cedar shelterbelt where turkeys trotted after late grasshoppers in the ragged grass. It all fit neatly into the narrow valley. Above the

THE NOMAD FLUTE

shed roof the low, worn river bluffs rose quickly and took their place against a blue fall sky.

We sat down to dinner at six o'clock—the hosts, the boy with his hair wet and combed, and myself, when suddenly a young woman I hadn't seen before joined us. There was a salver of fried ham and roast potatoes and baked yellow onions and applesauce and a dish of last-of-the-garden. The woman told me they used to have a good many guests at the house; they actually boarded an occasional hunter or party of canoeists descending the river. So they were used to newcomers at table and rather missed the visitors. She had her black hair pinned up with a barrette. She talked well, floating a bright, three-dimensional conversation. Her husband was quiet corroborator, smiling and nodding. The boy looked off at whatnot while he chewed. The young woman was silent. She must have been twenty-five, cast in a thick, insular morph that radiated both isolate vigor and mysterious inner doings.

The ranchwoman filled me in on things in general. They had a married daughter in Missoula, in addition to the boy—he broke his reverie briefly to send me a twitch of a grin. We soon discovered that we shared a common origin, the woman and I, back in Ohio, and in a few moments had narrowed it down to a startling degree. She had been raised in a town of 15,000 just half an hour from my native village. Within the stroke of three sentences we were each poised with our forks halfway to our mouths—she knew my hometown rather well, had had a good friend there and had visited frequently. I knew the family of her friend in a general way, knew their house, not far from my parents. There was a moment of simple disbelief and childlike suspicion before accepting the coincidence and releasing the frank glint of mutual wonder and connection in the eyes. The husband chortled and the boy looked up.

The woman had left Ohio in 1949, moved to Wyoming shortly after high school to stay with relatives. There she had met and married—the man nods slowly, yes, by Johnny, he was there. They then came to

THE NOMAD FLUTE

the upper Missouri country in Montana and ranched not far from their present home. They took over the ferry operation (it was one of a handful of state-subsidized ferries in the bridgeless remote of the outback) when the husband injured his back. They still ran a few white-faced cattle along the river. They sometimes chafed at being tied down by the ferry from April to October, but on the other hand, as the woman put it, it was "more social than pure ranching."

We talked for two hours after dinner. Now we had connection, and when I lay in bed that night I found myself thinking of the quiet residential block in my hometown that the woman knew so well forty years ago. I conjured it as I dozed off, the very block of small white houses with titmice in their trees . . .

*

The next morning after breakfast I walked out and down to the ferry landing. Traffic was heavier than usual, they said, with the bird hunters coming and going to and from the public lands, loads of men from Billings or Denver with dog cages and cases of dark rum in their campers. One group got out of their truck to pose for a photo on the ferry barge before heading south.

I wandered back away from the river toward the barns. I glimpsed the strange girl going into the garage, but when I passed the open bay doors she had disappeared. I walked around the small barn and the cattle lot behind it and then passed the little cottage bunkhouse. There was an old man sitting in the yard oiling his work boots and I stopped to say hello, eventually sidling in through the weak wire gate to his yard. His name was Harold Soldier and he worked for the ranch doing anything that needed doing. He was familiar with the western Montana town I lived in, had been there once or twice for basketball tournaments when local teams made the grade. We smoked and chatted and watched squadrons of ducks fly up and down the river. There was a small garden patch browning in a corner of his yard and when I left

THE NOMAD FLUTE

he invited me to take one of the pale softball-size watermelons lying there—"But if it kills you, don't blame me."

At lunch—the woman made me a tiny, photogenic tuna sandwich —my hosts told me about Harold. They had known him for more than thirty years. He was a Gros Ventre man from up around Hays and could fix about anything broken on earth. He was in the army at the tail end of World War II and a year or so after it was all over he brought back a wife to Montana: a Belgian brunette whom everyone said was a gypsy. The ranchwoman remembered her but hadn't known her long. Harold and his pretty gypsy wife settled into their new life working at a far-flung ranch way up on Cow Creek. The girl didn't quite know what to make of it, but once curtains were up and Harold rigged a phonograph for her to play her Django Reinhardt records she made it OK for a while. Her accent soon became famous around the territory and all the Indian veterans of the European theater made a point to stop and say hello and talk of places in the war. She worked hard at everything, cooked and washed and ran a stringy flock of chickens. Carried endless water and fought the 'hoppers, but the Django bop eventually thinned on the wind and it was just too much for her. She disappeared one day after three years. Nobody could figure it out—she was clear of eye and strong of teeth and she seemed to care a great deal for Harold.

And Harold Soldier, poor man, was completely baffled. He felt no malice whatsoever and what pain there was came forth as a strenuous effort to comprehend and explain this almost preternatural severance. During half a year he would shake his head slowly, looking at the dry earth, and ponder it and tell the ranchwoman how much his wife wanted to speak French again; she missed it badly and often chattered in it to herself, and Harold proffered the theory, born of some late cloud-mooned night, that she had run off to Canada for that very and noble purpose.

A few years later Harold moved down here and went to work full time. "He'll be here tomorrow for Sunday dinner," the woman said.

THE NOMAD FLUTE

"He eats with us every Sunday. He's welcome all the time, but that's the way he wants it."

That evening the ranch couple and I sat down for a drink before dinner. The woman was spruced up in a nice dress, strong and calm and quite beautiful. After a while she said, "I can show you something from back home," and left the table to fetch a dulcimer and set it on the low table before her. It was a crusty old thing that had been in her family a good while, she told me, having been carried over the mountains to Ohio from eastern Pennsylvania. She teased it a little and finally broke into a halting pretty tune that clanged and bonged about the halls and crannies of the house. The husband smiled good-naturedly at the odd sound in his ear. The music was anachronistic and lovely in the late-afternoon stillness. When she finished I said I could almost smell the honeysuckle and I think she knew what I meant.

The strange girl was back for dinner, suddenly there standing behind her chair. She was spruced up a bit too and the puzzling time-lag sensation was stronger than ever. Her hair was plaited and coiled on her head. Her eyes were a serious midsummer blue beneath dark thick brows. Her nose was slightly upturned, with frank functional nostrils. The cheekbones were high and Slavic and she bore faint, downy, Idaho-shaped muttonchops to her jaw. She stood, gazing away, with a composed vacancy. Her other-century look was accentuated by an odd assemblage of clothing of timeless cut and grade: neat, clean, but somehow out of kilter, "Albanian," and then seamed stockings and blocky heavy-heeled patent shoes. She responded when spoken to during the meal, but the dense magnetic field was never broken.

I retired to my room early and lay down with my window up. *A German Idyll* by H. E. Bates. Later, just before sleep, I heard a party blow their horn for the ferry and minutes later the muffled clank and bustle of the engine as it crossed to pick them up.

Sunday morning the boy was assigned to drive me out to see old tipi rings on the bluffs three miles downstream. We took his pickup as

THE NOMAD FLUTE

usual. He had opened enough in my presence by now to sniff a rudimentary laugh when I made a joke or crossed my eyes at him during meals. He maneuvered the truck along a rough track and finally pulled up at a level knoll and parked amid a dozen tipi rings of pale stones like fairy-ring mushrooms melting in the grass. It commanded a fine view of the valley and we spooked two whitetails from the brush below.

Later I took another smoking stroll around the ranch grounds, thinking to walk up the road a ways. As I passed the small barn I saw the girl duck into its doors with her arms full of something and I decided to follow. I was curious to speak with her alone, to see what she was like on her own. I turned into the barn within a single minute after she had entered, but she was nowhere to be seen. It was obvious after a glance around the place that she had seen me coming and had either fled or was hiding, perhaps watching from a mow, so I walked out and on across the yard.

Old Harold was in his chair again so I stopped for a chat. I sat on his steps while we listened to his portable radio bringing in weekend football scores from across the nation. Harold annotated an occasional town or region when it struck him: The Bluffton score reminded him of a Mennonite conference he attended there long ago and the Kansas score he associated with a great niece who studied nursing there. And in Philadelphia he had once spent a few carefully inlaid days unwinding from boot camp. At one point the boy drove by and gave us a businesslike nod. Harold said, "That boy ought to go to a picture show."

Eventually we walked over to the house together for Sunday dinner. They ate that meal in midafternoon, the way I like it. The strange girl was absent and I took the opportunity to ask about her, casually, but the woman simply said, "She needed a place to live." The woman wore a slim peach dress for the Sabbath and again there was that pedigreed something in her pointed aplomb and her tossed-back head. Harold and I demolished the better part of a huge beef-and-turnip pie and a deep plum cobbler.

THE NOMAD FLUTE

The lady was feeding waxwings, a flock of Bohemians that showed up on a quick north wind a week ago, and after dinner and our separate ways I slipped into my room and poured a jigger of whiskey from my flask and sat alone in front of the bay window for half an hour watching the beautiful birds feeding on raisins in the yard. One group would flutter down from the tree to feed for a moment on the ground, to be replaced, gently, by another in a near-constant flurry both gregarious and civilized. They were located on the west side of the house and caught the five o'clock sun—svelte, immaculate birds down from Jasper or Lake Louise, dropping from the trees soft as ash, gorgeously detailed and perfectly painted, all the fine points radiantly and lovingly *there* . . .

Late that night I was awakened by a faint door slamming and had a silly inadvertent vision of the boy in plaid pajamas slipping along the hall and into the strange girl's room, and then the sleep-hazy conclusion: "So that's what they've got on their minds."

The next morning everyone was busy with Monday business. I gathered my things and by half past ten the service-station man was there with my fan belt. I said goodbye to Harold—he was meticulously coiling friendly old scrap wire—and walked to the ferry to say goodbye to the man. I offered him money for my board. He refused a cent, but then said, in an afterthought way as I turned, that he could use an old-time number-seven iron bean kettle if ever I ran across one.

I found the woman in the west yard broadcasting raisins for the birds and we had a warm goodbye that brought the humble coincidental glint back to our eyes. I said I would stop again when out that way and I drove slowly off through the grounds thinking how much better it all was than a simple bridge over the river. The girl with Albanian muttonchops was elsewhere as usual. The boy was backing a tractor out of its bay as I passed and he responded to my honk with a matter-of-fact index-finger salute and a quick spit over the rear tire.

*

THE NOMAD FLUTE

The following spring I traveled east for Easter with my family. It was a cool bright Sunday wet around the ears and the village maples were vivid with red blossoms showing like mulberries against bare branches and leafless blue sky.

There were relatives about, the small house was a-jostle with several persons too many, squeezing by one another in the short hallway and taking turns at the loo. For the midday meal we had a ten-pound fresh ham grazed with garlic and basted with stale beer. When we all gathered around the long drop-leaf table my father bowed his head abruptly and set his face, closed-eyed, for the paschal grace.

"Dear Father in heaven, we thank you for the blessings of this day and the promise of this season. We thank you for health and good food upon our table. For family and loved ones to share this holy time. Help us to make the most of our opportunities and to appreciate the beauties of this life and grant us the strength to do thy will. We ask it in Jesus' name. Amen."

Then he rose and put the "Russian Easter Overture" on the record player and set to carving the chestnut-colored pork. Throughout dinner he clowned for the cousinage and razzed his younger brother with shadowy references to chasing country girls through summer dusks sixty years before. Every quarter hour, as the wine went round, he broke into a bar or two of "Roaming in the Gloaming" and grinned mischievously at my uncle, who shook his head with a blank helpless look and the entire table tittered and stirred.

After the meal a few of us adjourned to the side yard to take in the afternoon. My mother and I ended up alone in the wooden swing sipping California brandy. From the small yard partially enclosed by young elms and catalpa trees with wild grapevines hanging from them, we overlooked the back lawn with its fierce new green and its kitchen garden half-spaded where robins hopped, and beyond, the dull red-brick buildings of the village square. Jonquils were on the verge of blooming and a single yellow tulip raised its head.

THE NOMAD FLUTE

We talked a little, but mostly we listened to the new April goings-on, the various robins caroling about the neighborhood and titmice whistling high in the trees. I could hear three cardinals (a bird I never heard in the West) in full song, calling from three different directions and planes. I placed them instinctively in trees of yards I knew from long ago: the far one, two blocks off, beside the house the Groves girls lived in twenty-five years back; another over by the one-time Ronda Rathburn home on Vine Street; and the third straight south, in the maples showing their uppers just above the community library.

The latter treetops struck me, when I looked off that way, hit me with it all again: they stood along the muddy block the woman at the ferry had spoken of, and I told my mother again how strange the meeting had been, how casually it surfaced and jelled.

"She is a beautiful woman," I said.

"She always was a beautiful girl," Mother said. "I remember her. I met her at the Harveys' once or twice. She came from a very good family."

After a moment of shooing away an early insect, she picked it up again. "She left in kind of a hurry," she said, giving me a look I knew well, a quick, dramatized scowl-grimace with an eye roll worked in, conveying deep commiseration with just a trace of censure.

My eyebrows rose spontaneously. Just then my father called from the window above us announcing that he was about to play his time-worn "Crepitation Contest" record for the cousinage and inviting us inside.

"I think we'll pass this year," I said, and when our proper silence was restored my mother filled me in in a low, slow voice.

"It wasn't too long after the war." The girl was a banker's daughter over in Martin. She had just begun college at a hoity school nearby. She was going strong with a prominent Methodist preacher's son. One October night—I was already picking up a strong imago of 1949: smoky autumn light on the mothball fleets, Miles Davis doing "Godchild"—

THE NOMAD FLUTE

78

one October night her parents and some of their tuxedoed friends came home from a social outing and found her with the boyfriend in his car, parked in the driveway with the motor running. Carbon monoxide had got them. They hadn't a stitch on when they pulled them out. The girl was unconscious. The boy turned out to be dead.

One of my cousins came striding around the corner of the house, still grinning from Round One of the crepitation contest. He wore a jaunty yellow boutonnière and carried the brandy bottle mock-hidden inside his suit coat. He always had the finest timing in the family. We laughed and held out our glasses saying, "Yes, I do believe I will."

THE NOMAD FLUTE

NEAR MICHAELMAS

Two men stand in a village park one hot September. They stand quietly, tall and slender, side by side with their heads down and hands clasped behind their rumps, in the cool spray of a lawn sprinkler. Flocks of shiny grackles feed methodically on the light-green manicured grass nearby.

A police car has slowly circled the park and now pulls up near the men. Two officers climb out and amble across the lawn. When the wet men see the policemen coming they step softly out from the hose spray and into the shade of a hackberry tree.

"Good afternoon, gentlemen," one of the officers says. The two wet men grunt politely, nodding.

"We're looking for a dog," the other cop says. "An Irish setter. A red dog. Have you boys seen anything like that?"

The two men shake their heads quickly.

"OK," says the cop. "The way it is, the owner of the dog saw a man with a red shirt on fooling around with her dog just before it came up missing. We noticed you're wearing a red shirt. That's all." He nods toward one of the men.

"Yes," says the man. No more.

"Do you boys live around here?" asks the officer.

"Yes," they both answer. Then one says softly, "Red Shirt." The other says, "Lost Dog."

The policeman nods and glances at his cohort. The two wet men are obviously stone sober; their English is a little weak, that's all.

"OK," says the cop. "This woman who owns the animal, she thought maybe someone walked off with her pet . . . So you haven't seen a red setter dog running around then?"

One of the wet men looks up, points at his friend and says, "Lost Dog."

The officer chuckles and glances at his cohort again.

The cohort speaks up. "Where have you boys been this morning?"

One wet man says, "We just came into town this morning."

"From the reservation?"

One man says, very softly and politely, "Red Shirt." The other, "Lost Dog."

Both cops grin, lift their caps and run their fingers through their hair. One of them steps back and gazes at the red-shirted wet man.

"Well, I guess there's likely to be six or eight fellows walking around in a red shirt on a Saturday morning."

The wet man in a plaid shirt yanks his thumb at his own chest and says quietly: "Red Shirt."

The cops laugh.

The wet man in the red shirt touches his hand to his own belly: "Lost Dog."

The cops laugh again. They think the game is getting good, whatever it is. Then the wet men laugh a little, getting into the spirit of the thing, looking back and forth quickly from cop to cop.

One of the wet men, still laughing lightly, asks the policeman for a cigarette. The officer pulls out his pack and gives the two men smokes and lights them with his lighter. As he puts his cigarettes back in his uniform pocket he asks, as if he had almost forgotten, "Where are you boys planning to spend the night?"

The two men nod together, saying at once: "Red Shirt/Lost Dog."

The policemen stand and look at them. Finally one of the cops slaps

NEAR MICHAELMAS

his hands together, turning and glancing about the park. "Well, screw it—let's go scout around a little more." They say goodbye to the two men and walk back to the patrol car.

They felt good, friendly, relaxed. Cosmopolitan even. Their verbal assets had been subtly frozen; autumn seemed imminent even through the strong late heat.

NEAR MICHAELMAS

THE END OF JOHN SADDLE

John Saddle had been having bad luck for a while now. It began when he was booted from the town of Flicker. For years since the Second World War there was a tent and shanty Indian camp on the north edge of Flicker. It stood in a broad grassy field just beyond the stockyards. Lots of people came down from South Dakota to shop in the Flicker stores, and when they came in those days they usually set up tents and stayed to enjoy themselves for a time. There were fifteen or twenty tents that liked it there well enough they became permanent citizens. John Saddle was one of these. He lived four years down there and nearly called it home.

Then one summer the community leaders of Flicker decided the tent town was getting out of hand. It was a bit larger each spring, they noticed, and there were more and more idle shantytowners killing long sultry days on the street corners. So one afternoon a group of businessmen collected a dozen moribund cars donated by the Flicker auto dealers and drove them out to the tent camp and told the people they could have the cars for their own if they packed up and drove them straight north to South Dakota and didn't return. All but one of those worn-out cars made it back to the reservation and even ran for a week or two thereafter. The one that guttered out on the Slim Butte road was John Saddle's; he had to unpack his belongings and pile them on top of the old Chevy just behind. And so he lost his Flicker home and his new vehicle in one midsummer swoop.

Back in South Dakota John moved into an empty cabin in the hamlet known as Number 9. Local jokesters called it Sioux City. It was a decent muddy little village out of the way of things, with deer heads tossed on the roofs to weather away. John lived there a full year and made it OK, but his luck, to his mind, never got any better. He sat there in Number 9, eating light but never complaining, and then one day he died, rolled off the old kitchen chair in front of his cabin, where a neighbor girl saw him and ran for help.

They carried John Saddle down the dirt street to the community hall and into a small back room and laid him out on a cafeteria table. In a few minutes the village medic arrived and soon the neighborhood priest. They looked John over and listened to his chest and then straightened up and pronounced him dead. The medic went off to call a physician to certify the event and the priest conscripted two Christian women from Number 9 and sent them to bathe the corpse and prepare it for eventual burial. The women undressed John and put his clothing in a plastic bag and covered him with a U.S. government sheet.

They gathered their towels and basins and returned to the little room with a bucket of hot water. They were speculating whether the water was too hot to be used on a corpse and wondering if it mattered at all, when they opened the door—and, lo, there sat John on the edge of the table with a sleepy look on his face, idly scratching his lower back. The women hollered and one scurried for the priest, and soon people from the community-hall offices were coming back to peek in the half-open door. The priest trotted in and whispered with John, asking him a question or two he couldn't answer, and insisted he sit still with the sheet and a green army blanket around him.

In half an hour the doctor drove in from a nearby town. He listened, scowling thoughtfully with his chin in one hand, to the story of John's

THE END OF JOHN SADDLE

revivification and examined him thoroughly, then pronounced him fit and functioning normally. The people in the hallway looked at each other wide-eyed. The doctor and the priest conferred briefly in a far corner. John put his clothes on and thanked everyone in the room. He stopped by the coffeemaker in the front office and drank a quick black cup, then walked slowly outside and down the street to his cabin, with everyone in Number 9 watching secretly from their windows.

John stayed inside for two days, sleeping and gathering strength, before he walked back into town and down the street to check his mail at the post office. It didn't take long for him to see that things had changed since his unorthodox solo flight. People avoided him in the town, crossed the street hurriedly to escape his path. He felt the sudden irrational sour of the social-caustic that first hour out and knew that his polestar had changed, and all the world with it.

John was viewed by his townmates with a virulent form of the suspicion provincials hold for widely traveled neighbors. He was, since his one-hour ellipsis, considered foreign, spooked, and even touched. Always a minimally social man, as his image curdled in the eyes of Number 9, there was no net to hold him. Months passed and John's outcast life fell into a lazy neglect. He conversed with no one, hardly even the postmistress when he stopped there. He began to frequent the garbage cans behind the community hall in search of scraps. He became the shepherd of stray dogs; half a year after his false death he had eight mongrels living with him and every new moon seemed to bring another. His one social occasion was a visit to an old man he had known all his life. Once a month John walked four miles to his friend's rural home and the two of them would adjourn to a sagging engineless Oldsmobile parked off behind the house. There they could sit in peace, away from the grandchildren, and talk a bit for half an hour.

It wasn't much of a life, John knew, but it meandered on, off-key but steady, for two years, and he had almost come to accept it as normal, when one summer day the sheriff and a deputy drove up and an-

THE END OF JOHN SADDLE

nounced that there was a rabies scare in the county and John would have to give up his dogs. They herded them, all sixteen of them, into a paddy wagon and drove them off somewhere to shoot them in a gully. The whole episode reminded John again of his rotgut luck.

Now, without his fawning watchful dogs, John cared for nothing much. He decided to give up his cabin in Number 9 and move into a half shack on a hill across the creek, where he would be less bothered by his fortune and its social stigma. He put up his old wall tent from the shantytown days and lugged his few possessions up there and put his kitchen chair in the shadow of the tent. There were a few scraggly wild plum trees at the edge of the hill and a blanched tailing of household trash from previous tenants trickled down toward the creek. There were a hundred small marrowbones and a thousand bottle caps trampled into the dirt of the yard.

John sat there all alone every day with the look of a calm shipwrecked man. All because he had dived and resurfaced. He didn't even visit his old friend anymore. The village dwellers could see his tent up there on the hill. There was one old lady who dropped off a sack of potatoes now and then. When cold weather came, John moved into the half shack and stuffed the cracks and soon had a low-profile rustcolored mutt sleeping under his table. There was an abandoned country church half a mile downstream from his camp and he walked down there twice a week to pull boards off for firewood. By spring all four walls were stripped naked to the studs for seven feet above the ground and John figured he had come out even.

On a warm April day when John was loafing in his kitchen chair watching the plum blossoms on the hillside trees, a shiny car pulled off the road and drove back toward his tent. It was John's half sister from Rapid City and his nephew from California. They were driving around visiting relatives on the reservation. The man hadn't been home in nine years. The two got out of the car and stood a little uneasily after saying hello. They looked on and off at John in his chair and

THE END OF JOHN SADDLE

the stained wall tent whiffling in the breeze and the cedars on the hills beyond.

Now John hadn't spoken for four or five days, but he had something he wanted to talk about, and this was an unexpected opportunity. He cleared his throat and with his eyes on a marrowbone told his guests that he had finally had some luck. Just last week he had gone over to check his mail as usual and the postmistress handed him a large envelope from some sort of Grand American Sweepstakes. The envelope looked almost like a telegram or newspaper headline and it had his name printed in big letters and said right there in plain English that John Saddle of Number 9 was a big winner in the thing—maybe even a millionaire, or at least a cabin cruiser or a fancy car.

"I hope I get the money," John said. "I'd rather have the money. The letter said four to six weeks. I'm going to build a nice big house right here on the hill with plenty of room for anyone who wants to come and visit, and always have good things to eat."

Late that afternoon John walked into town to check his mail; he was keeping a closer eye on it now. Returning home he found a single English walnut lying beside the road. It must have hopped out of someone's grocery bag. John picked it up and took it home with him in his shirt pocket.

Back at his table, John ate a slice of bread with Karo syrup on it. Then he fished out the walnut and looked it over and shined it on his sleeve. He cracked it carefully with his hand axe and spread out the meats and picked through them happily, chewing them up slowly fragment by fragment. He lay down to bed that evening still dislodging an occasional morsel of nut from his teeth and chewing it up with appreciative little bites. And then, shortly after midnight with the plum blossoms dancing, he died again, and stayed there this time.

THE END OF JOHN SADDLE

TOTEM

Roy turned east onto Route 20 and leaned back to get comfortable. It was good to be on paved road again. He was off and running for three or four days and that made him happy.

He laughed again thinking of Dick that morning. Roy had seen him shortly after leaving home; as he approached Dick's ranch lane he noticed him walking out toward the road with a rifle. Roy pulled up near the mailbox.

When Dick got near enough Roy yelled. "Whadya do, find a big snake?"

Dick said, "Naw," and kept coming until he leaned in the passenger window of Roy's car.

"Naw. I tell you: There's a dead steer lying over there that's swellin' up and stinking so bad I can't even sit in the yard after supper. It's right upwind. I figured she'd be blowin' pretty soon, but she hasn't. Thought I'd come down and put a hole in it and get it done with."

They talked for a few minutes and Roy drove off. Several times that morning he thought of Dick out there shooting at the bloated carcass from a discreet distance. He thought of it again now, accelerating onto the highway, and wished he'd brought a six-pack of beer with him. It was getting hot.

The hotter it grew the flatter life in Wyoming settled; spread and flattened and sank. The Rattlesnake Range shimmered off to the south—uranium country, baking and fuming. Only the big hawks had an option and sailed high up to tilt and drift. Everything else curled up, flattened, and closed its eyes like a man trying to hide and sleep at the same time.

Roy drove through Hiland, where a pathetic pontoon rusted steadily in the weeds, and tiny Waltman, hiding and sleeping, and then he saw the handful of buildings ahead that comprised the hamlet of Powder River. Roy always slowed when he saw that place ahead, set himself in a certain way each time he passed through the town, once or twice a year. There was a thing there that set him off, jelled him. He never really anticipated it, but he knew it when he got there and welcomed it as an atmospheric change, like a small gust on a heavy day.

It was a simple enough thing that set him off: a remnant sign of a defunct roadhouse that hung from a tall pole above a rotting parking lot. It read: Romeo and Juliet Café. It wasn't any sort of casual speculative whimsy that stirred him. He knew the rectangular concrete-block place from thirty years ago when he was in high school and lived forty miles to the north and west. The high-school kids used to stop there for hamburgers on major outings.

The Romeo and Juliet wasn't named by an itinerant Shakespearian or even by a jerkwater wag. Romeo was a man of Basque descent; his father had ridden a train in to the edge of the Bighorns for a shepherding job. Juliet was a large-hammed Wyoming woman.

The particular scene Roy thought of as he passed through the village was senior prom night, 1954. Three couples, including Roy and his date, met at the Romeo and Juliet after the dance. They drank beer, screwdrivers from a bottle, and sloe gin as they drove to the place. They ate hamburgers at the counter and talked loudly in their suits and formals in the bright inner light. Then they decided to go out along the Powder River to a place they knew, to drink a little more before going home.

Out there, at a long-abandoned farm site, they stood around the cars

TOTEM

in the warm May night listening to car radios and getting mildly drunk. To this day, when Roy heard the word *love* in a song he associated it vaguely with a feeling of buoyancy like the one he felt that night on the upper Powder River in his charcoal-gray church suit with a red carnation and his big black Florsheim shoes.

He remembered that night as strongly as any scene in his life. Of course the annual drive-by reinforced it regularly, kept it green. Other than that, he remembered very little from his past because it was not given to him to do so. A few faces, a fishing trip or two. If one pushed him he would eventually recall the day a pair of turkey vultures vomited on him in his uncle's Indiana woods when Roy blundered beneath their nest tree.

But the prom night was his primary polestar, the single reading from which he continuously receded. The six kids drank in the '54 moonlight. They walked around the old home site with their screwdriver bottles in hand, exploring sheds and the bank of lilacs.

Roy and his girl were holding hands and strolling along a rickety windrow of cedars and elms, when they came to a concrete shell sunk into the earth; an old root cellar perhaps, four or five feet deep, the concrete shining silver in the moonlight.

They walked dreamily along the edge of the pit. Roy was just beginning to think of things romantic when his date glanced down into the corner below and jumped back with a start—"Skunk!" she cried.

Now this was the part of the story that set Roy off and made him squirm in his seat and glance uneasily around the horizon every time. He had been a bit drunk that night, he knew that, but it must have been more than that. He had been lifted by a vodka-washed chivalry; he had astonished himself.

Tossing his screwdriver bottle softly to the ground, Roy vaulted into the cellar without a thought and attacked the cornered skunk with his big black Florsheims. He kicked the animal when it tried to scurry by him, knocking it back into the corner. The skunk released its spray,

TOTEM

but it was too late. Roy was on it with his big hard-heeled shoes; a quick one-stomp to the head and the animal shuddered and lay still. It had taken fifteen seconds.

Roy, now that the stench had hit him, the gagging bio-syrup caught in his throat, jumped out from the hole, cursing, and ran back toward the cars. His date was there, relating the story. They were swearing and guffawing in disbelief. Roy's suit was so saturated with skunk oil he had to take it off and throw it into the lilacs and put on an old mechanics overalls from his buddy's trunk. His girl drove the car home while he sat in the back seat, stunned.

That little chivalrous moment would become a minor legend in the area. Roy never knew that, but the tale was kept afloat by a recitation every few years by, perhaps, a rancher off to the east or a car salesman out to dinner up in Greybull. Roy would return in a couple of days to see about the suit. He would certainly retrieve the big Florsheims. He and the prom girl would remain friends, but nothing ever came of it.

Stupid, he thought now as he rolled east from Powder River. *Stupid*. He raised himself up from the seat enough to loosen the trousers from his groin.

The stink of the skunk brought back the stink of the turkey vultures in his uncle's woods. A skunk and a buzzard, he thought. What a team. It was the first time he had associated the two images, the first time he held them up together, one in each hand. It made for a burning, salty continuity he never knew he had. It was stupid unto greatness. He reached for a stick of beef jerky in his glove box. He would stop for a six-pack first chance down the line, at the Natrona store.

TOTEM

HOECAKES

From the Interstate exit ramp I walked down to the Yellowstone River and upstream till I found a small, willow-choked island not far from shore. It looked like a good, out-of-the-way place to sleep for the night. This was a trick I picked up in the 1970s in California when I was hitchhiking a lot. It was a time when several renowned mass murderers wielding machetes were on the prowl in the Golden State. At sundown in those days I often slipped out to the median between freeway lanes to sleep in peace under the Russian olive trees, or, on occasion, found a discreet island in the right river.

I pulled off my shoes and waded the cool summer current of the near channel. Immediately, I sensed the rustle of someone stirring back in the willow patch. A woman called out as I sidled through the brush and then I saw her kneeling in a sandy clearing and readying a small fire pit.

"I didn't want to scare you and set you off."

She was a muscular and somehow battle-weary woman with a good-natured face. She had chosen the island for the same reason I did.

"People used to say I was a pretty lady. Now, there are certain things I don't have to worry about anymore . . . but there are always a few characters looking for no good. Especially along the Interstates. I'm going down to Mildred—that's not very far, but I don't drive at night. I'll go on down in the morning. I'm not paying $65 for a dusty motel room."

She was making batter for hoecakes—"journey cakes," she called them—and had a pint-sized fire going and a dime-store skillet warming up. I tossed my sleeping bag back in a nook in the willows. We were eating, dusk was closing fast, when we heard another soft plashing from the river. We turned and watched as a young man pushed his way through the willows and into the weak firelight. He was an Indian fellow, carrying a shoebox, and said he was on his way to Miles City.

"I just smelled the food."

The woman fried another skillet of cakes, one after the other, wet them down with Karo syrup, and passed them around on paper towels. She liked to talk, and was telling us, as she worked, about her past two days with an uncle over near Seeley Lake, in the mountains. The man lived there, just north of town, for a long time. Some years ago, his neighbors suffered a blow. Two of their grandkids, three and four years old, were playing out in the backyard and managed to pry open the cover on an eighty-year-old well, and then, as they pushed and peered, fell down the shaft, both of them, and drowned in the water at the bottom. The grandparents were shattered, and when they decided to flee and sell the three acres and little log house, the woman's uncle picked it up for a song.

A year later, with the neighbors far removed, the uncle dreamed up a commercial scheme to suit his retirement needs. The sad incident at the well had become locally infamous. People still drove by, paused to see the site and shake their heads. The uncle got busy, fixed the place up, built a small gabled hut around the well and painted it daffodil yellow. Then he began to advertise it as a fortune-telling destination, touted it as a point of pilgrimage where, for a modest fee, visitors could spend a quarter hour in the hut at the edge of the well and proffer important questions to the tender spirits down the shaft, then lean in to

HOECAKES

decipher the answering voices. Faint merry laughter meant good-to-come. Muffled childish sobs boded misfortune in the wings. He was making pretty good money at it during the tourist season.

The Indian man listened carefully as he ate a second serving of hoecakes. After a moment of silence, he looked across the fire as if he had just seen me sitting there.

"Don't you have any stories to tell?"

I wished he had asked me to sing a song. I'd been getting a handle on "Who's Gonna Shoe Your Pretty Little Feet?" from the Lomax collection the past days as I waited for rides along the Montana highways. I thought fast.

"You said you're from Lame Deer?" He nodded. "I went to Lame Deer for the first time in 1958. I was twelve or thirteen years old. My father drove me from Ohio on a long trip west to visit the Indian country. Rosebud, Pine Ridge, Bear Butte. Then up to Lame Deer. We stayed around there for most of a week, visiting battlefields and talking to people.

"There was an old-time trading post on the main street called Cady's Store. They had lots of Indian crafts. Good stuff. I remember I bought a porcupine-tail hairbrush there. We stopped in most every day for a Coke or some such. There were always two or three very old Cheyenne men sitting on a bench just outside the door. Men with wispy white braids resting on their shoulders. One of them, stooped and quiet, wore a pair of sunglasses to ease his tired eyes.

"I never forgot those men. And one day twenty years later, I was driving along and suddenly I thought of the old one with the sunglasses, the quiet way he sat there on the bench, and I realized, just like that, something that happened to him when he was a young man, something that happened a day or two after the battle at the Little Bighorn.

"I was so shocked that I pulled off the road and thought about it for a while. And I did the arithmetic to make sure. If the man was about

HOECAKES

six years old at the time of the battle, he would have been born in 1870. And by 1958 when I saw him he would have been about 88 years old. That worked okay.

"So this is the picture I got all of a sudden, out of nowhere. A day or two after the Custer fight, when the Indian camps had moved off a short distance, this boy and a friend were playing down along a small stream, idling or looking for berries, when they happened across an American soldier lying sprawled out on the bank of the creek. The boys crept in, whispered and watched. They couldn't tell if the soldier was dead or alive. He was certainly one of Custer's men who had slipped away, wounded, from the battle scene and made his way slowly up the stream in the cover of the chokecherries.

"The boys watched from twenty feet, trying to see if he moved or breathed at all. They began to throw little stones. Finally, creeping in closer, one of the boys (the old man with the sunglasses) reached out with a long stick and jabbed at the blue coat, poked it as he would poke at a dozing snapping turtle. When they concluded he was dead, they went in and took the soldier's hat and pistol and holster and ran triumphantly back to the village, waving their trophies and hooting. Soon there was a crowd of people down by the creek, all standing and looking at the sunburnt dead man in the bushes.

"That's the story I picked up twenty years after I saw the old man by Cady's Store, noticed him day after day as he glanced at our '57 Ford turning the corner in Lame Deer."

The woman by the fire clucked a time or two in acknowledgment. The Indian man sat still for a long moment.

"Were there any mosquitoes around while you were out there?"

"I can't recall."

"Maybe you're right. Maybe you got something, a piece of memory, from that old man. Maybe a mosquito gave it to you. I knew a man who was bit by lots of mosquitoes up in Canada at a rodeo. After two days,

HOECAKES

he woke up and all of a sudden could talk Cree pretty good. The mosquitoes must have got it from the Crees and passed it on to him."

Then he got up, thanked us for the journey cakes, and left, going to thumb a ride on into Miles City. The woman said, as I was unrolling my bedroll back in the willows, "I don't know. Maybe I should go easy on the mosquito spray . . . I might be missing something good."

HOECAKES

SEA HORSES

—1915

A boy was walking lost in thought along the Cheyenne River, miles from nowhere, idly whacking at old weeds with a stick. The wild plum bushes were just blossoming in confectionary piles of pink-white all along the streambanks and coulees. When he reached the edge of the tiny Indian town, he saw men handling a herd of horses, moving them into a corral beside the little fairgrounds and the spidery skeleton of a decade-old sun-dance lodge. The boy turned out from the cottonwood grove and walked over to watch.

It was always good to see horses out by themselves on a hilltop against the sky. But it was also good to see a herd of them put together and the way they acted and the new looks on their faces as they mingled and swirled. Through the corral fence, the boy watched them, two dozen brown horses pacing and kicking up the dust. When one of the men walked by with a lariat in his hand, the boy asked him what they were doing.

"They're joining the army, somewhere. I don't know what army— somebody bought up the whole bunch."

The boy stood there a long while, leaning on the fence. He tried to picture the herd in some kind of uniform, fancy trappings, with some kind of soldiers on top. And he wondered as he watched the horses mill, why any army might not want a pretty bunch of pintos instead of these solid browns and duns.

The next morning when the boy walked by the place, the corral was empty. Nothing but piles of horse droppings all over the ground, with blackbirds picking at them. By the following day, two hundred miles to the south, if you drove out from Gordon, Nebraska, into the blue skies of the Sandhills, you could see the herd again, cornered up in a pasture near the rutty state road, heads high and ears cocked, looking around at the new country with wind in their hair. It might remind you, those fat-grassed rumpled dunes and their lush valleys, of the name and the place three long days to the west known as the Horse Heaven Hills.

For two weeks the big horse-contracting outfit broke the herd. They hired some of the Spotted Bear brothers from up at the Pine Ridge reservation, a family of famous horse breakers generation after generation. The young men stayed in the green and white bunkhouse and cut out four horses a day and took them off to a small rodeo pen and broke them, just like clockwork. All the ranch children went over to see the Spotted Bear boys do their stuff. When the herd was ready, the cowboys moved them slowly up to the south edge of Gordon and sat in the shade of a Chinese elm to wait for the train that afternoon. By sundown, the horses were hurried up a loading chute and into a stock car—all twenty-four in one slatted car—and moving east.

All the April night across northern Nebraska, with every now and then the flashing red lights of a highway-crossing stabbing in through the slat walls, and over a long narrow bridge into Iowa. Then into the daylight once more, gray light twinkling into the dark car, across Illinois, creaking and swaying, the horse droppings piling up on the straw-littered floor. Through the edges of Chicago, rain slapping at the roof, to stop at last at a sooty stockyard in Gary, Indiana. The beef and hog haulers led the horses down out of the car and into a pen for the night, where they trotted and whirled in the new air with train whis-

SEA HORSES

tles everywhere around them. Packs of boys from the poor neighborhood heard the whinnying and came over with slingshots and jackknives in their pockets to watch through the high metal fence.

Next morning the herd was back on the stock car, all the manure shoveled out by now and piled at one edge of the pens, where dozens of shiny grackles were poking at it, and rolling east across Indiana and into Ohio, swaying past Toledo with its glass factories and two-bit beanery/brothels; then the Lake Erie marshes, the duck-gunner clubs quiet and empty in the spring, stacks of decoys haphazard in the storage rooms; past Cleveland, still fat from the Civil War; and the long haul across Pennsylvania, creaking around the Allegheny Mountain curves as dusk settled in.

By the following noon the train had reached its destination, Hoboken, New Jersey. *Hoe-buck*, the "high bluff," and below the bluff the Hudson lapping at its piers. Here the horses were unloaded again and turned into a bigger pen. Now there was another herd with them: gray and brown and a few black horses, whuffling and milling. They stayed there three days, eating well and inhaling the strange harbor aromas on the wind, fish and coal smoke, hearing the ferry horns and the clanging buoys in the night.

Of course the school kids of Hoboken found them and walked down to see them on their way home from school. The night before the rested herd was to be loaded onto an England-bound ship, another person stopped to see them, just at nightfall. He was a stevedore of smudged ancestry who had worked the Jersey docks for years and was now expanding his mouths-to-feed repertory in the private hire of a one-time German merchant-marine captain. Stranded in the States when the World War broke out, the captain soon devoted his restless energies to running a cadre of secret agents making serious old-world mischief along the Atlantic seaboard.

The stevedore in the gloaming in Hoboken that night carried a

SEA HORSES

harmless-looking black lunch bucket as he sauntered down the side streets toward the stockyards. At the fence where the horses shuffled in the near-dark, the man removed a bag of sugar cubes that had been sent up from the Washington, D.C., basement laboratory of one Anton Dilger, the patriotic German physician who masterminded the plot. Dr. Dilger had painstakingly implanted each cube with a tiny tube of glanders bacilli. The horses snuffled and wolfed down the cubes as the agent strolled along the fence tossing them furtively into the pen. It was nothing against the horses, personally. Or against the United States, personally—the U.S. wasn't even in the war yet. The notion in the night was to set loose upon the fields of embattled England the glanders seed and wilt the various livestock of those greeny hills and plains.

By noon the herd was waiting on one of the Hamburg-American Line docks, smelling the strange waters and hearing the countless gulls overhead, and then led up the cleated ramp and into the ship's hold. Now the eyes were rolling. Two hours later they were off, off down the Hudson and out through the stately Narrows, Brooklyn on the left, and onto the Atlantic itself.

Days and nights were lost to them in the dark hold. Boys came by each morning to shovel up the droppings into wheelbarrows and leave feed in the troughs, and the ship swayed something like the trains. The fourth day out of Hoboken, an officer came below to look things over, then called for the ship's medical man. The news was simple and bad: Half the herd had greenish pus oozing from the nostrils, raw sores on the tender septa, runny eyes. The glanders was up and burning.

That evening, after a flurry of cables, just past nightfall when the ocean was quiet and smooth with wandering lackadaisical swells, smooth and solid as India rubber in the salmon-gray light, half a dozen men moved the horses to the lower stern deck—now this was a wide familiar sky with the stars coming on—dropped the barrier gates, and slapping and hooting drove them overboard into the sea.

SEA HORSES

PAGING CHARLES LOWBOY

The woman in the messenger-red coat had crossed the highway and given them the news. In the half hour since, the tall old man with the salami nose had been dressing: climbing slowly into his black suit pants and clean white shirt, rigging his cuff links and shining his long narrow shoes with a corner of the bedspread.

Elmer, a very old man who lived in the cabins across the highway, had died that morning just before daylight. Charles Lowboy was dressing to go to the family and sit with them in neighborly condolence for the afternoon and probably on into the night.

Now he stood beside his wife, bending to enable her to reach his necktie from her wheelchair. His vision was too far gone for the fine work. Hazel tugged at the wide tie and straightened the big knot and slapped at a speck of lint on his suit coat.

"Now don't forget," she told Charles, "Elmer's brother is related to some of those Big Legs. He married one of those girls from Hisle. Those Big Legs were connected with my mother's people a long time ago. My aunt married one of those boys. They lived over by Allen. You tell Elmer's brother when you see him; he'll know. That's Donald. Not Donald Junior, Donald Senior, from Hot Springs. You tell him who you are."

She turned Charles around to inspect his backside and then pulled him over her and straightened his thinning hair with a crooked arthritic hand. Her voice was strident with excitement but her touch was soft, had butchered many deer.

It seemed they went through this procedure every two weeks anymore. The woman knew the connections and the bloodlines and the circumstances-in-the-wings. Charles was the ambassador who attended the wakes and spoke for their family in his handsome dark suit, spoke softly in his faint, sweet Oklahoma accent. He always knew the details because Hazel briefed him well and he remembered it all because it was important to remember it all.

And now that they were old, Charles was summoned more and more. He was a workhorse of condolence. The white shirts were always kept clean and the black suit at the ready, and it seemed they got it out every two weeks anymore.

The woman followed Charles to the cabin door in her wheelchair and turned him around one last time and smoothed his pocket flaps and sent him off. He moved slowly across the yard with his walking stick. He hollered at a boy and asked him to help him across the highway. Hazel leaned to watch him from the front window until he was out of sight.

They lived at the "Shady Grove," an archipelago of superannuated tourist cabins in Belle Fourche, South Dakota. The cabins were arranged in two thoughtful, mirror-image crescent rows beneath tall cottonwoods. Between the two crescents an erstwhile gravel driveway loop showed faintly through encroaching grass.

Across Highway 212 was a nearly identical set of cabins, the "Mountain View," in a similar magisterial grove. The two sets differed only in color; the cabins on the west side of the road were white, those on the east a cocoa brown. But they were all of 1920 vintage, small, nearly square clapboard structures inviting in scale and intention. They had prospered for three decades in their flickering cottonwood shade. Tourist families could walk from the cabins to the Belle Fourche and the Redwater rivers to fish.

PAGING CHARLES LOWBOY

Nowadays they sagged a bit. The brown and the white paints were shabby pintos. The red-shingle roofs were ratty in places and the eaves were full of twigs and leaves. Window screens were often torn and curling. Old drainpipes and rusty lawn tools and the occasional castoff sink lay about the grounds.

The white world had abandoned the cabins years ago, but they were still weather-tight and they were still cozy in scale and pleasing as social architectural clusters. Most of them were inhabited, many by older people who had left the reservations, like Charles and Hazel, to find simple ease and good solid shade. A younger family or two were usually there as well; there were always children and grandchildren to stir the air and punctuate the midday naps. And the lines of the cabins softened now that there were people living in them full time.

Over the preceding decade the two clusters had taken on casual lineage affiliations as relatives heard of the places and their moderate rents. So the brown cabins tended toward a certain wide, loosely defined kin and their acquaintances, while the white cabins across the highway comprised more or less another.

In one cabin there lived an old silent man with one remaining incisor who worked in his yard carving cedar flutes that he sold to tourist shops. He continually smacked his lips as he worked, holding up the flute at arm's length, carefully sighting along it to keep it true.

Next to him lived a silent old man with a red nose, who covered all his windows with Rapid City newspapers and once a day crept down the three steps with his diamond-willow cane and circled the cabin one time and went back inside. Beside him dwelled an old half-Arikara man with a gray butch and one leg off at the knee; every weekend his daughter came and took him for a drive and ice cream.

There were old couples thankful for company, who kept their cabins neat and planted flowers by the stoops and small kitchen gardens in the rear and often sent food to the womanless men, and one large family with seven children that rented two cabins side by side to hold

PAGING CHARLES LOWBOY

them all and stretched a canvas tarp between them for a breezeway. Formerly, they could be seen on Sunday mornings walking out the drive and filing north at the highway toward the Catholic church. Then one day the Catholic father told them the kids must have new shoes to go with their school uniforms. Now they turn south Sunday mornings toward the Episcopal services.

There was a middle-aged couple who made painted dance shawls for powwows and a single woman with children who taught at a local kindergarten. There was a part-time auto mechanic and a night janitor and a café cook.

In the summer people came and went, took trips to visit family and fairs. Some weeks the cabins bulged with guests and there were new teenagers whispering at night along the rivers. Winters, there was the low talk and the hunching, the football on television, the long sitting with the inner dailiness, and cautious walks across the snowy yard to see the neighbors. The little colony had the rough harmonious weave of any enclave; the insular hum and percolation. It strengthened and grew and after a few years it was as if the Caucasian town existed around the cabin colony just to sell it beef and candy and white bread. 212 was like a river through it.

In the midst, Hazel was the busy archivist of woof and warp and due. She could catalog bloodlines and clan-character with the best of them and chant it like Homer. She clarified things for the colony, she kept track. Warm days, she watched it all from her front yard. During the depths of winter she beaded earrings for her grandchildren and hooked rugs. She tended the gas heater beneath a photograph of a meadowlark torn from a magazine and watched it all from her window. When Charles brought in a particularly graphic, risqué parsnip from his snowy little root plot—a mandrake-like parsnip with two legs and a prominent male member—Hazel would laugh and clean it up, wrap it discreetly in newspaper and send it by child messenger to one of her women friends across the road. Later they would see each other

PAGING CHARLES LOWBOY

across the way and wave little knowing waves and snicker like school-girls.

And Charles stabilized the cabins with his gentle humor and sweet diplomacy. He loved the children of the colony. He called one of them to him every evening and Sunday afternoons to read the comic pages aloud to him and describe the goings-on frame by frame, while he sat chuckling and nodding. On good days he would call the child back for a second reading an hour later.

He performed his funereal duties with a fluency that continually surprised himself. He was good at it; people liked to see him coming up the road. As a young man he had been skittish of that sort of thing; as a boy he had fled to the hills along the Canadian River near Watonga, Oklahoma, to avoid a funeral, and sat all the afternoon smoking in a hackberry tree.

But he learned. In the past five years he had been called all over the western Dakotas; twice to Riverton, Wyoming; and once each to Sheridan, Billings, and Colorado Springs. Everywhere he stood tall and half-blind and his words were soft and soothing. He learned, laboriously, like a heavy bird taking off from the ground. He always bore the pall left-side middle so as not to stumble and fall.

Lately when called to Rapid City he had taken to having a fancy cigar on the street in front of the big hotel and often managed to work in an evening at the dog track, where he sat quietly gazing at his shoes and stroking his salami nose, enjoying the ebb and slow crescendo of the crowd as the pack sailed from far side to homestretch. He learned to take pleasure from his duties, an honest, ambassadorial pleasure that he considered a healthy byproduct of all the sympathy and sad suction and demanding protocol of departure. He learned that what had at first seemed like the handling of tarantulas was more like a juggling of bluebird chicks. He observed it all with humble curiosity and an occasional anti-Rosicrucian chuckle, as every two weeks or so they took the black suit down from the closet while Hazel briefed him and off

PAGING CHARLES LOWBOY

he would go. Sometimes across the highway; sometimes catching a ride to Pine Ridge, or to Thunder Butte in the rain. A Minniconjou man run over by a locomotive. A young bull rider trampled in Cheyenne. An Oglala boy killed in Asia and that long, high, invisible flight back to South Dakota. An invaluable old woman who "slept away" on Pass Creek at noon on the Fourth of July.

*

There were breakthroughs from the cabin dailiness. There were visitations and uplifts, bracing verticalities in a part of South Dakota where they were scarce and sorely needed.

There was a gifted twelve-year-old boy over in the Mountain Views, a boy who picked up distant conversations via birds of prey. Walking alone beside the Redwater or from the railroad bridge abutment nearby, he gazed off into the distance and waited. Sooner or later a soaring bird would come into conjunction with a car or an isolated house many miles to the south and the boy would hear the talk going on in there. Eagles brought him the important transmissions: messages of vague origin and ropy, private innuendo. Hawks, and even crows, those birds that follow highways in search of carrion, sent him lesser news and ranker gossip as they went their crooked ways.

The boy picked up sweat-stained trucker talk and random lovers' whispers from the bottomlands. From the reservations off to the south and east he pulled in a spotty flow of everyday news that he passed along to the cabin people. When the Swainson's hawks soared he heard breakfast chat from out near Faith or Redowl, and crowded-car conversations from along the Hermosa road. And very rarely, a deep, slow, eagle-relayed voice from somewhere over the wilder Black Hills.

And there was Elmer Foot, the old man who just died across the highway. He started something vertical once, a few years back. One night he was awakened by a disturbance in the garbage cans behind his cabin. Elmer got up and went to see about it. There, half in and half

PAGING CHARLES LOWBOY

out of the streetlight, was a man rummaging through the trash. When Elmer spoke, the man straightened and turned to face him, tall, calm, and chiaroscuro. It was, Elmer said the next morning, the Lord.

A week later an elderly woman from the white cabins was walking home after dark with a loaf of bread. As she crossed the old bridge she saw a man sleeping on the ground, up under the abutment. She was startled and tried to tiptoe by, but the man rolled over and sat up. It was the Lord again, and he lifted one shapely hand and said to the woman, "Storms never last."

After that the cabin people were on the alert. They looked two and three times at strangers passing by that summer, and eyed the spry hoboes sunning by the rivers. No one was taken for granted; there were half-heard voices in the night and ghostly brushes with the Lord on both sides of the road. Charles chuckled and said, "I believe he's gone and moved into this neighborhood."

Cabin people appeared and disappeared over the years and countless scroungy lapdogs perished on the busy highway, but it was the gradual foothold and sunflowering of the colony that caught the hawk's eye, that the residents came and went by and looked up to as if it were in the treetops: the slow accretion of the social reef and its happenstance bivalve symmetry. Girls from the brown cabins married boys from the white. A girl swelled with child in the Shady Grove and people glanced slyly across the highway to the Mountain View. Given several generations, two dialects might well spring up in the camps, gently enforced by the highway-river.

And the seasons soared higher and higher now that people lived in them full-time, bent and hid and slept in them. Months mattered more than days, years more than months, and the sunflowering more than any single tale or thing.

Try as you may, Charles thought, it is in the treetops; it is always the no-one-man that steps forward from the chokecherry patch.

*

PAGING CHARLES LOWBOY

And there was another fine autumn Saturday showed up like a moon—a big full day to look twice at. The first golden cottonwood leaves twirled down on the cabin roofs. The day was almost the color of those leaves. Wild turkey feathers lay scattered about the grove and tumbled lazily when a breeze hit them. People moved about slowly, hesitantly, like the cool-stunned yellow jackets thudding all day against the screen doors as if they were drugged or happy beyond good sense.

Charles was napping in the bedroom with the radio down low. His long narrow shoes stood up like mule-deer ears at the foot of the bed. Hazel sat in her wheelchair sorting rags for rugs. A tricycle creaked steadily from a yard down the way. The old man with one incisor sat by his steps in the sun, finishing a cedar flute. Every few minutes he blew a long mellow note to test the tone. *Thud, thud*—yellow jackets against a screen . . .

Beyond the highway, the boy who heard from birds came back from a walk along the river and made a peanut butter and jelly sandwich while he told his mother some news. He told it in short robin-like phrases, each almost like a question: an old lady named Agnes Other Side was near death down on the reservation.

The boy's mother turned her boiling potatoes down low and put on her jacket and went out and across the yard. As she stood at the highway waiting for traffic to pass, Hazel saw her from her window. The old lady stirred and hoisted herself in her wheelchair. She strained and squinted so that her lips pulled back from her teeth.

She thought as she watched the woman crossing the road: "Who is it now? Maybe Rachel's brother's boy—he's been real sick down at Porcupine."

The old man across the yard blew a single, hollow thrush note on his flute. Then Hazel twisted in her chair and called over her bony-thin shoulder: "Charles! Charles, wake up!"

PAGING CHARLES LOWBOY

THOUSAND LEGGERN

She grew up in the Yakima Valley of Washington in a house immediately downwind from the big mint farms lining the river: a benevolent site that instilled in her early on a simple sense of the good life as one of regular, uplifting fragrance. Miles and decades after, she dismissed, with a firm, exile's superiority, the bouquet of the Dakota pines, when the wind was that way. Even the lubricative aroma of fresh-cut hay on August evenings bore no comparison to her ultimate touchstone: mint fields after an arousing rain.

She often taxied me around the Flicker country when I was carless and she usually worked the Yakima Valley somewhere into our day-talk; it was an emerald kite above a hard flat life. Today she was driving me out to see Oscar Whitetail at his home far up on Bear-in-Lodge Creek. He had promised to take me out one day to find tree mushrooms. The woman knew the territory well and told me stories in a staccato monotone as we drove, her eyes moving methodically from highway to speedometer to rearview mirror. She nodded toward a battered concrete shell of a building standing a hundred yards off the road.

"Fireworks plant. Someone screwed up every five years or so and the place would blow all to hell . . . There must have been a dozen men blown to bits at that place. One or two every five years. Someone slipped up for a split second and *bang*—that's the last of them. They finally gave up and closed the place a few years ago."

Beyond the thick-walled bunker relic I could see dust clouds where a herd of horses rolled in a good bare spot near the river.

We left the paved road after half an hour and drove back a series of tough gumbo tracks that rose and fell across the pine-speckled hills. One moment we were topping a grassy ridge and admiring the white bluffs twenty miles to the south. The next we were rocking through a deep draw where ash and box-elder trees thrived. I saw the heavy, half-green scent of chokecherry blow turn the woman's head for an instant as we rumbled by.

Oscar was sitting quietly against a tree when we drove into his place. He got to his feet when he recognized us and waved us in, but soon lost interest. It was the only time I had ever seen him drunk.

We went inside the house with Oscar's wife and sat at the table talking and sipping sweet coffee. The old woman bore homemade tattoos on her hands and forearms: anachronistic boys' names in the bay at the base of the thumbs; L-O-V-E spaced across the lower knuckles of one hand, pricked in with a safety pin fifty years ago on a summer night. On her thin arms the ink-blue initials and arabesques were distended and fuzzed by the years like amorous old carvings on aspen bark.

She was tending a large cast-iron skillet of curly thick-cut bacon and boiling a pot of corn mush on the stove. She told us shyly that Oscar was drunk for the first time since she had known him. Something had hit him and he went out and bought a bottle the night before. Now it was gone. We could see the lean dogs of the place gathered outside, rearing, maneuvering windward with their noses high, working to catch the bacon wafts.

Oscar came in while we chatted there. He approached me noncommittally, squinting a little. He laid his calm broad hand on my shoulder and spoke in a husky whisper: "I know you're FBI. I know damn well you're FBI." A moment later, while he stood waving gently like a tall pine beside the table, he bent again and said, to balance the intricate

THOUSAND LEGGERN

human equation, "But I love you, I love you." Then he went out to his tree.

I would come back another day and we would all walk easily through the stream bottoms looking for tree mushrooms in the box-elder groves, talking softly, dropping the mushrooms into brown grocery bags.

*

The woman from the mint country drove me back to town. When we passed a rural arbor where dances and celebrations were held, she told me a powwow story. Some years ago she guided an elderly professor to the annual July get-together at this place. The old gentleman had spent his entire life comparing various marginal modes of subsistence on the North American continent: migrant cherry pickers in Michigan orchards; Baffin Island seabird-egg gatherers; Louisiana nutria men . . .

He was passing through the Flicker River region and the woman agreed to escort him to this small *wacipi* for a look. They pulled in at midmorning and sat in their lawn chairs under the pine-bough arbor, fanning themselves with wide-brimmed hats, waiting for the dancing to begin.

By noon it had reached one hundred degrees, bone-dry and droning. The professor flagged. The dancing had not begun. They told him "One o'clock sharp." He wet his handkerchief and mopped his face and head. At one-thirty he walked to the announcer's booth and inquired again, a bit testily this time, what was the holdup, what was the holdup exactly.

The woman from Washington calmed him, poured him lemonade, and taught him a hot-weather trick of the old Indian ladies—placing his wet, folded kerchief squarely on top of his balding head and leaving it there to cool the pate. That, with its ethnological overtones, held him until two-thirty. The naming ceremonies and the family giveaways dragged on.

THOUSAND LEGGERN

At three-fifteen, still no dancing. He began to redden and rave, pacing behind his chair, throwing his arms about, raising his voice. The woman reached to soothe him, but it was too late. He broke away and stormed the announcer's booth with shouts of rage and indignation. He pointed at his watch and pounded on the wall. It was a terrible outburst that had the crowd on its feet, craning; vindictive, heavily educated spleen slashing at the salvationary roots of the host culture.

The woman and the Fox Society men finally gathered him up and put him in her long white car with a dowsing of cold water. Then she drove him, eyes closed and muttering, back to his motel in town.

And now she dropped me at my bicycle chained to a Chinese elm in the same hot town—merchants peeked from their murky windows— and I pedaled slowly out of the village and up into the cool pine-ridge haven just south. I made a quick camp and lay beneath an aromatic ponderosa until sundown, reading and gazing out over the long shimmering plain with a tiny jitterbug of badland on the skyline. But each time I looked too long I began seeing little groups of men being blown up into the air and down in a thousand smithereen confetti, men exploding from the earth like dusty geysers . . .

That night I dreamt I was riding down the Flicker highway and came to a rural mailbox (an actual, waking-world mailbox I have passed many times), its name in bright gold letters: DVOŘÁK. But this time I wheeled the bike into the lane and took off for it, pedaling hard, soon hitting a steep pastoral downhill that I shot, faster and faster with the grade, the naturally suspected "Dvořák music" now faintly audible from up ahead (wild wind in my face, my mind flashing "First white man to ever set foot in these parts!"), then louder, full-symphonic as I zoomed in around a meadow curve to behold the shady ranch house, the mythic music blaring, radiating from the grove like sunlight off windows, and the Dvořáks lined up out front, shading their eyes and waving.

THOUSAND LEGGERN

UNCLE AND SHRIKE

WITH SUMAC CANDELABRA

They were camped on the Arikaree River, six cars and six tents in a small palm of a place out of the wind. They had been there a few weeks judging from the camp sprawl and the flat of the grass. They drove old Cadillacs and Continentals showing rust along the running boards— one-time Tory clans from the looks of it. We—my uncle and I—were pitched up on a knoll directly across the river.

My uncle surveyed them with binoculars now and then our first days there, sized their little camp, and finally deciphered their license plates. And one morning we cut down through the brushy bottom and crossed the near-dry river to talk. They came from Pennsylvania and had been on the move for a year and a half now. They were jokey, good-tempered people; we could hear them laughing on and off throughout the day and every evening they built two big fires and played canasta or gin rummy on card tables set up tandem between them with greasy brown bags of popcorn on the side.

It was a good place for a spring camp—the cool well water and the river-bottom shelter—and it was far enough from the major highways that not everyone on the move showed up, although it wasn't unusual to find a new tent or step-van in camp when I crawled out from our lean-to in the early morning. Most of the passers-through would stay two or three days, shy and uneasy, visiting with the Pennsylvanians and my uncle, asking about places to summer, or winter, about places with good wood and water and no trouble, worrying about gasoline, asking how to eat chokecherries and what could be done with the hackberries that hung dry on their trees all winter. Then one morning after a prolonged breakfast and the shaking of the blankets they would load up and drive away. But my uncle and I and the Pennsylvanians stayed for a while. We liked it there.

My uncle had me for the summer (that's the way the family put it). He wanted to show me things, things, I know now, not everyone saw. Things he wanted to see again for himself while he was still able. He met me at the Cheyenne bus station in latter May, bought me a hamburger, then drove straight north for an hour and a half with a look of intense concentration on his lean old face. He said little until we made our first official stop at a bridge over a puddle-wide little flow through the eastern Wyoming grasslands. He walked me down through the ditch and over to the right bank of the stream. There was a cattail or two. We stood for a moment gazing down at it, then he turned to me with a wry grin and made the formal introduction: "Here we have the headwaters of the Niobrara River."

And then we began to drive. We cut east into Nebraska, utterly hurry-less, stopping often for this thing or that, camping where we felt like it in our tarp lean-to. In the Sandhill country south of the Niobrara we drove out each evening at sunset to any given promontory to sit there in the car with sandwiches and a warm thermos watching the fireflies come on in the lake valleys below. I had never seen fireflies before—the sandwiches lasted a good long time. The third night out we hit it right, an entire vast oblong valley was pulsing with a collective phosphorescence so dense the black oval of the lake stood out like ink from the flashing lightfield around it. My uncle, after a while, poured another cup of coffee and told me the story of Benvenuto Cellini and the lizard: How Benvenuto and his father were sitting quietly before

UNCLE AND SHRIKE

the fireplace one night when a beautifully colored lizard darted from the woodpile, so beautiful and so gratuitous that the father reached out and struck Benvenuto across the cheek to ensure that the boy would never lose the moment and its unexpected brilliance.

It was a noble story, I remember thinking; I liked the warm orange hearthglow in it and the sense of aesthetic chivalry. When we finished our suppers a few minutes later and were having a last gaze at the flickering valley, my uncle reached over through the dark of the car and gave me a quick, halfhearted cuff on the back of my head.

Life was quiet on the Arikaree, save for the occasional thunderstorm blasting out of the west, when everyone ran to their cars to wait it out. My uncle was a great reader. He carried a duffel bag of old paperbacks in the trunk, as well as a grocery box of particular favorites on the back seat. The first day in camp he had found his official reading spot under a clump of chokecherry saplings and he moved his chair around it to stay in or out of the sun as the thermals dictated. On cool mornings he took short arthritis-slowed walks along the river, invariably bringing back a specimen or two from the outerworld: a feather or an odd stone or an old coyote turd dried unto nothing but silvery mouse hair in a neat peristaltic braid. He arranged them on the folding table in a kaleidoscopic still life. When he wasn't walking or reading or napping in the shade he often sat silently for great lengths of time staring far off and muttering intently.

There were no boys my age in the camp across the river, but I made friends with a girl named Tina who was somewhere near twelve. We played catch with a rubber ball, and later marbles, a free-form sort of marbles called toss-and-chase, a nearly pointless game that led us far from camp, often out of the river bottom and up the hills until we would look out over the Arikaree prairies and be startled to find ourselves there in the midst of all that afternoon light and air and just stand for a moment with our cat's-eyes in our hands. For supper my

UNCLE AND SHRIKE

uncle made macaroni with oleo and chopped salami or sardines, or corn mush with a can of tomatoes stirred in, and we ate and talked a little and watched the night come in.

One morning there was a strange car just upriver from the main camp, wedged into the edge of a thicket as if to hide, with an old green tent by its side. An hour later a man and a woman could be seen shuffling around the site, and then a boy about my size. But they stayed to themselves all day and seemed to avoid even looking in our direction. The following day I wandered up the river toward their place and surprised the boy fiddling around on the muddy bank. He was a ruffled, edgy sort of lad wearing abundant corduroys with the cuffs turned up half a foot above his sneakers. He hurried off into the trees before I reached him.

The family stayed on the Arikaree for five days and never approached our camp, or the Pennsylvanians either. My uncle thought their license plate said Maine. I saw the boy idling privately through the bottoms once or twice. He seemed to carry on a continuous conversation with himself, gesturing eloquently or waving one diplomatic explanatory hand like a gypsy in a phone booth. Some of the younger kids from the Pennsylvania camp said they had approached him and tried to make acquaintance but he growled at them; that he had a bad tooth that he sucked on malevolently and blew the stink at them as he backed away into the bushes.

None of these people had houses anymore. Just the cars and the tents or trailers. Some of them had relatives with homes somewhere, whom they could visit now and then and store excess belongings in a barn or shed and pick up their mail twice a year. But none of them had houses anymore. They moved from camp to camp on a shuttle of need and whimsy. They were used to it by now and most everyone in America was used to them. Winters they hugged the Mexican border and the Florida panhandle, Lake Mead, and the Salton Sea. Summers they pre-

UNCLE AND SHRIKE

ferred the hinterland western camps because they were usually far from complications and seldom crowded.

My uncle and I had been on the Arikaree two weeks. The folding table had saucers and bowls full of specimens by then. An ancient key, a magpie cranium and a rock resembling a prime lamb chop and assorted prairie grasses. Early one morning I was drinking my coffee alone at the table when I heard an unaccustomed sound not far off behind a plum thicket: a steady series of small percussions that sounded like a temperamental cap pistol in the still morning. *Tap, tap, tap, bang. Tap, tap, bang.* I finished my coffee and walked quietly to the thicket and around one edge until I saw an old green Ford Falcon station wagon that had obviously pulled in during the night. It had canvas-wrapped gear and a spare tire lashed on the roof.

With another step I saw an old man sitting Indian fashion on an open sleeping bag in the sun. He was hunched over a flat stone, deeply absorbed in working his way through a roll of caps, striking them one by one with an egg-size cobble. I could smell the old familiar burnt powder hanging in the cool air. Then he sensed me and looked up.

"I haven't done this in a long time."

I stood quietly until he finished the roll, then I told him who I was and where I came from—the other side of the plum patch—and squatted down to watch him from a courteous distance. He took another roll from his shirt pocket and draped the loose end across the stone. He seemed to enjoy the audience. He said he was going to California to see his sister; she still had a house and a yard full of flowers on the outskirts of Sacramento. The man was tall and thin. He had white eyelids, like a magpie, that flashed each time he blinked. But the caps were the main thing at the moment and neither of us said much while he tapped and banged away. When he finished the second roll he stood up and gave one great satisfied clap of his hands and sent me back to my camp with two sugared doughnuts.

Late that afternoon my uncle and I walked over to see him. We

UNCLE AND SHRIKE

chatted for half an hour. This time, maybe it was the time of day, the newcomer seemed distant and memory-sick, but to me he was so far an adult of possible interest. He was still there the next day, and after supper we walked over again and sat with him into sunset eating malted milk balls and drinking coffee.

He was garrulous this time. He told jerking stories of the old days on Lake Erie, stories (there were mallards flying over) of duck- and goose-hunting camps on the marshes east of Toledo. As a teenager he had worked with the head decoy man at one of the big duck clubs, the indispensable man who raised and trained the live goose decoys, keeping them "just right" between half-wild and half-tame, grooming his small flock to sail forth from their holding pen at just the right moment and swing out over the gray bay to the wild flocks-of-passage and coax them back to the shore, where the gunners were congregated in elaborate underground bunker-blinds, smoking cigars and sipping whiskey until the signal bell rang and they trotted off to their shooting posts and readied for the incoming flock. In the low firelight he conjured handsome images of legendary decoy broods, each bird with a name, ranging day after day in perfectly choreographed maneuvers high above the lake, controlled from afar by a fingertip wizardry in the mind of the trainer.

Then, after rinsing the coffeepot, he sat down and launched another story, his eyelids flashing. A story with different colors this time. A man and his twenty-year-old son were hunting ducks on Lake Erie in November. They were settled in a blind far from shore; they rowed a skiff out to it and tied it under the camouflage. About midday a storm blew in out of nowhere. Before the men could react their skiff was torn loose and gone. They were caught in what was soon a blizzard. The son decided in desperation to wade in to shore before it was utterly hopeless. (The storyteller's voice had dropped to a hoarse curmudgeonly whisper.) So the young man struck off in his hip boots for shore. He made it fifty yards before he foundered, sank to his thighs in the bay

UNCLE AND SHRIKE

muck and couldn't go on. And there was his father watching from the blind, just able to see the boy through the snow, thrashing and shouting as the water rose and the—

My uncle jumped to his feet. "I don't care to hear any more of this story." He pulled me up from the ground, saying goodnight as we walked off into the dark.

Back at our camp he was moody and restless. He perked up our fire and paced at the edge of the light, tossing my rubber ball in one hand.

Finally he stopped and said, "He had his hands all over that story." He was thinking hard as he spoke. "That's not the way it's done. When you tell a story you treat it like you would a person. You don't put your dirty hands all over it just to make someone shiver or run scared."

He was leaning heavily on the table, thinking it through bit by bit. "You look at the world and the people in it and you think about it with words. It goes back and forth between any person and the world, with the words in between. And to get it right, to see it right without being a four-flusher or a fool, you have to slow down, and to do that you have to slow your words down."

He paced a while more, tossing the ball, then came to sit beside me.

"The Arapaho word for blackbird is *hitecouceiiwanahuut*. The word for turtle is *niiceciana baaba*. For chickadee, *ceciitcenihiin*." He made me repeat the chickadee word twice. "These words are long and slow to say so that they will teach a person to be patient in the brain, patient in the talk, so he will have room each time he pronounces them to see and hear how the words fit into the world, how they throw a little net around things and bring them back in to the mind. They teach a person to use them and what they stand for with respect—and to keep their dirty hands off things that don't deserve it! . . . Dog fennel! I'm going to bed."

He wanted to show me the head of the Smoky Hill River. We packed up on a cool cloudy morning and drove up out of the breaks. The Penn-

UNCLE AND SHRIKE

sylvanians were still there. Tina and a few adults waved back at us as we crested the hill.

We drove south on the smallest paved roads we could find—gravel roads ate up the tires—weaving back and forth across the Kansas-Colorado border through the high plain that lay dark and ill at ease under matte cloudlight. By midday we came to a narrow bridge over the river and my uncle pulled off the road and sat for a moment looking off. Then he got out and put a few things in a mesh potato sack and we walked off over a spent fence and upstream along the river for a hundred yards.

The Smoky Hill at this point was little more than a rill, even though it was June. It swung wearily through the grasslands, two, maybe three feet wide, its banks bare save for an occasional runty willow. But my uncle walked right up to it and turned to me and announced ceremoniously, "The headwaters of the Smoky Hill River," and gave me the same sly boyish grin he had used back on the upper Niobrara. Then we sat down in a stand of last year's burnt-out mullein stalks on the north shore and ate Velveeta cheese and tangerines.

We knew there was a camp down on Ladder Creek not far from the town of Modoc, Kansas, and after my uncle napped for half an hour beside the Smoky Hill we drove down there. It was a small flat place with a few box elders and a water pump in the middle of a huge mud puddle where scores of wasps and damselflies came calling. Three cars and a large tent sat at one end of the grounds.

The camp was a dull one except for the several riverbends and their thinning trees, but we stayed for a time. The people in the big tent were on their way to a small chapel somewhere in Nevada to see an icon of Christ that wept real tears each day at sunset accompanied by a grievous band of pigeons on the eaves outside. My uncle was in the midst of a fat book and wanted to get through it before we moved along. And he had spotted a ranch pond just up the road with an inviting "No Fishing, Don't Ask" sign tacked to one of its trees. Each evening at dusk we

UNCLE AND SHRIKE

walked over there and he slipped through the fence and threw in trot-lines baited with bacon rind. In the morning I would hear him return-ing before I was up from bed, carrying a stringer of nice bullheads, which he tethered in a Ladder Creek pool until suppertime, when he skinned them with pliers and rolled them in cornmeal and fried them and everyone in camp stopped and sniffed the air. One day he caught a snapping turtle, which he traded to an Alabama family for grapefruits and a jar of blackstrap molasses.

I explored the little river in both directions, whiling away the warmer and warmer days, climbing trees and reading Robin Hood. One morning I discovered a newcomer lying in the sun beside a muddy pool downstream from camp. She was a stout white-skinned woman with cropped tow hair. She rolled over when she heard me step through the brush and put one hand over her eyes to look.

Finally she said, "If you'd've been here ten minutes earlier you'd've caught me buck naked." She had a deadpan, farmer sort of voice.

It was a startling image, I knew that instantly, and that I would walk many miles out of the way to avoid seeing this person buck naked. She was stocky, strong, and very pale, a negative out-from-under-the-stone pale. She wore denim clothes and had tiny chewed nails on short-dig-ited hands, pale blue eyes reminiscent of a too-hot sky. She was most certainly tough as dirt and unshakeable—beyond doubt an adult of possible interest.

She was a dogcatcher from a rural county in Missouri. She had been to Oklahoma for a funeral and was lazing here on Ladder Creek for a while before the final run home. This was the first vacation she had taken in ten years, she said, not counting the opening day of trapping season, which she took off annually to get her muskrat traps deployed. She was driving her dogcatcher truck, she told me, with seven homeless dogs in the back because she was unable to find anyone trustworthy back home to feed them for a week.

She was lying on one side, propped on her elbow on a beach towel.

UNCLE AND SHRIKE

She exuded through her faint eyes and blank-white skin a primitive pastoral aplomb that almost attained suavity. Her center of gravity was low and calm, with a fleck of cunning that could have survived, even thrived, at a fashionable cocktail party. As I said goodbye and turned to go she cleared her throat and repeated her opening sentence verbatim in the exact pitch and tone. "If you'd've been here ten minutes earlier you'd've caught me buck naked." That night as the moon came up—we were eating bullheads and cottage cheese with grape jelly on it, and my uncle was saying, "Two dollars for cottage cheese! Hell's fire! When I was a boy we gave it to the chickens"—we heard her truckload of dogs crooning from across the river.

I visited her camp the next forenoon and every morning thereafter. Her name was Trixie. She always wore the same denim pants and jacket over a gray work shirt. Looking back on it, I suppose she was thirty-five or forty years old. One day I found her loafing in the shade of her truck, cleaning her nails with a jackknife, leaning against two huge sacks of dog food. She said she was about to run her dogs, if I cared to see it, and got up to unbar the door of the cage.

The seven mutts poured out from the truck and swarmed around her, a hodgepodge of reds and browns and yellows. She picked up a thin bamboo cane, the kind you might win at a county-fair game, and waved it over the animals once and they were instantly quieted. "They know better," she said. "I do this twice a day, rain or shine." Then she sent them off with a gutteral "git" and we watched them course in remarkable coordination around the wide flats north of the river. If they moved too far away she called and waved the cane and the pack responded. They reminded me (or maybe they simply remind me now) of the trained goose flocks working their remote-controlled chore-life over Lake Erie. The dogs hullied right or left, fore and aft, as she commanded.

I returned next day to watch them again. Trixie told me on the side how to catch a mink and blow eggs and take a live skunk from a trap.

UNCLE AND SHRIKE

That last afternoon I saw them run, when the dogs were back in their cage and the sun was just in the treetops, Trixie sat down and looked at me a long time with her flat blue eyes and asked how old I was. Then she began to talk in a low country-store kind of voice, the lilting provincial voice that charms and fascinates with its cardinal sureness and its lexical world of absolute jerkwater certainty. She began tossing out blunt, seemingly random tidbits of confidential lore from her hometown in Missouri. She knew a farm boy about my age who was getting sexy with a milking machine and got stuck in it. She looked at me matter-of-factly for a sly moment to see how that registered. She knew a man who could squeeze milk from his own nipples. She knew of a man, a highway patrolman, who had three balls. The stories got fancier and fancier, but her coded vocabulary was so coy and so far beyond mine—she was bandying rapid-fire about so-and-so's cooter, japus, or mojo—that I was never exactly sure I was getting the right picture. She went on and on, pausing long sacerdotal seconds between each folkloric tableau, all in a hypnotic monotone so flat she might have been calling a bingo game—until my uncle whistled me over for dinner.

She left early the following morning. She would be home in time to run her dogs before dark. Like all of the people that summer she had loomed and faded suddenly, but she left an abrupt imprint all her own. I realized much later that she was a scion of peasantry held over from the age of the Bruegels. I would no more have cared to meet her again than I would have cared to see her buck naked in the first place. But for several pubescent years whenever I heard mention of Missouri I thought of her briefly, of her cartoon village and the sideshow menagerie of people in a state of constant, furtive semi-arousal, with something like a toy-train whistle sounding far off behind . . .

Then my uncle finished the long book he was reading and we packed up. We drove half a day south into the Gila-monster country, bought groceries, and then curled easterly and found an almost empty camp

UNCLE AND SHRIKE

on Pawnee Creek not too far from the town of Jetmore. We set up our lean-to in the lee of a thicket, as always, and had several quiet days to ourselves.

My uncle insisted on waiting a short time between books, so he sat a lot along Pawnee Creek, gazing off at the skyline or an old cotton-wood for hours. He would come to find me sometimes where I was playing alone or annoying an anthill. He would squat for a while watching, reach out and stroke my head one time, then get up and walk nervously away, slapping his thighs in rhythm to some inner Dixieland type of tune.

I was ill at ease and even frightened when he sat so long gazing, sailed out so far. It left me too much alone. A few years earlier I had visited him at a time when he still had a small house. It was May and he was making his beloved garden in the same old backyard spot, and I helped a little. Only that year I gradually realized he had lost control of it. He measured out and hoed his wobbly furrows and then forgot to plant the seed; or planted one row properly, then proceeded to cover the rest of the unplanted furrows in the section, tamping them carefully with the back of his hoe. At the end of the week no one had any idea what, if anything at all, might come up where.

If I went to join him in his reverie, as I often did on Pawnee Creek out of fear and loneliness, if I went slowly to him and sat on the earth near his folding chair, he would gradually come back home, stir a bit, drum his fingers on his knees, and mutter a sentence or two about a red-haired girl from Tennessee he dated years ago: she was musical, a singer; she had "elf ears." One afternoon he came back detailing a favorite incident from the family past, the fact that his mother had stood before Geronimo as he made his mark on scraps of paper and sold them to tourists at the 1904 St. Louis World's Fair. And then he would come all the way back and stand up and clap his hands three or four times and say, "What I wouldn't give for a bowl of Michigan blueberries and an Indiana musk melon!"

UNCLE AND SHRIKE

There was no bullhead pond at Pawnee Creek so we were back to macaroni and variable rice stews. When the time was right my uncle pulled a Thomas Wolfe novel from the duffel and started on it for what he said was the fourth time. He called me over now and then and read me a long sinewy sentence or a favorite passage as he sat within a small dome of lantern light.

Then we started east, moving a little faster than usual. We were headed for the Kaw River, a camp just west of Topeka. We drove short, easy backroad days once we left Pawnee Creek, but we camped at each place for just a night. My uncle wanted to get to the Kaw before the summer got too far along. We put up at the Cheyenne Bottoms near the Arkansas River, at a damp camp on the Little Arkansas east of Hutchinson, and then at Cottonwood Creek out from Emporia. I might be forgetting one. We always paused for a nice long lunch by some stream or other and then a nap for my uncle, and stopped religiously to back up and look at dead snakes on the road, but we kept moving, in our way, toward the Kaw in order to get there before the summer boiled over: he wanted me to hear the eastern bird songs.

We drove into the Kaw River camp on the Fourth of July. It was a big camp, almost like a town. It went for a good ways along the river. There were all kinds of tents and huts and trailers, with makeshift alleys threading through. There were more trees on the Kaw than anywhere else we had been and everyone had their shade to rest in.

We took a walk through camp after we were set up and stowed. There were cars from all over the country. Some families were hawking things like tires or tarps or parched corn. None of these people had homes anymore. They were strikingly neither happy nor sad. That evening just at dark about half the camp climbed the hills south of the river and sat silently watching the tiny fireworks on the horizon going up out of Topeka and some of the small towns to the north.

There were fish in the Kaw and at suppertime the whole camp

UNCLE AND SHRIKE

smelled of them frying. One family was selling lemons. Three consecutive mornings my uncle roused me before daybreak, handed me a quick breakfast, and led me by the elbow to a sizable uninhabited grove downriver. We stood leaning against a cottonwood and waited quietly as the first light came. Then the birds in the river trees began to sing. My uncle nudged me in case I'd forgotten why we were there. First one tree, then another, and another, until the entire congregation was in full voice around us.

"These are birds you'll never hear in the West," he whispered. "Listen to them while you can."

We stood there for half an hour each of the three mornings and then walked back to camp. My uncle fished a little in the Kaw and I explored the neighborhood. There were plenty of boys to throw the ball with. Sometimes we saw cars of people from Topeka, probably, drive up onto the hills above camp and sit there a while looking down at us all. It was hot and dusty; then it rained. There was a fight one evening after dark, and one day they brought in three teenagers knotted up sick in the back of a pickup. They had eaten jimson weed and were in bad shape. The parents jumped in the back of the truck and they rushed off to find a hospital.

But my uncle wasn't feeling very good. He had lots of spells that week. He would wander off suddenly to the riverbank and sit there looking in that way that left me far behind. I tried to keep him in as close as I could with my usual tactics, easing over to sit beside him, or asking a trivial question, or, finally, clowning in front of him, walking elaborately backwards to and fro across his field of vision.

And he recited more of the odd windborne little stories as they came to him. One about his high-school girlfriend, a country girl he hadn't seen since 1927 until he attended his fiftieth class reunion, and was standing talking with old friends when the door opened and there she was—"Lissy"—with her husband and a face full of wrinkles and stove-

UNCLE AND SHRIKE

up hands. She recognized my uncle and turned and ran from the building and never returned.

And one he told half proudly about a sad farm widow with children he had talked out of suicide during dark days of the Depression when he was employed as a relief worker, his first job. I carved him a backscratcher from a willow branch.

But I could see he was traveling farther and farther away. He slept a lot there by the Kaw, as if that place, the farthest extent and turnaround point of our summer, was also a sort of apogee for his inner orbiting. I watched him as he napped on a bedspread under a tree. Now and then he would click like an electric oven going on and off. I thought hesitantly about his life, of his many wanderings and manifold interests. Well-schooled, he had finally taken a job with a hatchery, driving truckloads of new chicks here and there about the prairie states. Driving, because he loved elemental motion; the prairie states, he told me, because he could read a good bit at the wheel.

I pondered as I watched him in deep-ocean sleep just what exactly becomes of all the learnings, the lifetime of lore and burnished, relished detail. What would happen one day to all his brief jokes and off-color puns and spirited wit and simple love of earthly things. What would become of "Dog fennel!," "Finer than frog hair," and "Oh what a bag Dad had"? It was as if the whole affectional inner life, delicate as an ear, was slowly leaking while he slept and disappearing, slipping into the Kaw, then the Missouri, the Mississippi, and off. And I was afraid for us both.

But other days he would be right back in the world, determined to figure its particulars. He drove me over toward Topeka one morning. A man had told him about a great stormfall of trees in the valley, aftermath of a blaster blow last spring. Many of the downed trees were sycamores, the man said. That excited my uncle; he wanted me to see the great white boles. We spent half a morning moving through the

UNCLE AND SHRIKE

wreckage of the storm. It was odd to walk familiarly among the bright upper branches of the large trees, admiring the intimate dapple of their sky-limbs at rest. My uncle was quick to point out that the sycamores were all fallen in a uniform direction, aligned almost magnetically amid the drab jumble of the non-sycamore mess, and I could sense his silent groping to explain.

Shortly thereafter we left the big-city camp and started back west. We camped a rainy night at a pull-off somewhere near Hollis, Kansas, and the following day found a pretty camp on a curve of the Republican River. There was a threesome of old Airstream trailers set up there with lots of people in them. They had their old folks gathered in a small snow-fence pen, sitting on folding chairs and pitting chokecherries and dropping them into a kettle.

My uncle was bound to finish the book he was reading before we parted, so we stayed on the Republican for a week. Within two days there was a pile of buffalo gourds stacked like cannonballs on the table beside a snakeskin and a giant black beetle. It was chicory season, the "blue time," and we took short drives in the late afternoons to see the pools and swales of the off-blue blossoms with the lowering sun on them. And there were bowls of sugared wild black currants after supper.

When the John Ruskin was finished and returned to the duffel we headed out for our final camp. My uncle decided it would be fitting to go back to the Arikaree River for a couple of days. We drove up the Beaver River for a long way and then cut west to our old camp. We set up in exactly the same spot we occupied in June. The Pennsylvanians were gone, the girl with the bag of cat's-eyes was gone; grass was growing back where they had worn it down. There was a family camped across the way. Californians. They were busy all day hanging and tending white cloth sacks in the lower box-elder branches. They were trying to make some sort of cheese.

UNCLE AND SHRIKE

My uncle and I just rested, paused in a formal tacitly agreed-upon way. We watched the magpies ride the wind down a long steep hill over and over, flying slowly back up to the top to do it again, like sledders with their sleds, then sailing effortlessly down in scalloping, rollicking swoops. In another day or two he would take me to Cheyenne and put me on a bus for Reno and he would drive back to his bachelor hotel in Ogallala where he was the only non-cowboy in the bunch. But he got along fine. He slept on a bedroll on his fire escape at least six months of the year. His room, I knew, was stacked with books belt high all around the walls.

We had driven a nice big watermelon of a loop on that trip and we were both pleased with it. We didn't discuss it much, the trip or its being almost over, but my uncle did give me a sheet of paper with a list of his ancestors' burial places—sleepy, saggy-fenced rural graveyards across Indiana and Ohio and down into western Virginia—and requested that if I ever in my life got that way I might drop a peony here or there on his behalf.

Our last morning in camp, after we loaded up, my uncle took a slow stiff-legged walk up into the Arikaree hills. I sat on the fender of the car and quietly moped. He was gone a good while and I was beginning to feel frightened underneath the mope. Then I heard him holler and saw him far up on the hill, hollering and waving for me to come up.

I knew he must have found something good. I hurried up the dry slope and down through a gully head and over to where he was standing grinning beside a small thorn tree. Hung about the branches was an assortment of small creature carcasses—mice, shrews, and a small bird or two impaled carefully on the thorns.

"A shrike tree," he said, beaming. "I haven't seen one in years."

It looked like a sort of bedeviled Neanderthal Christmas tree. My uncle leaned in from all sides and stood on tiptoe to examine the specimens. He pointed at a broken chickadee on one of the limbs, looked at me, and enunciated slowly: *ceciitcenihiin*. That was the very climactic

UNCLE AND SHRIKE

thing he had been searching for the past few days, the perfect casual but cabalistic closing of the summer's circle.

We went over every carcass on that shrike tree, studying them, lifting them carefully with a sharp pencil, on that hot dry hill above the Arikaree, and by the time we were finished we had both shaken our mopes and lost our silly fear for the world and we drove away toward Wyoming.

UNCLE AND SHRIKE

GRASSHOPPER FALLS

There was a dog of note living along one stretch of the Paint Creek highway. You would see her, a calico half terrier, every summer day working the backwater reservation road. She survived entirely on her own, subsisting on grasshoppers and other insects struck down by passing traffic. Of course she had to compete with the neighborhood birds for the bounty; she learned to use them to locate prey the way fishing boats key on swarms of gulls at sea. Sunday mornings she traveled a mile down the road to a country church and gleaned the grasshoppers from the gathered cars' grilles. But she was otherwise along the upper stretch, combing along the berm with her nose to the ground or sitting on her thin hips beyond the ditch waiting alertly for cars.

The Lakota family in the new house not far above the terrier's range had just discovered an old man near starvation in a shack back in the canyoned hills. The family had been back there in their pickup truck— it was rough country getting in and out—gathering berries the day before. They all knew the once-blue shack at the edge of a stream; they passed it every year on their berry run. But none of them knew the old man sitting almost in a stupor on the ground outside, leaning against the wall.

The man seemed too weak to even speak. He was dark and shrunken, his long thinning hair pushed back over large ears. He looked solemnly at the family from one face to the other, sat flat and listless against the shack and finally closed his eyes. The pump in the yard worked. Inside the door the mother of the family found a coffee can of water and a washbasin holding a handful of berries. There was a wooden crate turned upside down with a package of limp saltines and a box of Bluetip matches on it and a hairy cowlicked blanket spread on the floor.

The family leaned over the old man and talked to him slowly, asked if he was sick, if anyone else lived in the shack, would he like to come down with the family and find someone to help him out. He shook his head at each question and closed his eyes. Finally the mother left a ham sandwich and a Pepsi and three cigarettes on the ground beside him and told him they would be back with food as soon as possible.

And now today they were all trying to find out who the old man was. They asked everyone who lived along the Paint Creek highway; everyone knew the shack, but had never heard of anyone living up there for twenty years now. The mother called people around the district, asking for advice, asking if anyone had heard about an old man all by himself up in the canyon hills.

They sent Hamilton and another boy back this morning in the pickup. They carried the old man a bucket of soup and a loaf of bread and a box of donuts and a muskmelon and a bag of smoking tobacco. They found him sitting on the floor just inside the shack. He looked at the soup a long time and finally began to sip it with a large arthritic spoon. Hamilton and the other boy sat with him a half hour and then drove down the hill.

People had heard about the old man by now and began to stop by the family's house to learn the details. There was a good crowd there when Hamilton got back, men and women standing around the living room drinking coffee. One of them was inquiring about the old man's appearance. The father described him: a little bit of a man, kind of stoop-shouldered, long white hair going bald on the top. The people

GRASSHOPPER FALLS

listened carefully. One old man seated on the couch (he might have fit the description himself) coughed and asked, "Does he have all of his fingers on both hands?"

The father of the family said he thought so, and turned to Hamilton as he entered the room. "Did you see if the old man has got all his fingers?"

The boy said, "Yeah, he's got them all."

The man on the couch nodded slowly and settled back in his seat.

"If he won't say anything, tomorrow we can call the Elderly Council and report it to them. Maybe they know if anyone is missing."

"From the look of it he's been up there a long time," the mother said. She was making a fresh pot of coffee. "I wish Edna was here. I bet she would know who he is. She knows everybody west of the Missouri River."

"We should let Edna know about it. She might know the man right away."

So they asked Hamilton if he would ride over to see Edna and her family on English Creek and tell them about the man and what he looked like.

"Take the three-wheeler," his father said.

It was a long ride cross-country to Edna's place, up and down hills and across two creeks, so Hamilton sat and ate a lunch before he started up the three-wheel cycle and left the yard.

The boy was a quiet, ponderous fifteen. He was just showing signs of an early plumpness and wore large dark-framed glasses strapped to his head with elastic. He loved solitary errands more than anything. He loved their blend of solitude and prescribed destination because he tended toward the contemplative end of the constitutional spectrum and often was faintly alarmed to find himself sitting stolidly for long periods under a tree or beside a river, wondering about things. He wondered about water and ice. About the unbending purple of the hare-

GRASSHOPPER FALLS

bells. About the muscle of souls and the gristle of opinion perpetually halving. He wondered about the flight of birds, wondered if the big cottonwood groves by the rivers filtered the air of the spiritual acridity of human malfeasance the way they took the carbon monoxide from their lungs, the way vultures cleaned the roads. He wondered why some days he was sad as a Jain. This pensiveness would make him proud later in his life; he would cultivate it as a proper metaphysician, a thinking man, but at age fifteen it sometimes annoyed him, like the bulge of superfluous belly above his belt. But it was always there, a quiet background music of ponder almost like a shadow, and his favorite time of day was still sundown, when the colors faded and the lavenders took over and softened the brittle borders between things. And lately he had found a comfortable, sensible way of wondering. An experienced thinking man in the vicinity, a Hunkpapa man, learned and bent almost double, had explained to him that the philosophical life was like the workings of the woodpeckers, their resolute daily searching and prying among trees for worthwhile things. The man had picked up a twig and tapped with it against a tree trunk, imitating the unobtrusive staccato of a woodpecker at large. He told Hamilton to do the same when he felt like thinking about things; it was a good way to warm up for a mull.

Hamilton drove up the dirt road climbing behind his family's house and over the pine-clad ridge, slowing as he dropped down the other side and the road dwindled. A small cloud of white dust followed him. It was a bright August day and everything he saw appeared clean and well-intentioned. He began humming and thinking about the sacred, the *wakan*. He saw that the sunflowers in their swales were *wakan* by virtue of their golden gregariousness and strong necks, and that the flocks of black-and-white buntings flushing up beside the road were *wakan* by the grace of their social two-toned unanimity pretty as piano keys.

He forded the creek at the bottom of the long hill. People called it

GRASSHOPPER FALLS

Grasshopper Creek. There were two mallards there in a pool below a little riffle-falls—*wakan* because they knew how to dress fancy and live invisibly at the same time. Then he was on a narrow road climbing gradually through grassland and scattered pines, a faint dirt road with sweet young sage and white mallow vine trailing along the fenceless edges—and the kingbirds hawking above him were *wakan* simply because they partook of such a day and place, grew from it and larked through it making a cantankerous and indispensable noise.

Within this thought-world of hills and streams, the boy was also thinking of the old man they had found. A man without a name, or with a name that nobody knew. Hamilton had watched him closely for the half hour while he ate the soup that morning, and now the boy found himself remembering something a young man—another thinking man he saw now and again at sweat lodges—had told him several months ago. Of a sudden the man had turned to Hamilton in the last of the sunset as the fire was roaring and popping and said quietly, "No one wants to be born. We're all like those people starving over in Somalia. No one asks people if they want to be born. We just wake up and find ourselves here."

The boy arrived at the second creek—English Creek—and crossed it at a gravelly shallow. He met a man walking along carrying a dead hawk in one hand. Hamilton stopped and the man held the bird up by both wings to show it off like a butterfly, speckled red and gold and black across the shoulders, *wakan* because the sun was on it.

Another mile down the creek Hamilton saw the house where Edna and her family lived. It was a square old stucco under steeply pitched roofs with a good many shingles blown off. Hamilton shut off his cycle and walked to the front door. A crewcut man was working on a car engine near the porch. Inside, Edna and her husband were sitting on a soft couch talking with two boys and a handsome young woman. Edna brought him a cup of coffee.

After a few minutes Hamilton shifted his feet and let go of his mes-

GRASSHOPPER FALLS

sage. "You know, we found an old man yesterday, way back in the hills. We were getting berries, and found him sitting by that old blue cabin back there. He didn't have hardly anything to eat. He doesn't say anything to anybody. No one knows who he is."

The old people had stopped everything to watch the boy.

"We took him back some food and left it with him. He ate some soup and smoked some cigarettes. My mother wants to find out where he came from so she can tell someone. He doesn't say a word."

Edna's husband finally asked, "He hasn't got any social-security card or nothing in his pockets?"

Then, a moment later, Edna: "How old is the man? What does he look like?"

"He's old," Hamilton said. "He's little and stooped over, with white hair. He wears a red and black flannel shirt."

Edna: "Is that the old cabin on Sweetgrass divide? Along the big breaks?"

"Yes."

"He didn't say nothing? Not even in Indian?"

"He never said a word."

Edna thought for a minute. "Is he a dark-skinned man?"

"Pretty dark."

The two teen-aged boys and the girl had gone back to whispering softly among themselves.

"Has he got all his fingers on his hands?"

Hamilton looked up at the old woman. "Yeah, he's got all of them. I saw him rolling cigarettes."

Edna was considering, with lips pursed. "Maybe he used to live back there a long time ago . . . Maybe someone didn't want him and took him back there and left him."

After a while she turned to her husband and said, "Maybe we better go over there. We better go and have a look at the man. Maybe we can

GRASSHOPPER FALLS

figure out who he is." The husband agreed and Edna went off to pack up some food for the stranger.

Hamilton wandered out to the porch where the young people had moved. The girl was home from college for the summer. She had long hair in a ponytail that hung below her hips. She was smoking and talking to the boys.

"We should change all the names of places back to names our people called them. These whiteman names don't mean anything."

She looked over at Hamilton and smiled. She wore long dangle earrings from Oklahoma that stretched her earlobes a little with their weight.

"They named everything the same—Mud Creek or Dry Creek or Castle Rock. They don't know what land is."

She told them how Indians in Canada had changed the spelling of their tribes' names to make them Indian words, not white words. "And the Omahas changed their name to U-ma-ga-hagh. It's more of an Indian word."

The boys nodded and smoked. Hamilton asked her, "How do you change the names of everything when they already have names?"

"You have to make a new map. The Chinese people and the Russians are always changing their names around, to make the words look more like people say them, not like somebody else came in and said them. They change the maps. First it was Peiping, then Peking, and then Beijing. They have people working on that all the time."

Edna and her husband came out with a bag of things. The young people decided they would ride over to Paint Creek with them, and a minute later the man working on the engine decided he would too. Hamilton said he would rest a short while before riding back over the hills.

"Sure, go ahead," Edna's husband said. "In the house or out here, anywhere you want." They all got in the car and drove away.

GRASSHOPPER FALLS

The boy stood with his hands in his pockets and watched the car ease out the lane toward the valley road. His errand was completed and he was alone again. He looked around, then began to stroll the yard and off among the outbuildings, through the pigweed and past the car with its engine hanging from a gantry. There was a mean-looking hen with a brood of chicks that surely never asked to be hatched—they tore through the world omnivorous and slashing.

Hamilton wondered who the man with missing fingers might be. But he was tired of all the questions and the wondering. Edna could take over for a while; she was a good thinking woman. She would figure out who the man in the shack was and that would be taken care of. For today, Hamilton was tired of it. He would just as soon have a set of purple summer sucker-kisses running down his neck like most of his friends that year.

He would take a little rest. He walked over to the corral and leaned on the fence looking at the horses. As always, standing alone near horses made him think of his great-grandfather. Henry Feather had been a famous bronc hand known all over South Dakota. Hamilton had heard all the stories about him many times. Henry was the ace horse-breaker for a big outfit around here and down into Nebraska. Early this century they sold herds to the Mexican government, and during World War I they had a big contract to furnish cavalry and artillery horses to the French and Italian armies. They sent a lot of horses over there.

The boy walked over and stretched out on the ground under a little tree. He could still smell the corrals. His great-grandfather once rode twenty broncs in a single day. Stories had it that Henry always wanted to know where each of the bronc lots he worked with was headed for; winked and said he taught the horses a little different for each country. Hamilton drowsed. He had a plan of his own: he would think and study and acquire knowledge until he was thirty-five or forty; then he would quit, take it easy, maybe go to live in California for a while. He

GRASSHOPPER FALLS

didn't know if an old Indian man without a name was all that different from one with. But he knew exactly where Henry Feather was buried. He was buried down the road in the hamlet of Lowe, in a patchy-grass and sagebrush cemetery off behind the Catholic church. His brown and gray horses were scattered, far from the meadowlarks, in little pieces all over France.

GRASSHOPPER FALLS

PIE FOR BREAKFAST

From the café counter I was watching a boy out back plinking at something up in a tree with his air rifle. I hadn't slept well—it was deer season in eastern Montana and the high-school girls drove by the little motel until what seemed the middle of the night, honking and bluff-whistling at the out-of-town hunters gathered in the parking lot. I watched the boy in patched baggy jeans and a brown jacket fire his BB gun nearly straight up in the air and then stand there with his mouth open as if he were waiting to catch a high-lobbed piece of popcorn.

Then I ordered bacon and eggs and a slice of pie, and the young man down the counter did exactly the same, and we began to talk.

"I haven't seen a true lemon pie in ten years."

I knew Ida hadn't made the pie as soon as I saw it sitting on the serve-up. It was too generously full and too fancy around the edges. She set down her cigarette and leaned through the cook's window and told us her sister was visiting and she had made three pies to earn her keep.

It was a wonderful pie, the kind with whole unpeeled lemons in it, sliced thin as paper and cooked with lots of sugar and eggs into a custardy mass. Ida said her sister would only mix it in a yellow bowl. The man at the counter liked it too, and around his last forkful told me about a fresh fig pie he had run into in California, another custard-style pie with chopped figs in it, served cold. He had a small notebook on the counter and carried half a dozen ball-point pens in his shirt pocket.

A pair of very old men came shuffling into the place, talking loudly. They were bent up and deaf and slow on their feet, one-time ranchers, but it was obvious they were longtime friends and they were immensely happy to be out together. A boy was with them, keeping an eye and moving obstacles from their path. It might have been the boy who was shooting the air rifle. The two men sat side by side along one wall and conversed in hoarse intimate shouts.

I was telling the man at the counter about a cider pie I had sampled once in New England, an honest enough, timber-less pie, and Ida came out front with smoke twirling from her nostrils and talked about the transparent pies of northern Kentucky, from up along the Ohio River, and I remembered a cane-syrup pie I picked up at a bake sale near Thibodaux, Louisiana.

A UPS driver and a ranch couple were now in the café. One of the old men was bellowing gleefully into his cohort's ear: "I WAS OVER COURTING THIS GIRL ONE AFTERNOON. WE WERE SITTING ON THE PORCH AND I SAW AN OLD TABBY CAT OUT ON THE LAWN WASHING ITS FACE REAL NICE AND I SAID TO THE GIRL 'I BET THAT CAT'S DOING SOMETHING YOU HAVEN'T DONE TODAY' AND BY THE TIME SHE LOOKED OVER THERE THE CAT HAD TURNED AROUND AND HIKED ITS LEG AND WAS LICKING ITS HINDER."

And the young fellow at the counter was going on about chess pie, how it should be made only with buttermilk, and that if you go far south and add a handful of chopped dates to chess pie you've got Jeff Davis pie. Then he jumped, understandably enough, to Robert E. Lee cake, a lemony yellow cake layered with a lemon-curd filling and served cool, out on the veranda.

We got up to leave together. The two old men were still wiping their eyes and blowing their noses after the tabby-cat story. The UPS man

PIE FOR BREAKFAST

had wolfed his eggs and gone. I asked Ida how long her sister would be with her, just for reference on the pie futures in case I got through town again soon.

In the parking lot I noticed the man had boxes of books and tabulation in his backseat. A geologist? Anthropologist.

"I'm working on a project around here. Something that's never been done before, as far as I know. I'm doing a study on what you might call White Indians."

I shaded my eyes with one hand.

"I mean people who really jump into it, pretty much give up their own cultures, move west and settle on a reservation. I'm interested in how they go about it. How they penetrate, what happens deep down in their private lives, their language, their daily habits, the works. I'm locating people now and want to stay in touch with them for a period of years, follow up on them.

"The last time I was over here I interviewed a woman living in a cabin up north. She's about twenty-five. From Philadelphia. She was mashing chokecherries with a stone hammer, drying meat in the sun. She was making pemmican. Hadn't been off the reservation in two years."

"No pie."

"No pie."

"Have you met the kid over around Lame Deer, a blond kid with braids?"

"No." He had his notebook and one of his pens out.

"You might want to talk to him. He dresses 1865 every day of the year. Leggings, breechcloth, otter-braid wraps. I don't know his name, but he's not hard to find. Look for him in front of the big grocery store on the highway. Or south of town, down by the powwow grounds. I see him down there a lot, sitting back along the creek by himself."

PIE FOR BREAKFAST

MEN IN SHADOW

Not far from the Cannonball River, not far from where it disappears into the shackled Missouri, full summer in place. The bright sky, the drumming perpendicular heat, the dust-heavy sunflowers along every road and byway, the heedless grasshoppers, cardboard beer cases smashed in the ditches—have driven the old men, three of them here, into the cool thick shade of a haystack, a tall trefoil of three huge round bales now forgotten as though misplaced and never found, slowly melting toward one shapeless preindustrial toadstool mass.

The men were at ease on their haunches, leaning against the stack. They had taken off their straw summer Stetsons and set them, each, on the dry ground just off their right knees. It was first-class shade. They could see the small highway not far off, the occasional cars slowing a familiar iota for the old stop sign, and a blanched peach-colored house long empty on a distant treeless knoll. Nearer at hand in the sunflowers and tall grass stood an unknown and unowned mortar-and-wattle hive of a thing, a cracked mud-colored wasplike oven or kiln, also melting, belt high under a spindly summer-fey elm.

When a young boy with a popsicle idled up on his bicycle, instinctively edged in under the shade for a moment muttering a little approximate tune to himself, the one old man began to talk. He talked to the other men but thought of the boy while he did.

"I was walking across from Shields the other night. Coming home from my brother's. It was dark already, there wasn't much of a moon. I got to the creek there at the log bridge and stopped for a smoke. I sat down on an old tree stump right there and smoked. Pretty soon I looked across the other way and there was someone over there— I couldn't see anything but their cigarette light up when they smoked on it. I said something out loud. Nobody answered. Just the cigarette burning in the dark with somebody smoking it. So I sat there and finished my smoke, then got up and walked to the bridge. I passed right by that person—from here to that sunflower. I looked as hard as I could but there wasn't anybody there—just that cigarette. It was still there, going on and off like a firefly when I looked back across the bridge."

The other men said nothing. It was six hours till dark. The boy's mouth was coronaed popsicle red all the way around when he pushed off silently, as gradually as he had arrived, and pedaled in an unhurried reflective weave away into the bright sun.

The man on the right—if you stood and faced them, the man on the north—was Eldon Hat. He sat beside his Stetson in the shade. Two days earlier he had received a visitor from Atlanta, Georgia, and it was still with him in a lingersome way, like smoke in your hair or gasoline on your hands.

Donald Hanks had flown from Atlanta to Minneapolis to Bismarck, North Dakota, with the sole purpose of finding Eldon Hat. They had been in the Second War together, shoulder to shoulder through some nasty business, and hadn't seen each other since. Donald wasn't sure even where Eldon was living, if he were living, but he came to North Dakota to find out.

He rented a car at the Bismarck airport and drove south along the Missouri. He glanced at its gulls, then stopped at the store by the Cannonball turnoff to inquire if Eldon Hat was still around. They sent him

MEN IN SHADOW

up the little road along the Cannonball River. When he got to the half hamlet of Shields he stopped a woman on the road and asked again. She gave him high-pitched directions abstract as ice, but he recognized the house immediately when he got there.

Eldon Hat was resting in his kitchen. He saw the two horses in the yard look up and off toward the road together and his blind deaf dog get up to circle slowly in place and he knew someone was coming to see him.

He recognized Donald Hanks by his huge body and oversized to-tempole grin. He was glad to see him. They shook hands for a long time, then went to sit on two straight chairs in the shade of the sky-blue house. "My wife is at work." They were old men who knew it, one slight and slow, the other large and full of awkward sprawl; his chair braced and groaned. They had exchanged one friendly pair of letters in the spring of 1951, and were about to talk for two hours.

"I'm seventy-two come September," Donald was saying. He had a handkerchief in his hand to catch the runnels from his brow. "Forty-four of them went to Waco Scaffolding. Atlanta branch."

Eldon figured for a moment. "That makes you fourteen months older than I am."

"September 9, 1916."

"The third of November, 1917. I've lived here all my life."

"You remember Dave Finney."

"Sure I do." Out of Frankfurt, Kentucky. Lanky, long oatmeal-textured face. A good man, called everyone "Buddy." Professed to love whiskey. Constantly cracking his knuckles. Prayed on his knees every night. He died in a factory explosion in 1975.

"You remember Aaspaugh?" Harry Aaspaugh. "Goosey." Dover, Delaware. Quiet. Always talking quietly about the Bay. Bluefish. Crabs. Gigging frogs from a canvas canoe. Then the big fry, all you could hold. Beer and a half-peck of lemons. The flattest feet they ever let in the army. Left tracks in the shower room big as a grizzly. Laughed at the

MEN IN SHADOW

drop of a hat. But goosey—jumped three feet if you touched him anywhere between the belt and the kneecaps. Worked for Procter & Gamble. Died of heart, 1980.

And Eddie—Eddie Bainge, with the Barlow knife and the black hair all over his body. He never came home. Buried outside St. Lo—or was it St. Crieuc de Ton?

"You remember Carl Jones." Wichita, Texas. Smoked Lucky Strikes (green war pack) like candy. "Bones" Jones. A high-cheekboned lonely distractedness, an innate noblesse oblige that kept him leaning. Loved every woman he ever met. Could eat enough for three men. A little older than the rest. He went back to Texas. He died in 1969. Used to sing "I dream of Jeannie with the light brown hair" all day long.

"I thought that was Ebersprecher."

And J. T. Murray. He's still alive. Still in Oakland, California. He never misses a Christmas card. "Hurry" Murray. A great poker player, but quick on the uptake: Irish impatience under blinding blarney veneer. "Hurry it up will you!" Lavishly proud of his city. Lived there all his life. Still lives there, all dressed up, talking about the big blue bay.

And Ebersprecher. Zoltan Ebersprecher. Wibaux, Montana. "That's not too far from here." A master belcher. Could also bugle like an elk and walk long distances on his hands. A hundred and fifty pushups. Always singing "Cecilia" with a theatrical lisp. Became an engineer. Dropped dead in Denver, Colorado.

"What about Zook?" Zook died two-three years ago. He went back to Cleveland after the war. A perpetual squint. Dennis Albemarle Zook. Crazy for baseball. Worked for some big department store. Laughed at the drop of a hat. Went back during the landing at St. Lo and pulled some leg-shot kid out of the water and got him up onshore. Saved his life.

"I thought that was Jones."

"No, that was Zook."

"I could have sworn it was Jones."

MEN IN SHADOW

"I'm pretty sure it was Zook."

Zook or Jones. Maybe Jones, probably Zook. Winner take all the cicada shells.

They had finally covered it all as best they could and got up from their chairs. Donald Hanks had cooled in the recollection, his big face was shiny but dry. Eldon took him for a little walk around the place; showed him the two horses with dream-spittle on their lips and the single pink hollyhock beside the gate. There was a clothesline with denims on it and an abandoned pit toilet with an elm sapling growing out from under it. He showed Donald a pile of deer skulls along the fence, then nodded toward a swale in the adjoining field.

"I had two sons lived over there. One and then the other. Eldon Junior and then Everett. They were good boys but they took to drinking. One of them got drunk one night and let the house burn down around him. Couple of years later Everett put a house up there. The same thing happened to him about six months later. Two fires in one place." He turned back toward the house.

"I'm awful sorry to hear it, Eldon."

"After that happened I almost forgot all about the war."

Donald went to his rented car before he drove away and got a video camera from the back seat. He asked his friend to stand outside the kitchen door. He shot Eldon for a full minute standing uneasily with his arms hanging limp and his eyes off over the fence somewhere. Donald panned slowly to the left, getting the rest of the house, the two chairs in deep shadow, and then the horses asleep on their feet and the valley where the road ran beyond. A pause, then back slowly across the house to Eldon, who hadn't moved a muscle, and on to the right, the other half of the yard with the outhouse, the old wooden fence, lagged a moment at the field where the boys had burned, the gentle lift of the grassland and yucca above—then on out, panning to the hills southeast, sweeping the whole half circle, slowly across the heat-shimmied

MEN IN SHADOW

southern skyline, the southwest with a trace of the Cannonball visible way off, and back, bearing back in, the horses again, the edge of the sky-blue house, Eldon, with one hand now in a hip pocket.

One of the men by the haystack got up to go home. The heat of the day was breaking. Eldon and the other old man, the man who had seen the ghost smoking at the bridge, sat a while longer. They had known each other since 1922.

"Did you hear about Mickey Mouse getting a divorce from Minnie? He said she was fucking Goofy."

Yesterday Eldon had thought about the war. Not much at all today. Less the war than kind Donald Hanks who had come all the way from Atlanta, Georgia, with a good bit of it stuck in his teeth.

Eldon was pretty sure it was Zook pulled that boy onshore. And just then, right through the Minnie Mouse joke, he was remembering a split second of the day he got back from it all, a welcome-home parade down at Fort Yates, not too far from here. There was a brief dusty scuffle: a dog nipped a child. A band with two tubas was playing.

II. AN AUGUST THIRD

I stopped at the high point of the hump road—a solitary breezy place I was fond of on the gravel road crossing the Porcupine–Wounded Knee divide. I got out to stretch and go to the bathroom in the ruddy bluestem and look at the Black Hills off to the west.

Early that morning I had pulled into a desolate ranch house a hundred miles to the south to ask directions among the unpredictable back roads. It was a lovely site tucked against a protective rise. An elderly woman answered my knock, a petite pink-cheeked lady in an apron, a sweet American Swede with uplifted eyes working diligently through thick glasses. She invited me in. Soon we were seated, the two of us, at

MEN IN SHADOW

her lacy dining-room table. She brought me a saucer of cookies and a tall glass of milk and told me her story: her early homestead life on that very ground (a tractor shed out back had been their dugout home the first several years); the premature death of her first husband; the sad unraveling and slow demise of a second, leaving her twice alone there. She began to weep, daubing with an ironed hanky at her nose. Then I caught it and began to choke up with my mouth full of macaroon—and then we pulled ourselves together. She advised me on my route and we said goodbye. But I thought of her more than once that day and stopped the car and stretched and threw imaginary fastballs.

"Are you choking your chicken?!"

By the time I turned and located the voice through the sun the men were laughing. It was a good surprise. They were back in the shade of cherry bushes in a sharp ravine below me. They were all chuckling as I walked down the grassy slope to see them.

The heat was like a slurry in the air. But these men were experts. Their cherry patch was situated at the head of the ravine, just where it first split the hillside open. I had to scramble down three feet to get in under its shade. And there they sat in the almost shocking cool of their shelter. It had the feel of a hut or a lair; there was plenty of headroom and elbowroom. Chokecherries dangled around the edges. The men's expertise meant they sat erect and alert, neither sleeping nor restless. I knew John Door. One of the others had a jug of shadow-cool tea. We all wore faded wash-worn shirts with thin spots and bramble tears in them. We all shook hands.

Below the cherry patch the ravine dropped and deepened between steep white walls. Ash trees and dark cedars grew from its narrow floor, and farther down tall cottonwoods on their tiptoes, their crowns brushing and just breaking the upper coulee walls. It was dense and sunless as a cave. From down there somewhere a man called out in a hoarse voice, then I could make out people stirring in a cedar's shadow maybe thirty yards below us.

MEN IN SHADOW

"They're drinking down there," John said. "You should have been here the other day. It was real hot. We were sitting here and all of a sudden this big fancy car comes over the hump, just rolling along, and then it pulls over real fast—right up there where you stopped. There was a man and a woman in it and they jumped out and started peeling off their clothes and then they crawled in the backseat together. They were in a big hurry. They must have been awful hot around the collar." The other men chuckled affirmatively. "It was a big Cadillac or something like that. I don't know where they were from. They had blue license plates. Joe says Iowa."

Another day they had seen a car stop and a priest get out and drop to his knees in the thin grass and pray with his clasped hands extended and his head thrown back as in the Gethsemane illustrations. It was a provocative road.

We heard a coarse grunt and a brief thrashing of limbs. A large man was making his way up the ravine toward us. He was having a time of it, helping himself along with saplings, and when he arrived he was winded and stood heaving for a good while, casting long breakers of beer breath over us.

I had seen him before, more than once here or there about the rez. I didn't really know him, but I remembered him well. He was a corpulent, noticeable man about sixty. Most of his days were spent loitering conspicuously, helplessly, in public places—gas stations, grocery-store entryways, post offices—with his trousers sagging and his shirttails flying lose. He was desperately social, yet socially formless and chameleonic in a needy omnivorous way. He stood season after season, moist-lipped, watching orphanlike and longingly up and down the streets. But when he was drinking he had a notorious mean and manipulative side to him. Enough so that most people called him "Haywire." He had mastered the aggressive whine and the surly kowtow. He was given to using the prehistoric past as a sort of scenic, penny-ante and lucrative leverage. One day in front of the grocery I overheard

MEN IN SHADOW

him working on a white couple with cameras around their necks; he had one arm around the man's shoulders and was going on in a lugubrious voice about his hard-pressed ancestors planting beans along the Missouri River a thousand years ago. The woman had tears in her eyes.

And now he stood holding on to a cherry branch, staring at me with a breathless, bruised St. Bernard look on his face. John skillfully tried to distract him, prodded him with brisk empty repartee. The other men were obviously uneasy in his presence; among other things, if he lost his balance and toppled down the hill he might well take a good part of the cherry patch with him. Finally he said something. "This woman goes to the doctor. Comes home and tells her husband everything is OK. He says, 'But what about your big fat ass?' She says, 'Your name wasn't even mentioned.'" He fastened an open-mouthed glower on me for a long moment, then went back down the hill.

We sat talking. Now and then the jug of tea went around. The floor of the cherry patch was comfortable, picked clean and worn soft by the layering of summer days. The men hung their caps on the same twig pegs every day. The afternoon relaxed and uncoiled. I realized this was what I had wanted to do all day. It was better than river driving, better than bank fishing. It had a sensible side-step dignity to it that made it seem ingenious under fire.

Haywire bellowed down below. We knew it was directed more or less our way. Seconds later he bellowed again and John reached behind him for a paper bag and pulled out sandwiches for all of us. It was some sort of lunchmeat and cheese. The whole thing was saturated with a virulent and cloying perfume.

"Who made these?" I asked him.

"Aida. She made them before she went to work. She works at the government office. She gets all dressed up and wears lots of perfume."

"*Whew*. They're good though."

While we ate, John began telling me about a local incident that people were following. A religious man on the reservation had agreed

MEN IN SHADOW

to instruct three Caucasians in a vision quest. They planned it all carefully. They were going up on Bear Butte, doing it right. They would fast for four days. This all happened about two weeks ago.

He was interrupted by the big man—we heard him thrashing in the understory and then he was coming up the hill. He was drunker by now, more surly. Maybe he smelled the sandwiches. He took hold of a cherry branch and stared at me. The other men shifted and cleared their throats. I felt responsible for this unpleasant burr in a lazy, temperless day and wished Haywire were far away in some other well-insulated ravine. He addressed me in a lathery voice.

"Sioux chief and white general meet out on the prairie to smoke the peace pipe. Chief smokes, passes the pipe to the general. General takes out his handkerchief and wipes off the mouthpiece, then smokes. He gives the pipe back to the Indian. Chief takes out his knife and cuts off the mouthpiece, throws it away. General says, 'Why did you do that? White men are clean, Indians are dirty.' The chief says, 'No way. You are the dirty ones. Indians go to the bathroom outside. White man shits in his own house. I blow my nose on the grass. You blow your snot in a rag and carry it around in your pocket. You ruined my best pipe.'"

Then he slid back down to his friends in the cedars.

The tea went around. John resumed his desultory tale. The three vision questers had given the Sioux religious man two hundred dollars apiece. All three bought expensive buffalo robes from a man in Rapid City. The religious man put them in a sweat lodge, then took them up on the side of Bear Butte and got them situated in a propitious spot. They talked for a while and prayed and smoked. Then the religious man left them alone. Said he would come back for them in four days.

Haywire was roaring down below. I envisioned him fumbling to load a .30-30 with wild-plum pits. Joe stepped out of the patch and walked off a civilized measure to go to the bathroom. A pickup truck slowed on the gravel berm; its dust cloud drifted through it and away.

MEN IN SHADOW

A boy yelled from the near window: "Is Morris in there?" John told him no, he hadn't seen him today.

"So after four days the men are waiting on the butte. They hadn't had anything to eat for the whole time. And the religious man didn't show up. They waited and waited. He never showed up. Finally they walked down by themselves."

Someone else was scrambling up from the cedars now—a slim little man wearing cowboy boots outside of his jeans. As he walked off toward the road, John yelled after him, "What's Haywire doing?"

"He's passed out," the man answered over his shoulder. "He's passed out cold." It was good news close at hand, a minor victory for the durability of the day. We all recrossed our legs and got comfortable.

"Those three men didn't have their car or anything. They went to a ranger station and finally got a ride into Sturgis where they had parked. They asked everyone they saw about the religious man. Nobody knew anything. The three men began to get mad. Six hundred dollars. After they rested up and had something to eat they drove down here and started looking for that medicine man. They went to his house. Nobody knew where he was; he hadn't been there for several days. They went to Pine Ridge, went to the tribal office. They even went down to Nebraska to the bars looking for him. They were getting madder and madder. Nobody had seen that man for days. He was just gone. Gone somewhere with the money . . . Joe says Santa Fe."

The episode had overnight become a bit of local folklore: the three men prowling the reservation in search of the medicine man, their candy-red car with ski racks on it—every day or so people saw it somewhere between Wanblee and Oglala, driving slowly and watchfully along the roads, or parked in amateurish surveillance behind a barn.

Haywire and apparently all his comrades were sleeping; there was a cushiony silence from the lower ravine. A hawk went by, glinted in a

MEN IN SHADOW

lessened light: the afternoon was fading, falling away. No one talked for half an hour. Piñon jays were stirring, crying somewhere up on the shady side of the ridge.

Joe looked at me with a savvy new-phase-of-the-moon look on his face. "You should come with us. We're going over to White Horse Creek for a feast. A cattle truck ran off the road over there last night, rolled off that steep hill. The driver told the people over there they could shoot all the cattle that were hurt. Now they're throwing a feed for everyone."

Day makes night. I drove. I could still taste the wild perfume on my teeth. I would have whistled something from *Aida* if I knew it. It was an evening—the very word—an evening whose sky in an hour would have that untouchable cool-down melon color streaming through its trees; you could see it coming. And I was with experts. We were headed for kettles of beef simmering on cottonwood fires. There would be tubs of canned corn and macaroni salad. Poorwills calling. Under a moth-battered yardlight, a card table of frosted yellow flatcakes. Urns of coffee. John said I could always sleep at his place.

III. BACON, FLOUR, SUGAR, TREE

LeTurner was always a nook-and-cranny man. He required a fundamental privacy: as a boy he had run off from the reservation boarding school ten times. It was a state record by a hair. They always found him a day or two later in deep, fey concentration—as if he didn't see them standing there looking down at him—in some little-known nook or pine-needled cranny near the family home. And this day seventy years later he was in out of the sun below a twenty-foot cottonwood, sitting in a slight hollow in the grassy glacis. It was an uncertain tree, dog-legged and slight of crown, its midday shadow was modest for two grown men, but they managed, LeTurner and another man, an approx-

MEN IN SHADOW

imate peer in things north-central Montanan, and squinted out over the plain.

It was a hot day. Twenty years ago, maybe even five years ago, Le-Turner would have walked up the slope on the slalom a mile or so into the cool pines that sprang up there and continued black and aromatic up across the flanks of the Little Rockies. But now he was too old and so was the other and they sat happy enough near the Fort Belknap road in the shade of the tree with a blanched church sign nailed to it. There was a dead porcupine on the edge of the road, and then the sharp blue shadows of the Judith Mountains on the skyline eighty miles southwest.

They hadn't known one another more than two or three years. They began running into each other along this road and then began to share the shade of the cottonwood when hot days caught them together and they had no other destinations. They sat and spoke of little gnat-like things. LeTurner was a small wiry man. If people looked twice at him it was to verify his bandy bowlegs or the fancy yellow flicker feather in his hat. He said little, kept his teeth clenched with his full lips hanging open, and was partial to Sen-Sen candy.

The other man had heard a story about LeTurner, just a murmur, but enough to catch his ear, of a sharp-edged incident far off behind him, long-finished but notable—less than some, more than others. Just a muddy whisper of it—but the facts of the matter were that in the summer of 1928 with Calvin Coolidge at the helm LeTurner Lake and his wife and baby were living happily in a little Indian town, in a pleasant cabin-house on the windward side of these very mountains; they looked up and saw them every day. It was a town of twelve or fifteen homes set on dirt streets with an occasional hard-pressed tree. LeTurner was eighteen. He did wage work on nearby ranches and came home and played with his child. His wife was a good-looking woman with thin shanks and fine long hair. She worked two or three days a week up in Demo Crossing, a mixed-blood and white town eight miles

MEN IN SHADOW

north. She cleaned house up there for a half-breed man who ran a mercantile and made good money and smoked thin crooked cigars and stood around with his thumbs hooked in his pant waist.

In the latter half of July 1928, the merchant began to tumble for the woman. He was a one-eyed man called Borgne. His squinting gave him an on-running harsh grimace, but he was really a harmless, moony sort of man. And he fell for the girl. He watched her all day long, followed her from room to room, tried to talk with her while she worked. This went on for several weeks. People in Demo began to notice the way the merchant stared at her and followed her into the yard while she beat the rugs and shook the blankets.

Then one day he showed up down in the woman's cabin town on one of her days off. He pulled his Model A off the road and got out and leaned against the car, smoking a cigar and gazing at the woman's house. Then he drove away. But people saw him, that time and the next, and began to sense what was going on, and the more he drove down there the more they began to get nervous.

LeTurner had no inkling what was going on until his brother called him over one afternoon and said, "I think that Borgne man up in Demo is sniffing around your wife." LeTurner asked his wife about it when she got home that night. She said the merchant was looking at her all the time, but she didn't think there would be any trouble. LeTurner sat and pictured the dusty streets of that town eight miles north, just barely there, with the trees of the big river at its far edge, and wagons tied at its curbs.

That night most all the residents of LeTurner's community knew that a car pulled up along the road and sat there for a long while in the dark with its engine running. Next morning at first light LeTurner walked over to the place and found two black cigar butts ground out in the dirt. That Borgne hadn't sense enough even to cover them up as any decent dog would have.

LeTurner told his wife to wait for him in the cabin, then walked

MEN IN SHADOW

over to his brother's house at the edge of the village. His brother was in the yard drinking coffee with a tiny new pup riding in his shirt pocket. He helped LeTurner put the team to the wagon and watched him drive away.

LeTurner took the old low road north. It was rough and dusty, paralleling the newer high road about half a mile west of it. The two routes joined about a mile below Demo Crossing where a store and gas station stood, its new planking still bright raw in the morning sun. The merchant Borgne wasn't home, LeTurner saw his big car was gone and the doors shut up tight. An old man on the street told him the merchant had taken his Model A out to the dump with a load of cans. LeTurner found him there, just sweeping out his backseat with a whisk. The merchant stopped and watched the wagon coming up pretty fast. When LeTurner set the brake and climbed down with his rifle the merchant looked at him like a hound in a tight corner, but then something changed and he stood up straight and tall as if he were getting his picture taken, and that's the way he was when LeTurner shot him.

LeTurner drove back on the high road. He pulled the wagon up before his door and pretty soon he and his wife were loading their belongings. They didn't hurry. They wrapped things right and stowed them securely in the wagon bed. In an hour they were ready and drove calmly out. His brother walked them to the big road with one hand on the wagon rail; he was still carrying the red-and-white pup in his shirt pocket.

They drove south twelve miles and then cut up a shadowy mining trail and climbed into the Little Rockies. They followed a small stream up, crossed a low pass through the cooked-out end-of-summer pines. They weren't running. They weren't in a hurry. They had everything they owned right with them. By late afternoon they reached a narrow valley in the eastern half of the range, a pretty place with no one around and red willows along its creek. They slept under the wagon and next morning put up a wall tent and made a tentative camp with

MEN IN SHADOW

the tent stakes not hammered in all the way and set their minds to waiting and seeing.

Three weeks went by, they were into a sweet September, and nothing had happened—no sheriff and deputies rode over the hill. Three weeks. LeTurner didn't know what to think. This place wasn't much of a secret to anybody around here. He wondered why nothing had happened by now. He shot a deer. The first quick snow blew through. And then he decided to go back over the mountain and find out what was going on.

He traveled openly, calmly, but timed things so that he arrived at his brother's house just after dark. He could see them in the lighted kitchen sitting around the table with the litter of pups wrestling on the floor. He stood inside the door and talked quietly with his brother. "What's going on back here? Nobody ever came after us. Did the Borgne man die?"

Two cousins had come over to the house by now.

"He died. He died right away. They buried him over at Havre, that's all I know."

LeTurner asked his brother to go with him to the gas station up the north road and see if they could learn anything. They took the wagon with a young brother-in-law riding in the back. LeTurner pulled the team up off to one side and sent his brother in to buy tobacco. "Make sure he really died." He could see him inside standing by the counter talking with the proprietor, another half-breed man heavy on the Cree side, and a knowledgeable loiterer a bony akimbo near the crackling stove.

He was back in a quarter hour, standing beside the wagon wheel in the dark telling LeTurner what he had heard. LeTurner sat sideways in the seat with the reins wrapped around one thigh.

"He died right away. I told you that. They buried him over in Havre."

MEN IN SHADOW

"What's that sheriff been doing about it?"

"Nobody knows anything about the sheriff."

"Seems like he'd be after me by now if that Borgne died."

"Seems like he would. Maybe he heard you were gone to Canada."

"Maybe he did."

"Ernie said someone was saying you might be down in Riverton, Wyoming."

"Who said that?"

"I don't know. Somebody just talking about it. Nobody told any lies."

The loiterer left the station and walked away and the screen door finally slammed behind him. The brothers drove home and LeTurner slept on the floor for a couple of hours and then started back to his wife in the mountains.

He still didn't know what to think, and neither did his wife, but after another week they began to firm up the camp. They cut firewood and insulated the tent and one day the brother showed up with the provisions LeTurner had requested: sugar and flour and bacon and tea. They were almost forgetting about the sheriff and the town. They were in out of the wind, and then it was spring and the woman was heavy with child again, and they decided to turn some ground near the creek and plant beans and corn.

And the sheriff never came over the hill. LeTurner went back to Demo once more and talked a little in the nightfall and bought a sack of flour. He wondered now and then how a thing like that could happen and cast no shadow. He wondered what had happened to the State of Montana and the United States of America under Franklin Roosevelt and even the Dominion of Canada and the Mounties, if that's where they thought he went.

And that was the only thing he ever shot, that and a hundred deer. The next summer the brother and some in-laws helped them put up a

MEN IN SHADOW

cabin in the valley and the following spring a cousin moved down there and built one and there were children yelling around the place and wood smoke in the air.

A car slowed and stopped along the highway where the old men were sitting. A younger fellow got out and opened the trunk and began carving a big watermelon in there. He carried two thick slices across the ditch and up to the shade of the little cottonwood. The old men were happy to see it. They ate and spat the seeds starboard. The young man offered them a ride home. But it was too early to go home, too hot.

The little settlement camp in the mountains is still there, although LeTurner left it years ago when his wife died during the Eisenhower administration. Twenty or thirty people live there, grandchildren, great grandchildren, ravens overhead. Even a place to buy soda pop in the summer. Fifty years ago, as people started settling there, they called the place LeTurner, but LeTurner wasn't easy with that, thought it was pushing his luck, so they called it "Osier" after the creek running there. Nowadays they say it "O-seer." It's eighteen and a half miles as the crow flies from the foot of the cottonwood tree.

Borgne's people are all long gone to Havre and beyond. The sheriff is dead for quite a while and his people gone to Spokane and Boise, long gone. The town where the shooting took place has almost disappeared. The wind has it, plays with it like a cat.

MEN IN SHADOW

NORTHBOUND BUS

A man named Williams opened a coffeehouse a few blocks off the main street in Cheyenne, Wyoming. The coffee was good and strong, there was an espresso machine at the ready, and a chessboard folded on the counter with the playing pieces in an old White Owl cigar box. Williams wanted the place to be the real thing, a place for thought and discussion and perhaps, eventually, free verse aloud. But he was realistic enough to simmer a cauldron of soup each morning and lay a bed of submarine sandwiches in a case by the door to sell to neighborhood workers. After a while some of the railroad crews began to walk the extra blocks to fill their big thermoses with mocha java or minestrone for the long haul to Omaha.

But it wasn't a lunch place, he insisted, no luncheonette or diner. It was a coffeehouse in the grand tradition. Williams played long-running tapes of Stan Getz or Thelonious Monk and kept a volume of Carl Sandburg on the premises and a stack of stale *Village Voice*s on the tables as cloud seed.

It was a heroic struggle, wrangling up the thought and conversation, until the retired doctor discovered the establishment and began to frequent it late mornings for an hour or two before he walked home and turned his afternoon attention to liquor by the large glass.

The doctor was an intelligent, humor-blessed man who could keep up with Williams in intellectual banter, and he seemed to answer the coffee keeper's ultimate prayer. Dr. Todd had been a physician in Denver for thirty years, a good physician and a gentle man, until the drinking cost him everything. In the end, his wife took the two teenaged children back to Illinois. Then he lost his driver's license forever after a series of humiliating car accidents that left him sitting uncomprehendingly in the shallows of Cherry Creek or far up on a Blake Street sidewalk surrounded by drifts of shattered glass. And soon he lost his practice as well, gave it all up, sold his big brick house on Gilpin Street and retreated to a cozy bungalow in Cheyenne, Wyoming, to get by and drink in primitive peace. During the cold months he sipped Old Crow bourbon beside a sunny window; summers he drank iced Smirnoff vodka and nibbled saltines on the shady side of the house. He switched beverages each spring and fall with a minor ceremony on the day the clocks were changed for daylight savings.

He was lonely, and often sad, but remarkably steady in his new life. Once, sometimes twice, a year he took long solitary bus rides for diversion. At first his destinations were solid: the Ozarks in autumn, an art tour in Santa Fe. Then they became trips for their own sake, for the reliable panoramic passage of landscape and the inevitable sociality of the passengers on the bus. To Kansas City and back. A roundtrip on the San Francisco Scenicruiser Express with a flask in each pocket and a mystery novel on his lap.

So when the man Williams opened the coffeehouse the doctor was delighted. Every morning they managed, the two of them, to mount some sort of brisk discussion accompanied by Herbie Mann or Lester Young. Williams usually set the topic: international affairs, political mire, speculative philosophy. The Irish Republican Army. Ancient Roman mores. The death of Andy Warhol. They went at it like badminton, and they managed quite well. Now and then a secretary or a Union Pacific brakeman joined in. On days when the doctor was sluggish and bleary from the previous day's drink, Williams would skillfully urge him, prod him steadily into the topic until the doctor came over,

NORTHBOUND BUS

joined in with a "Touché!" or "That's exactly the point!" and dialogue was attained.

One day in the fall of the year—it was scarcely a week since he switched from vodka to bourbon—the doctor announced that he was taking a trip to Montana, to Billings, Montana, to look up a distant cousin. He had a ticket on the Powder River line and he pulled it out to show Williams. Dr. Todd hadn't seen his second cousin Betty in several decades, or even heard much from her of late. But he preferred not to telephone ahead, he explained. Why sabotage a perfectly good bus ride? If she wasn't there he would enjoy a steak dinner at a nice restaurant and come home.

He boarded the 10 a.m. bus at the Cheyenne depot and was pleased to find it crowded with passengers who must have got on in Denver. He felt a mild wave of nostalgia for his former home city and took an aisle seat toward the rear of the bus. An Indian boy slept soundly against the window.

The bus rolled north for half an hour before it began to make the local stops. Chugwater. Wheatland. Dropping the occasional stiff pilgrim or taking up heavily taped pasteboard freight. It was monotonous on a cloudy day when the colors were down. The Indian boy slept deeply. The doctor had a nip of Old Crow to keep him company. When the bus stopped in Douglas for a forty-minute lunch break, the doctor hesitated, then gently nudged the boy and told him it was time to eat.

In the café next door to the depot, the waitresses were cynically braced for the daily lunch-bus hubbub. The doctor ordered the noon special, roast pork and sweet potatoes, and carried it to a table and sat beside the Indian boy and his cheeseburger. The food strengthened Dr. Todd and he began to chat. "Pork and yams . . . I believe I could enjoy life in the South Pacific on one of those islands where they raise nothing but hogs and sweet potatoes. That would suit my fancy." He told the boy about butchering day back in the Illinois of his youth, told how they set aside the little tenderloins (they called them the "fish") from

NORTHBOUND BUS

each hog, and then, at mealtime, dropped them whole into a kettle of hot lard and ate them under an October maple tree. The boy thought, "Oh shit, this man is telling me his life story."

But the doctor wasn't telling his life story. That was the last story he wanted to tell. Back on the Powder River bus, when they were back on the highway, he asked the boy's name.

"Orlen."

"Orlen."

"Orlen Bay Horses."

"Orlen Bay Horse. That's a fine name."

"Horses."

"Bay Horses. That's a wonderful name. My name is Thomas Todd . . . I have always admired those grand family names you hear of now and then. Trueheart. Greathouse. Lovejoy. Even Armstrong. It seems to me it would be easier to move through life with a name like that to ride on. It seems it would keep the wind in your sails. Goodfellow is another one. And I knew a boy with the name of Birdsong. I always wanted to trade him, even up: Todd for Birdsong. That would have been a deal."

They paused in Glenrock and the city of Casper and the village of Kaycee. The doctor gazed appreciatively, elegiacally, from the window. Every now and again he took a discreet sip of bourbon, and occasionally commented on something to the boy, and later he presented him with one of the ballpoint pens in his shirt pocket. They could see the Bighorns out the left-side windows by now, with the evening sun raying out over them. Somewhere north of Buffalo there was a house in the dusky foothills with colored Christmas lights glittering on its eaves and lawn cedars.

"They're a little early this year aren't they?"

The boy looked out. "They're still up from last year I think. I see them like that every time I ride this bus."

The doctor was ordinarily adept at timing his liquor in public places. But this day, after the bus had departed Sheridan and full au-

NORTHBOUND BUS

tumn dark fell, somewhere near the Montana border, he stepped up his sipping, finished the right-pocket flask and began on the left, and the Bay Horses boy dozed, up through Lodgegrass and Crow Agency.

They pulled into Billings at 9:30. The doctor followed Orlen off the bus and into the bright lights of the station. A young man was waiting for Orlen, leaning against a whitewashed wall. The doctor had to stop and rest inside the door, set down his little gym bag on the floor. He was surprised to discover he was unsteady, even drunk. He had lost his timing and botched it.

He saw Orlen and his tall cousin begin to walk toward the door and he called after them. The boys came back to him shyly.

"I'm sorry, Orlen. I'm sorry to trouble you. I've had too much, I regret to say. 'Yo no soy puede mas.' Will you do something for me, Orlen? I'll pay you for it if you do. I'd like you to take this letter to my cousin. It's got some old family photos in it. She lives here in Billings, the address is on the envelope. But I've had too much. I think I'll take the next bus back to Cheyenne. Will you do it for me, Orlen?"

The boys glanced at each other. It was a clear-cut fifty-fifty proposition. Doctor Todd fished out two ten-dollar bills and held them out to Orlen. The boy considered for a moment, reached out and took one of the bills.

"This will be enough."

The doctor slept in a bus-station chair and then caught the midnight bus back south. He spent a full twenty-four hours in bed when he got home. But the following day, after an especially slow and hearty breakfast (he opened a tin of kippered fish to go with his scrambled eggs and sliced tomatoes), he walked gratefully the half-dozen blocks to the coffeehouse. He peeked in the window and saw that the tables were empty. Williams turned from his soup cauldron when he heard the door.

"Hail Atlantis! I missed you, Doc. How's Betty?"

NORTHBOUND BUS

COLD HANDS, HIGH WATER

Like many American highways, know it or not, that stretch of Interstate in central Wyoming has a shadow route paralleling it, a worn, way-of-least-resistance pedestrian trail a hundred yards to one side, like a secretive towpath along a canal, between Billings and Denver. The uncowed penniless, the shy underbelly, and restless minstrels use it.

I was stopped there at a pretty place on the bank of the Laramie River, a tree-lined semiprivate mile of valley in early summer. A river couldn't cut a better place. I pitched my tent and hid my bicycle in a willow brake as soon as I saw the spot.

It had been an abnormally wet spring. The valley hills shone with an aggressive, almost crayon green; throughout the day you could see the white rumps of pronghorns bright against the skyline grass. Cattle feasted in the bottomland on the other side of the river, up to their fetlocks in water, then dozed sated among the pale Russian olive groves. The new Hereford calves looked like gleaming buckeyes fresh from the shells.

I was washing up my plate and skillet the next morning when I saw a man coming along the footpath. He was approaching from the north, the same way I had ridden in the day before. He was a young fellow with a rucksack on his back and a fly-rod case over one shoulder. He walked right up as if he were expected.

He spoke a careful, well-prepared European English that immediately slowed everything down luxuriantly; his sentences reminded me of a waiter carrying a heavily loaded tray. He had come from Denmark ten days before, he told me, to fish the American West. And after half a decade of planning and daydreaming and setting aside money, he had chosen the Wet Year to buy his ticket. The wildflowers were everywhere extravagant, but all the rivers were unfishably high. He told the tale with a clownish cast, but I could see it was a sad one for him. He had spent most of his money desperately riding buses from stream to swollen stream. He had just hitchhiked despondently down from the Bighorn.

I had a tin of Spam and a can of white beans. We built a small fire and fried slices of the meat and then poured in the beans. The meal cheered him a little. We ate oranges and talked and I began to realize how deeply he was disheartened, rocked, by his bad luck. When he wasn't talking, balancing that precarious English tray, he was obviously flogged, laid out like a peony bush after a storm.

So when he dozed off under the olive tree I wrote a quick note and bicycled the three or four miles south on the footpath to a highway interchange and bought a pint of California brandy in the hamlet there and pedaled back to camp. I finally found him, spotted his vertical, extenuated shape, in the shade of an ash tree. Good God, I thought, he's hung himself. Then, as I approached, he broke the tableau, laughing, pulled the loose rope from the ash limb and walked to greet me with a broad smile on his face. I took it as an official release from pity or concern.

He had five days before he caught the train in Denver, so he stayed there on the Laramie with me. He seemed to like the place as much as I did. The highway was mostly invisible from there; we heard the occasional truck roar by. No one bothered us. One afternoon a man in a slouch hat walked by going north, carrying a dapper valise.

The Dane stood looking at the river a good bit, and cast a few times

COLD HANDS, HIGH WATER

to keep in practice, and each morning he borrowed my bicycle and rode to the highway to telephone a ranger station here or there and check on the various river flows: the North Platte, the Cache la Poudre. But he was essentially resigned to no fishing in the American West. We ate rice and spaghetti and oranges and took hikes up-valley to the point where ranches came into view. He was reading *Trout* by Ray Bergman and spoke frequently of his wife back home. She was a nurse in the National Orphanage, with blond hair trailing down her back. Next time she would come with him. He faithfully sent her postcards describing his days with subtle, poetic equivocation. And each afternoon, sooner or later I would return to camp from a stroll or from the latrine to find him in some sort of theatrical death scene, sprawled dramatically by the fire pit with one leg still twitching, or over on the bank of the stream with a grocery bag over his head. Then he would jump up smiling, brush off his short pants, and announce, "That was James Cagney in such-and-such," or "The last of the Romanovs!"

One day he showed me his packet of dry flies and nymphs, went through them one by one with great affection. "Henry's Fork only, this one. Tied by Rene Harrop."

"Do you know what you should do, Url?" He should get off the train, if he could arrange it, for a day or two in Ohio, call my friend Earley who lives there, and go fishing with him. It might still be smallmouth-bass season out there. He could see those pretty, quiet streams I grew up with: gravel-bottomed, heavily shaded with real trees, with big oaks and beautiful sycamores. The Shawnee creeks we used to call them. Cool, dark, quiet, with young cornfields just beyond the river trees and the pewees calling. Those smallmouth will take the kinks out of your line, too. Earley could take him to some doozies in a couple of days.

He said it was a good idea. The next morning he got up early, did five minutes' worth of perfunctory calisthenics, and packed his gear for Denver. I showed him on the map where to go in Ohio and gave

COLD HANDS, HIGH WATER

him Earley's phone number and three rice balls with chunks of Spam in them. We walked up to the rim of the valley together, then I turned back to camp. I cleaned the place up and started south that afternoon. It wasn't any fun anymore.

Three weeks later I called Earley out of itchy curiosity. Url had phoned him from some train station in western Iowa about one in the morning. They talked at length anyway, had actually made rather firm plans to fish a couple of days thereafter. Url had sounded enthusiastic, asked in great detail about the habits of the bass and what they might be hitting. I had a fleeting vision of him sprawled under an Ohio sugar maple: "Hector beneath the walls of Troy." But that was it. He never called again, never showed up on the banks of the Olentangy.

COLD HANDS, HIGH WATER

BUNKER WITH PINES

JT was hunting turkeys and I was along for the ride, for the Tongue River hills and an hour or two of his gruff wandering talk in vestigial Arkansas cadence, excitable and truth-careless as a child's, offhand as a belly rumble.

It was less hunting than it was shooting, or reaping; all the work, if you could call it that, the two-legged figuring, had been done well ahead of time. JT owned a marble-eyed blue heeler. He threw the dog in the back of his pickup truck and we drove away from his trailer home with his twelve-gauge shotgun leaning between us, across the river and up into the piney hills. He turned off down a lumber road along the ridge and settled in at five miles an hour.

Now he was hunting. When the dog smelled turkeys near at hand she began to jump and whine and scratch at the back of the cab and JT stopped the truck. The dog dashed off into the woods and rushed the flock, which flew routinely up into the trees to avoid the yapping nuisance, and JT shot one, often from the edge of the road, his heavy white body crouched bowlegged to take aim, hardly breaking the stride of the story he was twirling at the time.

When we crossed a narrow valley-crease in the hills, I noticed a poorly homestead set back off the road, a rough sort of place with a bristly, barricaded look to it: small dread-faced windows and heavy fences around a defoliated yard with no soft edges. "That's a funny outfit there," JT said. And he told me about them as he dropped into low gear for the rutted grade.

Like many great schisms, it began over a piece of rotten meat.

The family had moved up to Montana from Denver several years before. The man's name was Appadurai, he was of Indian—East Indian—descent. His family had operated a small print shop for years in Denver, a sooty storefront on lower Broadway among the wig wholesalers and cut-rate spaghetti parlors and tattoo salons. They printed every sort of petty odd job from wedding announcements to chop-suey menus, but their specialty had gradually become, since the 1960s, bumper stickers for automobiles.

Appadurai and his cousin ran the place, with an ever-shifting mix of distant relatives standing by. They cranked out bumper stickers covering the political gamut from Mao to Hitler, every strain of bigotry and erotic preference, every childish peeve and righteous cause; they touted sports teams, Paraguayan ancestry, and hatred of the state of Texas. They all rolled off the same press and went bundled out the back door into the same low-slung station wagon. Appadurai stickers caused a man to be shot at the wheel (minor flesh wound) in Missouri and a poor old woman (a devout pantheist) to be rammed viciously from behind at a stoplight in Roswell, New Mexico. Appadurai thought them up himself for the most part, rising early in the morning to daydream with his eyes half closed and scan the newspapers for volatile issues of the day.

Appadurai married a Cheyenne woman he met at a South Denver bingo game. They lived quietly by television light in a small half house a few blocks from the shop with their baby boy and a tank of nervous guppies. Appadurai's cousin and workmate lived alone not far away. The cousin was a murky, locked-in man, a notorious miser built like an ichneumon fly, with muddy red-flecked half-moons under his eyes.

BUNKER WITH PINES

He smoked contemplatively all day and much of the night and once a month fished alone in the lake at Washington Park, straight-faced as a heron, until he had enough in his plastic pail to make a grapefruit-colored curry.

One Sunday afternoon the cousin was sitting with the family at the Appadurai house. A popular uncle and three other cousins were there, too, and a woman friend with her hair rolled, long known to them all. They had eaten earlier in the day and were gathered in the kitchen chatting and smoking. The toddler boy stood in the midst embracing a table leg.

Appadurai was after something in the refrigerator, leaning and reaching, and discovered a dish of food wrapped in foil. Peeking cautiously under the wrapping—"Oof, these chicken livers are a year old!"

He moved toward the garbage basket in the corner, but the cousin, with a quick and waltz-like step, intercepted.

"Let me see, I might take them home with me for supper."

Appadurai protested, laughing, waving a hand. The livers were no good, they had been in the refrigerator for weeks.

"Just let me see them, maybe they are alright."

"They are green as grass. They smell bad. They are too old."

By now the rest of the family attended. The cousin was trying to reach past Appadurai to take the dish. Appadurai was holding it beyond his reach, still laughing a raspy defensive laugh.

"Just let me smell them. I tell you they are probably alright."

Now all the family was chuckling nervously. The cousin flushed and looked back at them as if he'd forgotten they were there. Appadurai took advantage and lunged to the garbage basket and flung the livers away and closed the lid and sat on it. He was perspiring across the brow. The cousin straightened and looked at him for a brief moment with a bitter expression of formally registered insult and dismay.

BUNKER WITH PINES

The favorite uncle raised a waggish eyebrow, unfolded his legs, and said from across the room, "You must be starving, nephew. I will buy you something for supper."

Three years passed. The print shop prospered. Appadurai decided to have his son's horoscope made in honor of the child's sixth birthday. It was by tradition a ceremonious affair. The Coming of Boyhood. The Winging of the Bird. Appadurai's cousin was the only person he knew who was qualified to prepare such a thing. After closing the shop one night, Appadurai approached him, petitioned him in a grand manner to take on the job. They stood before a hubcap clearing house. A full horoscope was complicated, studious work. The cousin would charge a hundred dollars. Appadurai nodded thoughtfully. The deal was struck.

Six weeks after, on a damp March evening, the cousin came into the back room of the shop where Appadurai was sorting and loading a box of bumper stickers ("Make Mine Pomeranian," bound for Southern California). The cousin waited quietly until Appadurai taped the box. Then he handed him a large brown envelope, took two fifty-dollar bills in return, and left the building. His viscera tingled and his palms were damp. He was so pleased with himself that he stopped for a cup of coffee and a scoop of ice cream before walking home.

No one knows what exactly the horoscope promised the boy, but it was bad enough that Appadurai closed the shop for three days and drew the curtains tight at home. By the second evening his normally even-keeled wife had contracted his shuddering terror and they sat on the couch with the boy between them, whispering over the details and shaking their heads. Two days later they packed up, took what money they had in the bank, and left town in the early dawn.

In Montana they settled in the little Indian house on land belonging to the wife's family. They doubled the fences and halved the windows, cut back the plum brush from the yard and strengthened the locks.

BUNKER WITH PINES

They live for the most part on the Cheyenne woman's government checks. They use her family name now: Pin Cherry, Cherry for short. Rarely go out of the house.

Just after noon we came back that road, came bumping down the hill with five turkeys in the back and the dog sound asleep among them. When we passed the house there was a tall man standing below an ash tree near the fence. He had a fat prairie dog on a harness leash and turned to watch as our truck went by. From a leafy limb above his shoulder a set of barefooted legs dangled in yellow pajama pantaloons.

"That's Appadurai."

"Who's up in the tree?"

"That must be Breece, the boy."

BUNKER WITH PINES

TAILWIND

The men left the car along the dirt road and walked down a pine-choked draw to the cliff, and there was the wide Tongue River valley off below them and a dozen sudden meadowlark songs washing up through the May air. The beautiful old river oxbowed at her ease through sweet hay meadows and sagebrush flats. Her big cottonwood stands were ashimmer with half-grown leafage wild with the sun and the low willows cast a soft red haze to the bottomland. On both edges of the mile-broad valley rose the bluffs with their own deep earth-red glimmering through the black pines.

The white man knew the way and went first down the trail and the black man followed. They talked in the hushed, ready tones of fishermen approaching water. Soon they were in the valley and rigging their gear and eyeing the strong spring flow of the Tongue.

"We can find walleyes down in here. They come up from the big dam. And there are always lots of crappies to get into." The white man was older. He had lived in the area for twenty-five years and was showing the black man where to fish. They worked at the National Forest ranger station down the road. They moved to the riverbank and walked along it, watching the water work. "I haven't seen a game warden in here in ten years," the white man whispered. "They say the last time one came around he found a bunch of Indian boys with a mess of illegal fish and a pile of young turkeys. They stripped him down and ran an eight-inch perch up his arse and left him there. He had to have surgery to get the damned thing out."

They began casting into a large hole at a riverbend where song sparrows skulked in the willows and jumped to the bush tops to sing. The men warmed to the fishing and grew silent, passing each other leap-frog fashion as one of them moved ahead to reach a new hole upstream.

The white man called the black man over to show him a murky slow-water pool where a school of carp were milling. "We don't want to get into those things," the older man said as they moved on. "I'll tell you though, they aren't bad eating if you treat them right. I was stationed in England during the war and I ate a lot of carp over there. I had a girlfriend near the base and her father was a fisherman. He'd bring home carp and be just as proud as if they were trout. They look at them different over there—gussy them up and roast them like a chicken."

He pointed with his rod to a nice pool and motioned the other man in toward it. He moved off a few yards and stopped to bait his hook. He wanted to talk a little more now.

He cast a minnow jig and told the black man about the English months, good in spite of the war; about the girl, and his voice had a lower pitch to it.

He had wanted that girl more than anything, had chased her hard. Had wanted that whole life, he supposed now. The whole English bit had hit him pretty hard, a boy from Montana.

But it wasn't just that. It was the girl. He was crazy after her, but he couldn't pull it off.

"Just couldn't get it into high gear," he said in the husky fishing whisper. "Marge has been a wonderful wife to me. But that girl was the one I wanted."

He reeled in a nice crappie and knelt to put it on the stringer. He was off into it now and enjoying it: he began to mimic a British accent as he chatted and the black man smiled at the sea change.

TAILWIND

"I say, that's the ticket," the old man said, climbing up the bank.

They fished along steadily, keeping the larger crappies and an occasional walleye. They stopped and walked out onto a broad sage flat where the old man smoked a pipe and looked up at the two-tone bluffs, red on the upper half and white below, and the darker hill-mountains beyond. Then they went back to the fishing.

When they rounded a bend they saw a blue tent on the bank fifty yards ahead and an Indian boy sitting on the ground beside it. The white man waved and after a moment of consideration said, "That's Tommy, I think. What's he up to, I wonder."

Soon they reached the spot and the white man talked to the Cheyenne fellow while he fished. The boy sat by the tent listening to Merle Haggard on a tape player. His camp was tucked neatly between a dense willow brake and the river, in the shade of a large cottonwood.

"You don't mind if I fish in your front yard, do you Tommy?" the white man said. The boy smiled and said no.

"You better get them while you can," the boy said. "Before the strip mines poison them all off."

"We won't let that happen, now will we, old chap," the man said as he flipped his jig across the stream. He was still flashing a British facet in his sentences whether he knew it or not. It had become the tenor of the morning.

The white man introduced the black man to Tommy. The boy shook hands with the man and grinned: "Red, white, and black—the American flag." He showed the two men a stringer staked to the bank; three nice catfish swayed on it.

"That's what I've been living on the last couple of days."

The black man nodded at the boy and moved on to fish. Through the willows he could hear Tommy and the old man's chat and friendly sparring: the soft northern clip of the boy and then the preposterous would-be British patter of the man, so incongruous it made the black man laugh aloud and shake his head as he fished. The last thing he

TAILWIND

heard was the boy: "Everyone knows the white man is possessed by the devil."

Ten minutes upstream the old man caught up with him, startled him as he moved to his side at a large hole bellying under a tawny earthen cliff.

"This is a good hole, Roger. There's always walleye in here." They stood on a sandbar baiting up.

"That Tommy is a good sort. One of his brothers was a bit of a rotter though. Tommy worked for me one summer clearing fire roads. He lives up in Billings.

"A bit of a Lothario, I dare say. Right now he's laying low—that's why the campout. Hiding from a Cree girl who's got the goods on him. He might eat a hell of a lot of catfish before that's all over."

There was a shift in the sunny air, a tack, and the brief crystalline chill of endless need and pull, of all the warm-blooded tonnage and its scattered muddy entrepôts. The white man had rigged his jig and moved carefully toward the upper end of the pool.

"Quite right," he whispered in a pencil-mustached little voice. "Off we go."

TAILWIND

SPANISH FOR VANISH

Yesterday I stopped at the Belle Fourche post office to send off post-cards. At the lobby counter beside me an elderly common man was struggling gamely to compose a letter on a small lined notepad. He murmured conversationally, word by word, as he wrote. It seemed to be a happy letter, though each phrase was a chore, each short paragraph a triumph that brought a twitch of smile to his lips. I believe he said, just as I was finishing up, "I dreamed about that old black dog one night."

*

Each evening all week I sat with early English chamber music in the summer twilight, returned to it each evening for an hour or more without thought or question, nothing intended, sat with it and a nip of whiskey or a glass of wine. I began with some recent discoveries from the early 1600s: the *Fantasia Suites* of John Jenkins; plaintive, creaking-ship viol pieces by Thomas Lupo; odds and ends from Thomas Simpson, with crickets calling from beyond the door. Then reimmersed myself in the old favorites: Orlando Gibbons. John Dowland. The complete *Royal Consort Suites* of William Lawes, that foggy-day half jig, that saltwater and catgut insinuendo.

It turned into an experience of unexpected reach. The distinctive similarity of the various musics, the unbending strength of their con-

ceded limits and agreed-upon tone, formed in the end a riverine channel of steady, utterly persuasive force. Rather than each standing alone
as a voice in the wilderness, rather than diminishing one another by
their mutual ground, the channelized style acted to deepen and enrich
the whole to an extent that after five or six days the exposure was thor-
ough enough that I began to sense within myself a simple working
knowledge of seventeenth-century Britain, an everyday familiarity as
of my own world, an intimacy both unassuming and powerful. I had
been unexpectedly rendered privy by artists firmly in milieu. John Co-
perario. Anthony Holborne. John Farmer. All facets were casually ac-
counted for. I knew both treble and bass, winds from all quarters. I
knew hanky and ha'penny, hawk overhead, bat in the gutter. It was a
full-dress nonverbal infusion. I drank it in like a tonic I most obviously
needed, and I was still braced and surprised by it this morning driving
out from South Dakota.

When I first saw the man through the heat shimmy a quarter mile off
I figured he was a Sioux man hitchhiking down from the reservation,
but at fifty yards I knew he wasn't. He climbed in the car, preferring
to keep his gear handy at his feet. He was a pleasant-looking, darkish
man in his twenties, I would guess. It was a hot northern Nebraska
day by now, but he wore a bulky long-sleeved flannel shirt and thick
trousers. His only luggage was a heavy wool blanket neatly rolled and
tied and stuffed in a clear plastic bag. A tiny billed cap sat atop a head
of dark and curly, nearly ringletted hair that looked almost Hittite, or
Assyrian.

As we started off I asked where he was going. He merely pointed
ahead and said, "Work." Every subsequent gambit fell flat and echo-
less, including (I assumed he was a Latino man) my tentative pidgin
Spanish. But he accepted a drink of water from my jug, and nodded.
There was a faint odor of licorice.

SPANISH FOR VANISH

We were passing through the shapely short-grass country. The man chose to gaze out the side window in silence, though the landscape didn't seem to engage him nor the open spaces to draw his focus in the least. It appeared to be a blend of shyness and preference, hands formally folded. Fine with me. Ten minutes into the trip I had given up on talking of any sort. I was entertaining those idle, scattered, heat-lightning notions that build up and flash on blank midsummer days. Suddenly the young man turned to me and waved one hand and pointed urgently out the window. I stopped the car and pulled off the highway, where he opened the door and leaned out, gagging and spitting over the berm stubble. Then he wiped his mouth with a big blue kerchief, nodded his head, and I drove on.

I began to wonder about him, where he came from, whether he was seriously ill. And the farther we went in the warm silence, the more I found myself speculating on his being in an almost involuntary way. It was a rudimentary social reflex, I suppose, seeping in to fill the speech void. I thought he might be a Basque sheepherder on furlough, hesitantly wandering out from the Bighorn Mountains. But Basques were few and far between anymore, I had heard. They had been gradually replaced by Peruvian shepherds. Well, then—he might be an itinerant Inca herder, seeing a bit of North America.

We turned south and gradually entered more agricultural landscape: mammoth grain operations with fleets of enormous trucks and combines red-hot in the sun, miles-long feedlots with black and brown cattle in the mud. But the man seemed to find little of interest in any of it. Even the stench of the feedlots didn't faze him. He signaled to me again on a long straightaway and I pulled over to let him vomit out the door in a patch of dusty white poppies.

As we drove on, my reflexive speculation intensified of its own accord. He might be North African, or Caspian. An Anatolian gypsy. He might be pursuing a lost love around the West with a panpipe in

SPANISH FOR VANISH

his blanket roll. If he could only just once get within hearing range of her—a few notes would fix it all! Or perhaps a sad young fourth-generation organ grinder whose monkey . . . Things were getting out of hand in a hurry.

I stopped once more, twenty or thirty minutes later, at a pull-off overlooking a vast stretch of the North Platte River, and the man gagged again while I gazed out over the hot hazy valley. Aristotle, the Macedonian, reported that hyenas lured dogs to their death after dark by imitating the sound of a man puking. As we dropped down toward the city of Scott's Bluff the boy grew restless, squirming in his seat and glancing sidelong at me. "Do you need a doctor? *Un medico?*" A quick shake of the head.

At the first stoplight on the far north edge of town, cattycorner from that Chinese restaurant, he waved his hand and reached for his gear. He needed air; he was on to me. He took a cherry Lifesaver, thanked me softly in noncommittal English and hopped from the car.

SPANISH FOR VANISH

TALK ACROSS WATER

Just after sundown three half-Crow boys with pellet guns climbed the rickety fire escape on a gutted old school building in Montana. It was a simple case of groundling-airborne grudge: nothing else to do that provocative time of day unless you were a singer of Sky Chanteys but go up there to the ratty flat roof and smoke and fire spitefully at the laggard last of the nighthawks veering through the pastel evening overhead and out of reach.

It was late October, clear and mild. Every scratch and whisper carried like talk across water. At one end of the little town a group of Indian kids were back again at the poor Dunkard's bedroom window, crouched in the fresh darkness to hear the man carry on. The poor Dunkard, a man of forty with a face like a scrubbed shoat and a touch of the walleye and a shock of red medieval hair, after thirty years of inadvertent near-saintly religious life during which he lived with his mother and existed, thrived, fattened even, on a serene two-tone vocabulary of a dozen German phrases repeated over and over as needed —*Gottes wille*; *Gott denkt*; *mehr Butter*; *Gott weiss, jawohl*—after thirty years of it he was stricken two weeks earlier with the Babbling Disease and except for a brief tight-lipped flurry of household chores in the early morning he lay all his waking hours on a turn-of-the-twentieth-century divan or stretched on his narrow bed unleashing a torrent of German–English blend even his mother could not grasp in full or slow. And the neighboring kids crept in below his window like cats and listened with an honest awe to his rapid-fire mix of tongues and tones and hymns rendered barnyard risque, while his mother rocked resignedly at his side through nightfall awaiting the curtain of sleep.

Far to the east that very hour, a boy with a book was committing to memory the various plumages of the eastern nighthawk, the fluid, almost lunar progression from "tilleul" through "Quaker drab" and "fuscous" to "vinaceous-buff," and envisioning the legendary pure-albino specimen seen one summer at Lynchburg, Virginia, streaking, talked about all up and down the coast, through their pastel 1886 sky; and a man was bent at desk stroking one earlobe, writing, "Suppose, of all the overlooked and latent Power-Whorls of this world, that Melancholy, born of long experience, distilled from generations of the complex relations we live within, proved in the end to be the most transformative and incendiary of them all."

And early next morning a middle-aged woman drank an extra cup of coffee and ate an extra donut for her day off and drove from one side of the little town to the outskirts of the other to pick up her elderly aunt. "It's Halloween," she said when the old woman was settled in the car.

"Then we had better hurry up and get home before dark." The aunt was a perky little woman whose eyes were mostly gone. You wouldn't know it to see her drink a cup of Nescafé, but her great-great-great-grandmother was among those women crushed by the fickle riverbank while they were digging paint clay one afternoon two hundred years before. The people named that stream after them, that temperamental tributary of the Powder where lark sparrows sing—River Where the Cliff Caved In on the Women—but even so, only a dozen souls on earth knew that old name now.

They drove from town and up into the grassy red and yellow hills. "It's a pretty day," the younger woman said. The aunt cupped both her hands around her one decent eye and looked attentively out the window. "Yes it is," she finally agreed. "It's like a summer day."

TALK ACROSS WATER

"Gee, we were busy at the hospital yesterday," the niece was telling. "They had a big fight over at the river. A whole lot of fishermen got in a fight and beat each other up. They brought six or seven of them in to get fixed up."

"Which river?"

"Over there on the Big Horn."

"What were they fighting about anyhow?"

"All those boats get out there in the river and they run into each other or get too close and get tangled up in the lines. Then they get mad and start yelling and then they start swinging the oars and everything. Some of them were cut up pretty bad, too."

"I never did like fish anyway. Not enough to fight about it."

"I'll take my tuna casserole and leave the rest."

"I never did like tuna fish either."

They were driving up a narrow dirt road by now. At the crest of the hill was a small cemetery. They got out and walked through the creaky gate and the old woman paused with her hand above her eyes and gazed around the plot familiarly, as if she had entered a room she hadn't visited for a good while. "Watch out for rattlesnakes." Then she hobbled over to the family stones and rummaged in her purse, set a package of cigarettes below each one and whacked once or twice with her cane at the weeds behind them.

The young woman took her arm and they strolled among the graves, reading the names, saying them aloud as if to freshen them, keep them on the air and on the continent itself.

"Billy Far," the niece read, and the old woman nodded as she did each time they came.

"Billy Far," she answered. "He was a good boy. Then his wife ran away with that soldier. First thing Billy did was start up a band. They played all around here, on the reservation and off. Played those real sad songs that make you thirsty. Beer-drinking songs. He had that band for a year. Everyone thought he was over his wife leaving. Thought all

TALK ACROSS WATER

those songs had got him over it. So he gave up the band all of a sudden. But then he started drinking real bad. He got drunk one night so bad he walked out in front of a train. Over by Hardin."

She told the niece once again about the Shirts, their two stones set a few feet apart with a chokecherry sprout taking hold between them. They had been married ten or fifteen years when Iris, Mrs. Shirt, told Delwin he had to get out. No reason given. Delwin moved out into an old garage a few rods down the hill and lived there the rest of his long life. Iris set up the gravestones for them, but put a little extra distance between them. Delwin never did know why she kicked him out.

"And this fellow—Willis Wagon—he lived over around Cat Creek. He was a holy man, I guess they call it. Knew all about the ceremonies. Tobacco Society and all those things. He did everything real slow, like the holy men are supposed to. Always moved real slow and careful. He used to walk out to the mailbox by the road and it would take him an hour to get back. His wife would start to worry about him, go looking out all the windows.

"Kind of funny—his boy was a stock-car racer."

A starling in the cemetery's single tree was luxuriating in the sun, squawking and whistling, mimicking a killdeer, then a nighthawk, a May meadowlark, a peacock yowl he had picked up over in Billings. The women walked hand in hand back to the car.

"Maybe we should stop at the Corners and get something to eat."

They parked at the rural roadhouse and walked across the parking lot. All the hackberry trees had dropped their curled-up leaves several days before and each step made a crunch and a crackle. They took a table near the door and ordered hamburgers. The waitress and the man behind the bar wore Halloween getups. The girl was dressed as a sort of ranch-hand vampire and the man wore a mask of Fidel Castro with an arrow piercing his skull, left to right.

The women were finishing their coffee when another Halloweener entered the place. He came shuffling through the door and turned

TALK ACROSS WATER

heavily to the customers, staring dumbly through a pustuled and warted neo-Neanderthal mask with wild monkey hair flying from it. He wore a greasy long bathrobe with burrs and chicken feathers on it, hanging open to reveal a huge lifelike phallus the size of a ballbat, swaying bruised and scar-mottled and heavily veined to the man's calves. The patrons at the bar greeted him with a Ha and a Ho. He finally began to shuffle into the place, slow and humpbacked, pausing at each table to gape at the diners.

The two women peeked at him sideways when he stood beside them breathing hoarsely through his mouth. The niece giggled into her napkin. The old one finally set down her coffee and cupped her hands at her decent eye and looked again. She began to chuckle and shake her head, and the man lurched on toward the bar.

"You can see better than you let on, auntie," the niece said when they were out in the parking lot.

"Oh my. He's going to put someone's eye out with that thing. Reminds me of my first boyfriend. It was always Halloween with him around."

Off to the east a full day's drive, a girl on a late-afternoon sofa was reading and stroking a Siamese cat: "Be assured the slightest fragment of birdsong is not uttered in vain. During periods of sexual calm, it is the tireless rehearsal for the great concerts of love."

The women drove back through the summerlike day. The old one cupped her hands once to see if anyone was home at a certain sumac-red house on a hill. As they walked up to the aunt's front door the niece told her, "Now lock your doors and stay inside tonight. Close your curtains tight. Tomorrow is All Saints' Day. It will be safe to come out then."

"I'll be alright. No goblins want to fool with me—except maybe some old skeleton. I'm going to be busy anyway. I'll be busy praying for that Halloween man's wife."

TALK ACROSS WATER

ECHOFIELD

The old woman had a job cooking all summer at the Catholic boarding school. Every workday her husband drove her halfway across the reservation and dropped her in her hairnet at the kitchen door at eight o'clock sharp. Then he drove a short ways up the dirt road climbing the hill behind the brick buildings and parked his car in the shade of a grove of trees. He waited there all day until three o'clock when his wife got off work. He listened to several different stations on the radio. He took short walks along the hillside and occasionally climbed up to look over the top of the hill. He swatted flies. Sometimes he picked a hatful of chokecherries or black currants. He took long, away-from-home naps with his cap down over his eyes. Every day at 12:30 his wife brought a plate from the cafeteria up the hill and they ate together and talked in the front seat of the car.

One warm day she brought a big platter of meatloaf and mashed potatoes and after she went back down the hill the man decided he had eaten so much he had better get in the backseat and stretch out for a real nap. He even took off his shoes. And pretty soon the kingbirds had him dreaming.

He dreamed a long, out-of-the-ordinary dream that moved around from place to place. There was a white man and his white wife, people the old man didn't recognize. The man had married this girl—she was a ranch girl—and taken her off to a big city where he worked. It might have been Omaha. The girl got tired of it after a while and the husband loved her so much that he took her back to the country and built them a nice ranch house somewhere around Kaycee, Wyoming. They had air conditioning and two or three big horse trailers and a swimming pool. They were all settled in and comfortable, you could see that in the dream.

The woman was crazy about paint horses. She was soon in charge of a pretty herd. She spent long days with them, caring for them and brushing their manes and tails. Her husband was proud of his wife's hard work with the paints. He told his friends she paid more attention to the horses than she did to himself.

One morning the man needed to talk to his wife about some important business. He knew where to find her. He drove his pickup down the valley and out along a wooded ridge overlooking the range where the painted horses were grazing. He stopped at the edge of the pines and picked up his binoculars to scan the herd and locate his wife. He spotted her right away on one edge of the meadow. She was standing with the big paint stallion, a wildish horse with pale-blue milky eyes. She had her arms around his neck and was hugging him and stroking his shoulders. Some of the mares were standing around them, watching. The husband was watching too, through his binoculars. When the dream turned around and showed him he had a terrible look on his face. The woman's clothing was folded in a neat pile to one side and the stallion was beginning to neigh and shuffle with his tail in the air.

The old dreamer jerked awake in the backseat of his car. He got up on one elbow and scratched his head roughly. The dream made him uncomfortable. He knew where it came from; it came straight from an old story the old people used to tell about the old days—a woman falling in love with a pretty red-speckled horse. It was a story lots of people had heard—the jealous husband would shoot the stallion and make more trouble—but never with white people in it.

It made the old man feel annoyed. He just wanted a little nap. Those

ECHOFIELD

ranch people might be people he knew after all, and that dream might be none of his business.

Maybe it was the meatloaf that got everything mixed up. He got out of the car and straightened his shirt and tucked it in his pants, then walked down to the mission faucet in his stocking feet to splash cold water over his head, three or four times.

ECHOFIELD

MEN LOOKING FOR WIVES

I often hunted cottontails along the White River west from Flicker town, over near old Fort Robinson. It was a wild, sunken bottom, shaggy with brush and box elders, with the strong narrow river twisting through, a stretch with history thick upon it and a good place to get away for an hour or two. I met my third wife down in there.

I was hunting near the stream one day in October just after the first frost had knocked back the weeds and mosquitoes, when a small plane came flying over low and then circled back a little lower. I could see the pilot was looking me over and I could even make out a broad Irish grin on his face. He made another thoughtful turn and flew on, just short of stall, to the east.

When I left the bottomland half an hour later and walked toward my car I saw the plane sitting just across a fence in a pasture flat, and a man about my age walking restlessly back and forth beside it, waiting for me. That's how I met Halfhill. He had seen me with my twenty-gauge working through the wild-plum tangles and he was instantly hooked by a simple vicarious bond, the boyish longing to be down there kicking up rabbits himself. Hooked enough that he rolled up his sleeves and helped me clean my game. We were friends from then on.

We flew all over the place. We were both divorced at the time and were free and easy. He would come to Flicker from the big city and pick me up and off we went. Black Hills, Sandhills, Badlands. Catfishing for a day over on the Missouri below Omaha. Or sometimes I met him at a mealy asphalt landing strip belonging to a desolate ranch, waiting and watching the sky, finally hearing the drone of the distant engine and hurrying to shoo the cattle off the runway as he circled in. And off we went, hunting ducks on the potholes or grouse down in Nebraska, or just looking over the open spaces like a lazy hawk, passing down low above the prairie lakes to see the swans and watch the pelicans flap a few yards.

One summer day he called and said he wanted me to fly up to Studhorse with him, up in northern South Dakota. He had set down there a few weeks earlier to gas up and had taken the loaner car into town for lunch. He'd seen a young Hunkpapa woman in the café and hadn't been able to forget her. There was a powwow going on up there this particular weekend and he wanted to go, wanted to see the woman again, a little closer this time, and wanted me to see her as well, I guess. It was a vintage Halfhill scheme, and he had even darkened his hair a little for the occasion.

We took off early Saturday morning from the Flicker airport and flew straight north to pick up the Cheyenne River and followed it down the edge of the Red Shirt Table and on up, over the pretty, far-removed forks and downstream above Cherry Creek, and then took a hard left to jump over to the Moreau valley, taking our time and enjoying ourselves, buzzing a coyote now and then just to keep them on their toes and climbing out of our way a time or two to plunge blind into a massive cumulus and burst out the other side into a flash of blue-sky sunlight. Halfhill was musing. "I'd like to find a good woman who doesn't give a damn and quit my job, move up here somewhere and run a little crossroads gas station."

We followed the Moreau down, flying low and slow, the horse herds giving us the quizzical eye, over Green Grass and White Horse to the matriarchal Missouri, cut north thirty miles and turned west up the Grand River, maybe the sweetest of them all, over Little Eagle, and

MEN LOOKING FOR WIVES

twenty minutes later we were banking above the village of Studhorse, everybody craning up at us, and then landing at the rudimentary strip with its tattered windsock and wind-shivered tin-roof port-of-Hunk-papa-call.

We tied down the plane and walked the half mile into Studhorse—the café with gas pumps and a car-wide post office—and out the half mile on the other side to the powwow grounds near the river. People were setting up for the one o'clock session, carrying in folding chairs and drums to the shade of the circular arbor, checking the PA system that crackled like a hickory fire.

Halfhill and I strolled around the modest midway having a look, he keeping a sharp eye out for the pretty woman. We were beginning our second go-round when a youngish man lurched out from a group of friends and hailed us. The muscatel was potent on his breath as he looked us over with a penetrating squint. He was a solid fellow, built like a linebacker. He stepped up close to Halfhill and stood in his face and commenced with the classic half-comical, half-belligerent, "Are you guys any relation to General Custer?" routine. Halfhill tried nobly to make civil small talk during the pauses. The man carefully introduced himself (he had one of those long-standing, mutated, coulee-and-coyote French names from the northern plains) to clarify the rules of the jousting, and eased gradually into the "What are you doing here?" direct approach, bearing down on Halfhill's pretty blue eyes while the onlookers toed a fine line between amusement and fear of flame, until after ten minutes of it the man's focus broke and we could slip away.

Halfhill was upset by the encounter, or, it appeared, by the fact the drunk had collared him in particular, he who had articles of reservation beadwork on his office wall and a Wounded Knee centennial sticker on the flank of his airplane. I theorized that the man could sense Halfhill was in the insurance trade, could sniff the eerie, speculative, Caucasian abstraction of the calling. He didn't see the humor in

MEN LOOKING FOR WIVES

it, and we decided to walk into town for a cup of coffee and a change of subject matter. "So they discovered this new fungus or parasite worm or whatever it was, that lives in the lower bowels—and they voted to name it after Harry! How'd you like to have a bowel fungus named after you?"

When we returned to the powwow an hour later, the singing had begun, the drunken defender was nowhere to be seen, the day had begun to warm. We circled the arbor several times. Finally Halfhill saw the woman, sitting across the way in a lawn chair with a group of family or friends. She was pretty all right. And then the jockeying began. We took a seat and Halfhill watched her earnestly, elbows on knees, stared meaningfully across the thirty yards of the arena, getting up every few minutes to stretch and tread about behind our chairs. He liked her stylish sunglasses and the way she talked and laughed and tossed her brilliant hair. When at one point she stood and left her seat, Halfhill sprang up and was off to try for a closer look. Maybe she had recognized his throbbing firefly gaze and was angling out to public ground for an interception and interview. He came back in ten minutes; she was with a crowd, he never had a chance.

The jockeying went on in varying intensities for an hour and a half. I was becoming increasingly aware that a majority of the arbor gathering, especially the men, knew what was going on, and that certain of the more proprietary of the Lakota men were growing annoyed at the heedless telepathic aggression of the thing.

The woman left her seat again, and Halfhill was off like a dog. When he returned, he was visibly, you might say morally, shocked by the whiff of tripe soup he had encountered at one of the food concessions, the carrion edge of it after hours under steady Dakota sun. But he had finally gained a close-up appraisal of the poor woman, and he reported in a weakening, peevish voice that "her legs aren't that great. She's a lot older than I thought." He made a consolatory trip to one of the portable pit toilets outside the arena. I turned in my chair and saw him re-

MEN LOOKING FOR WIVES

coil and slam the plastic door, then hurry back stung by the simmering latrine aroma. He was ready to throw it all in with a gruff "Let's get out of here."

We hurried back through Studhorse. Halfhill was taciturn, his stride hard and long. He stopped to pee curtly behind a chokecherry bush. "I'll wait and take a dump somewhere else."

When we came in sight of the plane, he stopped, cupped his eyes, and began to run. Three small Lakota boys were joyfully climbing about the wings and roof of the plane in a rare fantasy of their own. When they saw us they clambered to the ground and scrambled away top speed on their bicycles.

Halfhill was worried. He went over the plane inch by inch with a stern look on his face, checked the struts and tires and opened the engine casing to examine the wirings for foul play or incidental damage. Then we roared and bumped across the field and took off, curling west as we climbed. Halfhill usually made a sporty farewell fly-over and dip of the wing above the powwow arbor on such occasions, but not that day.

We flew in silence for half an hour. He asked me then to take the wheel so he could lean back and rest his eyes, and a quarter hour later, after we had drifted inadvertently up to thirteen thousand feet, he seemed his old self again. Soon he spotted a golden flat-topped butte below, dropped down to scout it, see if it was negotiable, and then back around to set the plane down on top in the thin buffalo grass with twenty or thirty yards to spare. We got out to unwind and have a look.

We walked along the oblong edge, looking down hundreds of feet at the rough and runneled buttressing at the base of the butte and tracing the distant web of Missouri-bound streams, and studied the Black Hills to the near west. The gusty wind was making the plane twitch on its moorings. "Did I ever tell you about the time Erica found out I had a girl at my house and she came over, pounding on the doors and

MEN LOOKING FOR WIVES

screaming? We were already separated, but was she pissed! I turned off all the lights and went up to the attic. We peeked out and saw her trying to bash out my taillights with one of her high-heeled shoes!"

But then he grew quiet again, began the head-down, hands-in-pocket pacing.

"You know, those toilets really make me sick . . . And that soup! How can they eat that? That stuff is going to kill somebody!"

"Nothing a pint of Tabasco wouldn't cure."

"I wouldn't bet my life on it . . . Come on, let's get out of here."

We walked across the tabletop of the butte, checking for dangerous rocks or hidden logs or dinosaur bones, then taxied back to one edge, revved up and roared across the level and took off with a memorable little drop—*woop*—as we zoomed off the southern edge.

Halfhill landed us at the Flicker airfield and went in to use the bathroom. It was early evening by then. I watched him depart and fly off toward Colorado. Something in the pale pinks and apricots of the sky and the early stars and the high-tailed beeline cut of the little plane against them made it clear to any person looking up: that man lived somewhere far from this place and he was going home.

MEN LOOKING FOR WIVES

YELLOW BIRDS

Marco the peddler drove in low gear down from the mountains and onto the plains. He had come across Washington and over into Montana, seeking the lower passes to spare his birds high altitude and unprincipled storms. He took his time along the way, parked his rattly Ford truck almost daily to fish a pretty stretch of river and to rest the stacked hooded cages of canaries in the backend. He rolled the tarpaulin from over them and they sang a great rollicking chorus for him as he fried his little trout beside the stream.

The summer of 1927 was near the peak of the canary craze on North America. The people in California had shipped the birds to Marco by train, Oakland to Portland, as they did once or twice each year, and he loaded the truck and packed his cardboard suitcase. This year he decided to try new territory, east of the mountains.

He had already sold a good number of birds in Washington and Idaho, mostly the traditional yellow ones, but an undertaker in Spokane had sprung for one of his rare and costly white birds. He was still carrying three dozen canaries, including a pair of the newly developed and high-priced orange males, painstakingly bred high in the Berkeley hills, and he was hoping to get rid of them before he turned back west, so he could travel home light and carefree.

Marco and his birds looked up at the peaks of Glacier Park and then started east on Highway 2. He stopped in every substantial town—

Browning and Cut Bank and Shelby—pulling up at the square, if there was one, and uncovering his charges for all to see. While he waited for customers he plucked a hatful of dandelion greens or lamb's quarters from the road's-edge public domain and slipped a sprig into each of the cages.

He spent a night in a tourist camp in Chester and the next in the town of Havre, spreading his bedroll half under the truck, as he often did, where he could guard his cargo against the local vermin. The next day he bartered a yellow bird for a tank of gas and a case of motor oil and continued east on the half-paved road. In Zurich he noticed a family of Indians near the railroad tracks, selling something from a cardboard box. Thinking it might be warm food, Marco walked over; but they were waiting for the high-noon train to offer raggedy time-softened bison horns found on the prairie to passengers from Chicago and Minneapolis.

It was time to clean the cages, a task he had to perform every three or four days to avoid an outbreak of disease. He needed a place, a small building or an unused room, to free the canaries for an hour while he scrubbed the cages down. Over near the town of Fort Belknap he began watching for a suitable site, and finally turned into the lane of a brown shingled house with outbuildings around it. He could see it was an Indian house; two children playing in the yard straightened and turned to look and someone peeked out from a slit in a curtained window.

A heavy-set man came out of the house and walked hesitantly toward the truck. Not a friendly man, but Marco knew what to do. He called "hello" in an offhand manner and moved back along the truck to untie and throw back the tarp from one corner of the cages, and the birds began to stir and sing a few exploratory notes. It brought the two children running over, and then the large man came up, and a young woman from behind the house.

The peddler began his tale and soon had fastened a deal with the family. For a yellow singing bird he could use the one-time bunkhouse

YELLOW BIRDS

over beyond the well to clear his cages and could camp there beneath the truck for the night.

When the family grasped in full what the man was about to do, word spread fast. The nine-year-old boy sprinted across the field to gather his cousins; another young woman with babies emerged from a grove of trees; and an elegant, very old couple stepped slowly and carefully out the front door of the brown house and proceeded with matching diamond-willow canes across the yard.

Marco backed his truck up to the bunkhouse. He kneed the rusty door open and went in to check the building for leaks. The single rectangular room was empty except for a broken woodstove, a few old Butter-Nut Coffee cans, and a seatless chair. The windows on either side were raised, but the baggy screens were solid.

He plugged one small hole in a windowpane with his kerchief and began to move the cages inside. A modest crowd circled the truck by now, and Marco slowed himself, began to enjoy the interest of the people. He showed the various cages to the onlookers as he took them into the cottage-like building, and worked a trace of the impresario into his voice. Even the frowning man was intrigued and finally talkative: "We've got birds like that around here—except they have black wings." Three teenagers on chestnut horses galloped across the field and leapt off their mounts in a whirl of dust at the edge of the crowd.

When Marco began releasing the birds into the room everyone surged up to look through the cobwebbed windows and through the cockeyed screen door. Out the birds went, and when they gauged the amplitude of the sunny room they all began to flutter and sing and dance about, and the people began to laugh and put their hands in and out of their pockets or fold their arms, the youngsters hypnotized, the elegant old man and his wife transfixed with a radiant gaze of open-mouthed delight they hadn't worn since the nineteenth century.

Marco took the cages over to the pump and began to wash them down with Boraxo and scrub them with a wire brush. A few kids came

YELLOW BIRDS

to watch, then returned to the canaries. The slender old man hobbled over for a moment, put his hand on his lower chest and said, "Assiniboine," with a brilliant smile. In an hour Marco was ready to recage the birds, and by the time the sun was low he had his truck parked where he wanted it, and his bedroll spread.

The Indian family brought him a bowl of beef stew. Then he took a pretty yellow bird in one of the tiny balsa-wood cages and walked it over to the house and gave it to the little girl and told her how much to feed it and how it preferred to spend its days and nights. The mother of the child suggested he drive down in the morning and try to sell his birds at the orphanage thirty miles south.

*

Marco was ready to turn around and go home. He knew it suddenly as he drove in the cool of the early morning, glancing up at the dark mountains on his left and off across the vast spaces on his right. He knew there were herds of caribou far off to the north and armadillos rummaging far to the south, but he was ready to go home.

In a short while he recognized the orphanage perched high on a muscular hill above the reseda plains, and a quarter hour later he came to the sign at the entrance. The institution was a tight cluster of interwoven two-story buildings with something of a cupola on the top. In the parking lot near the main doorway, Marco stood for a moment shading his eyes, taking in the enormous sweep of vista north and south and west.

A man came out and interrupted his gaze with a cordial old-world greeting. A kindly black-robed man with gray hair, wire glasses, and a large pointed goatee. He was the director of the place, Father Rinscento, and he was visibly happy to have company. He recognized Marco as a fellow Italian and listened amiably as the peddler pulled back the tarp and displayed his birds and gradually worked into touting their merits and the beneficence of their companionship. When

YELLOW BIRDS

Marco saw how the man enjoyed the effervescence of the birds in the quiet morning he made him the offer.

"I will give you a very special price for the lot of them. Think how the children would love them—music in the buildings all day long!"

"Well! I don't know where I could accommodate so many birds. What would I do with them all? . . . But forgive me, come inside and sit for a while. Have a cup of coffee with me."

Father Rinscento led the peddler through the silent halls of the main floor and up two brief flights of stairs, out into a bright octagonal room placed at the top western edge of the orphanage so as to command the highest point of the high hill. They paused in a sudden flood of light.

"This is the reading room," Rinscento said. "Though not many read here but myself." The room was lavishly fenestrated, with three long wooden tables set parallel in the center.

"The views, I must say, though, are theological," he continued. Each expansive window framed a different shadowy mountain range —the Bear Paws to the west, slung like gypsy tents, the Judith Mountains to the south, the dark, lumbering Highwoods farther off, almost secretive on the horizon.

The men walked outside, through a rudimentary loggia, and paused beside a small fish pond on a groomed graveled point overlooking the orphanage grounds. A few sheds, a ballfield, four dairy cows on a steep slope.

"A quiet place . . . Where are all the children?" Marco asked.

"In class at the moment. We are on half days now, for the summer."

"And what part of Italy are you from, Father?"

"The Veneto. Via Vienna. And now Montana. I've been here fourteen years. We put this place up seven years ago."

Father Rinscento shaded his eyes to survey the scene. "We might get a few peaches this year . . . I'm afraid the labyrinth needs tending."

They went into the reading room and sat down with coffee.

YELLOW BIRDS

"I miss the food, of course," the priest said. "Especially the olives. I designed this room on my own—perhaps you could have guessed—with very little experience in architecture. I suppose I was thinking of something remotely Tuscan, since I had a hill at my disposal. A view in Pienza, perhaps."

They talked quietly for twenty minutes, and the Father said, "But I will not detain you," and they walked downstairs and into the parking lot.

"Now!" Rinscento said, clapping his hands together, "What shall we do about these pretty birds?"

"Take them all, Father! At a very pretty price. They are better than a radio!"

And in a moment the transaction was agreed upon and the two men were unloading the cages, setting them off along a shady edge of the building.

"Put the two orange ones over here. I will keep those in the reading room. They will match well with my goldfish!"

Marco left the priest the remainder of the birdseed and half a pail of grit.

Father Rinscento watched the peddler drive away, waved when Marco looked back from the final curve of the lane, and stood for a moment tweaking his ample goatee. Then he hurried into the building, where he spoke for some time with his subaltern and the domestic staff. Before proceeding to his office, he went to the north-facing window of the reading room and looked out. He could see what must surely have been the dust-plume from the peddler's truck, far up on the Belknap road. Then he sat at his desk to catch up on the paperwork.

That evening at seven, while the two orange birds sang subdued vespers upstairs in the study, he sat down to a private meal, said a brief prayer before the broad platter of carefully braised small birds, and began devouring them gratefully, rapidly at first, then slowly, rever-

YELLOW BIRDS

ently, taking each one, not so much larger than a walnut, whole in his mouth as they did with the *ortolano* in the old countries, murmuring thankfully in three languages with an enormous towel across his lap.

Marco by that moment was unrolling his blankets beside the truck at the edge of Cut Bank town. It was awkward and empty without the birds. He wondered if he would even fall asleep that night.

He had thought of Rinscento often during the day's dusty drive. His scrawny peach tree and his labyrinth. He knew the priest was right about the olives, though. Marco's mother had prayed for good olives most every Sunday of her life.

YELLOW BIRDS

LANDSCAPE WITH FROG

I kept the flute beside me on the seat. It was fashioned from good cedar and rubbed to a high russet sheen. White buckskin thongs dropped from just below the air block and the far end of it swelled slightly to form a crane's head with small brass studs for eyes and the halves of the bill open, parted slightly and expressively curved. It was the finest specimen Dolores During ever sold me.

I had just left her little house up in the hills above the Dickcissel valley and was fielding the surge of light-hearted light-headedness that place always instilled. Dolores was a tall, hale woman of impeccably eclectic bloodlines from the upper Missouri River territory. Lakota, Belgian, Irish-Virginian, a touch of Red River Metis. And from that rich ancestral pool she had, by the time she was twenty-five, selected as her own the fine art of carving old-style bird-head flutes and moved home to the reservation. She picked up the technique and the ethereal patience from a Sans Arc grandmother and became perhaps one of the last of the masters. I stopped to see her twice a year, hoping she would have a flute on hand and unspoken for.

When I arrived at the Sweeney ranch, where I was staying for the night in the little-used linoleum-floored bunkhouse, I carried the flute inside and set it on the table while the Sweeneys and a ranch hand and I sipped beer before supper.

Everyone knew Dolores During, her Buick and her flutes, and each time her name arose over the years, someone sooner or later offered up an oblique shard of the long-running rumor that she had given birth decades ago to a remarkable offspring like no other, that was either, depending on who was talking, something more or somewhat less than standard human. I had heard such variable snatches of the story often enough to have given up any hope of ever knowing the truth of it, and often enough that my ears perked up inadvertently whenever Dolores dropped an obviously familial name: "Lonnie did this," "Carla said that." But on the other hand I never made a move to capture a closer look at the rows of family snapshots arrayed on a cupboard shelf.

Whatever the facts of it, wherever the little sweet-tempered trilingual yeti might roam or moon, Dolores was a hale woman, and the night I got to the Sweeney house I was too tired to take up the slippery-sloped subject again and I soon went to bed, thinking on and off of Albert Little Hawk early that morning when I had stopped to visit at his home. There was an Indian Affairs police car sitting in his driveway. Albert had shot a raggedy tomcat that belonged to his neighbor after the cat had terrorized Albert's hummingbird feeder for weeks, leaping from its hiding place to swat the little creatures from the air. And there was old Albert, sitting hangdoggedly in a chair, head down, hands folded between his knees as he faced the ill-at-ease tribal cop.

I was awakened about midnight by a slaphappy Dakota wind, and was surprised that I was still eye-to-eye with the Dolores During rumor, mildly fascinated from a safe distance by the nagging, almost zodiacal increments of the thing. But I was relieved a few seconds later to find myself shunted to another, sleep-rallied place, in another light-headed moment of similar bevel and tang, in a drastically different setting: I was passing through my Ohio hometown—this was the preceding autumn—and after a quick turn through familiar streets to see sugar maples locally renowned that time of year—the indomitable old

LANDSCAPE WITH FROG

Matthews trees, the Clem and the Curl maples a few blocks north—I stopped for a coffee to go at the diner on the square.

There was, as always, a large round table near the cash register hosting a dozen regular coffee drinkers who every morning gather to hear and spread the village news. This particular day there were two or three men among them that I recognized and I stopped to say hello as I left the place.

One of them was a talkative country boy turned tireless businessman about my age named Seaton. Amid the banter, he called out to me across the table, "How's the groundhog business?" And immediately proceeded to inform his colleagues that, as a boy, I had made a pretty penny or two purveying woodchuck flesh on the sly to a regular clientele from central Ohio cities, had a flourishing little black-market business going come summer. I listened in amazement, through the good-natured chuckles and cigarette smoke, as the oddly innocent, groundless words left his mouth and formed cocksure chain-linked sentences above the drip-stained cups.

As I drove from town, the epistemological vertigo hit me. My God, I thought, how does it all keep going? How does the spoken world hang together in any form at all under such a built-in rule of memory-bumble and involuntary shape-shifting?

I knew what the man Seaton was talking about. I can remember the pathetically brief occasion perfectly, can see the deep dark green of its 1956 trees . . .

My three cousins and I were riding our bicycles out from their farm home one Saturday afternoon. Early July, from the shape of the willows and the glint of the sky. We pedaled down the rural road for three-quarters of a mile, then turned west on a smaller gravel lane lined with dusty fencerows and pastures just beyond the fence with dusty ironweed in them. We stopped, as always, at the shaky one-car bridge over the creek, the Kokosing River as the maps showed it, and kickstanded our bikes to look for mink tracks in the mud or spy on sunfish gazing

LANDSCAPE WITH FROG

dreamily out at the sky or check for the blacksnake that frequented an exclusive sunny corner below one of the concrete bastions. Maybe we broke off slim willow switches for our dirty Schwinns, and rode on.

We soon left the sunny, brushy fencerows and the open fields and entered the dense cool of a woodland that made a tunnel of the road. Deep within the forest a few stubborn trilliums still bloomed in the moist dark, and as we stood there for a moment we could hear a fox squirrel bolt across the woods floor to an oak.

Then we pedaled on, out of the woods and back into the warm sun and the lackadaisical tillage, young corn and a few calves, until we reached as much of a destination as we ever had: a flimsy, tractor-wide lane curving through a grove of leggy locust trees. It led to an erstwhile farm site with just a single ramshackle barn left standing. The place had a pleasantly evocative blend of domesticity and mild decay. We leaned in the door to check the rafters for barn owls and flipped over a dead starling to see what was transpiring on the other side.

When we came from behind the barn, Dean Seaton was riding up the lane. He lived a mile or so from my cousins' place and we got together once or twice a summer to play an hour of baseball, or go to his woods in search of raspberries, or fish in his cattailed pond. He was a red-haired, witty boy, nattier than most farm kids, always blowing small quick bubbles with his gum.

We decided we would knock down some green walnuts from the tree and pitch them up at the barn roof to hear the clang and rattle. Later we split into two groups and threw them back and forth over the barn. Then as we were idling, fooling with the bikes, a car drove slowly down the road, went on a ways, turned around and came back to stop at the end of the lane. We were watching it, then the horn honked and a window went down. We could see a black man stick his head out and yell hello.

Dean said, Oh, he knew who it was, and jogged down the lane to the car while the rest of us sidled in about halfway. We heard them talk-

LANDSCAPE WITH FROG

ing. The men wanted two groundhogs. They asked Dean if he could get them two groundhogs by tomorrow noon. Dean said he probably could and the man at the window smiled and said, "Put 'em in a cool place," and the car drove slowly away.

As he hurried back to get his bike Dean told us over his shoulder that the men were from Columbus. Once a summer they drove up here looking for groundhogs to cook for Sunday dinner. They had found Dean along the road a couple of years before and he had shot them a pair of woodchucks, and maybe last year, too, he thought.

But now he was all business. He jumped on his bike, said "Abyssinia!" and rode off to get his .22 rifle. He suddenly exuded a sharp-edged transactional air we had never known before from one of our own generation. We watched him disappear, pedaling hard, into the shadow of the woods.

The next day when we got home from Sunday school we changed our clothes and fed the calves in a hurry and jumped on our bikes. We rode straight to the old barn, didn't even glance at the bridge. As we were passing through the dark wood a car met us and passed in a cloud of dust. It was a different car from the day before and it was too dark to see if there were black men in it or not.

When we emerged into the light we saw Dean coming down the road, riding along comfortably, jauntily, with one hand in his pants pocket. He stopped long enough to tell us the uncomplicated denouement while the four of us stood around him straddling our bikes and squinting. He had shot two woodchucks—one yesterday and one this morning. The men from Columbus had just picked them up. Dean reached into his dungarees and unfolded and refolded a crisp five-dollar bill, then hustled off down the white gravel road. "Abyssinia!"

And that was that.

And it must be one of the more breathtaking laws of psychophysics that the personal memory-truth turns over, molts, at least once a dec-

LANDSCAPE WITH FROG

ade, in the manner of the epidermis, spawns a bevy of versions that, each, drift happily through stages of a poetic ontogeny like a swallow-tail or a frog. I still don't know about the Dolores During case, but the rendition of the woodchuck business we heard in the diner forty years later was a fancy late-stage variant, wherein the moribund frog sprouts clumsy wings and flaps haltingly over the pond a turn or two before crashing into the restful muck.

LANDSCAPE WITH FROG

ONE SUMMER BY THE RIVER

Each evening for fifteen years Henry Swainson has packed his redwood easel and a holster of paints and hobbled down the half-mile path from his home to the east bank of the Missouri River, smiling and licking his lips. He has painted the Dakota landscape for more than fifty years; stretched oils, hand-size acrylics, and quick charcoal cartoons lean three and four deep along his humble studio walls. Canyons, badlands, ghostly buffalo herds plodding the coulees . . . But at sunrise on his eightieth birthday he decided in a flood of liberating clarity to give up all subjects but one: sunset over the big, bulling river.

It might sound at first like an old man's fatuous surrender. But Henry is a gifted tonalist, neither a dabbler nor a dupe, and his decision was a masterful sharpening of focus and a conservation of energy worthy of a desert mammal. He loves awakening each day to find the Missouri still there, dependable as a dog. He loves its bulldozer sureness, its interchangeable gulls and random flotsam, and most of all the colors it begs from the Dakota sky. And every evening finds him there, accordingly, painting from a fertile trance where adoration flirts with and bleeds into dotage, singing aloud to himself on the breezy shore—"I Remember You" or "The moon was shining bright upon the Wabash."

That particular summer he was searching almost daily for an elusive shade of blue that he had never noticed before, a blue that visited the western sky for a brief vesperal moment just above the bands of apricot and flame. Henry mixed and matched and remixed and made notes on the hue as one might make notes on an exceptional wine. It was neither periwinkle nor royal nor kingfisher blue. It had morning glory in it, but also flax and jay and a subconscious pulse of winter-heron that bordered on lapis. All summer he worked at it. And he would find it eventually, this season or next, strike it one evening while singing "Just One of Those Things." He already had a name for it: "True Old Mandan Blue."

*

That was the summer the young people in the little Indian town began to dress like the old. It came on gradually, like weather or blossom. Took root on an afternoon much like this one, maybe, somewhere in the makeshift village set on a hillside on the west bank of the Missouri, the gulls sailing. The young people—sixteen-, eighteen-year-olds— began watching the old. On one corner a boy stood studying the two old men walking carefully down the street. Studied the hitch of their gait, the hang of their worn clothing. At the edge of town, where you could look straight down and see the river below, a dawdling brother and sister watched a rheumatic old man labor across a lawn to examine a chokecherry bush; he moved with a lurch, then a tiptoe. Lurch, then tiptoe.

Blocks away, a group of girls began to notice the old women in their kerchiefs and heavy sand-colored stockings. They all turned their heads at once and began to notice, biting casually at their fingernails or idly stretching a strand of hair. And, on a day like that, without collusion or program or even worded thought, the thing was set in motion.

*

It was also the summer they found the dead German man along the river ten miles north of town. A tourist-photographer from Stuttgart,

ONE SUMMER BY THE RIVER

he had, it seemed, been murdered in the night and his head cut off and presumably thrown into the Missouri. An old woman had discovered the corpse early the following morning.

The police chief in the little town took the report and drove up to the scene of the crime with a deputy. They stopped first at the small house of a man named Robert Onions. The house was a hundred yards or so from where they found the body. Onions came out to meet them. He was a man nearing seventy years, tall and lean, of good nerve and bountiful inner life, who spent a great deal of time nowadays sitting by the river. He had noticed nothing out of the ordinary the night before. Maybe a car door or two slamming at some point, but that was not unusual. The place they found the headless man was a small parking area at a crumbling one-time boat ramp. People used it all the time for swimming, drinking, propagating the species.

"Beatrice. She can tell you about it."

Beatrice Voice, an eighty-three-year-old utterly blind Hunkpapa woman, had discovered the body. She lived in an old house with seared elm trees just upriver from Onions, fifty yards beyond the boat ramp. She was sitting on her porch beside a headstrong trumpet vine when the police drove up.

"God bless you boys. I've been blind since I was forty years old. I was working at the trading post in Mobridge and that cleaning lye splashed in my face and I went blind three days later. I only remember a few colors. But I hear pretty good. Better than most. I can hear a baby cry on the other side of the river on a clear night.

"Last night I woke up and heard some loud music. It must be a car radio. Then I heard people yelling. It sounded like some kind of a fight started. Banging around, hollering. Then it got real quiet for a while. Then I heard someone start to chopping and hacking away and I knew right away they were cutting through bone. I could tell by the sound of it. Like butchering a beef. I know that sound my whole life. Then I heard a kind of a splash, a kind of kerplunk like a watermelon, then

ONE SUMMER BY THE RIVER

the car drove off. Sounded like an old car, not running real good. *Ping-ping-ping Chang! Ping-ping-ping Chang!* That's how it ran.

"When it got daylight I walked over there right away and poked around with my cane. Rotgut bottles all over the place. And there was that body over next to the bullberry bushes. I could feel it with my cane and I could smell the blood. I know that smell all my life. That's when I sent for my granddaughter and had her call you up right away. God bless you boys! My name is Beatrice Voice."

*

That week the young people began showing up in town dressed like old people. Just a few at first, Delano and his sister Eliza, and one or two of their friends. They walked down the street, went to the store and the post office, the usual daily things. The boys wore baggy secondhand trousers held up with suspenders over faded white shirts. Old dusty clodhopper shoes, or outmoded narrow dress shoes dating from the 1930s. The girls wore pale, thin print dresses with shawls over them, and black, lace-up Model-T shoes.

The Marine Corps recruiter from Aberdeen was one of the first to notice. He was in town on his quarterly rounds, sizing up the Indian boys as they played basketball or baseball or shot fish with .22 rifles from the creek bridges, looked them over good with a toothpick flexing in his teeth. Every year he found one or two of the right heft and stature and talked to them for a long time on each of his visits, took them off to one side and talked to them in a low avuncular salesman voice about becoming a U.S. Marine and, if they timed it right, being able to wear the fresh-pressed uniform down the aisle at high-school graduation. When he saw the first of the young people dressed like the old he looked over at the café waitress and rolled his hazel eyes: "If you say so!"

A few days later there were more. They showed up in small groups at any time of day. Some had driven matter-of-factly to Bismarck to shop in the thrift stores. They had soft old Stetsons and well-worn

ONE SUMMER BY THE RIVER

sportcoats, old bolo ties and neckerchiefs and antiquated sunglasses. Girls came down the street under parasols three times their own age.

It was no simple prank. It was an odd, almost atmospheric mimicry both harsh and thoughtful. A mime that came on without premeditation, like flowers on a bush. If you asked them, the young people might have said that Delano and his sister were probably the source of the idea; from them it spread quietly but surely, without smirk or smile or even consultation. It was an instinctive generational reflex the young people couldn't explain themselves, and didn't try.

And the old looked on with a cautious attention, like fox, or deer. They watched the mime gather and rise with amused intelligent eyes. The old clothing inspired a mild worldly nostalgia, as if the particular parasols and suspenders themselves were recognized after a long absence. It was an unsuspected but welcome phenomenon they appreciated and were curious about but left alone, knowing it wasn't theirs. Robert Onions watched the girls go by in calico dresses and Model-T shoes, saw Eliza in the blue one, and said to his crony in the shade, "She makes me think of Lottie Teal."

By the middle of July it crested. On a Saturday noon the little main street was full of people, as it was most Saturdays, but now the mime was on in full flower. The west side of the street was crowded with the young in their old outfits, going about their normal Saturday business. On the east sidewalk the old walked slowly along or rested out of the sun, watching. The mirror image was in place. Some of the thoughtful elders, like Onions, knew there was a glint of parody and mockery in the mime. But not enough to matter. There was also a hint of lying calmly face-down in the yearling grass in resignation, not to see the sky and clouds go streaming by.

By now, whether they knew it or not, the young people had adopted the slightest stoops and gaits of the old, the tilt of the frail boneage. The old people noted all the details with relish. "She dresses like my

ONE SUMMER BY THE RIVER

aunt Carlotta used to dress." Robert Onions was looking and thinking, enjoying himself. Finally he walked slowly across the street and up to Eliza in the blue calico. He removed his Stetson and formally presented himself: Robert Onions.

"People think Onions is an Indian name, but it's not. My great grandfather was half English. Canadian. Onions is an English name. There are still people over in England named Onions."

Beatrice Voice was there, in the hardware shadows. She had a daughter with her to describe the mime. "They're trying to straighten things out," she decided. "They had better be real careful."

It went on all morning. Onions walked back across to the shaded side of the street. "They're trying to shake things up. The years and the people. They're trying to break up the logjam."

*

The bereaved German parents were still there. They were staying at the Royal Motel in Bismarck. They refused to return to Stuttgart without their son's head; they would wait if it took all summer.

The police were milling without a clue. They had garnered no information from anyone since Beatrice Voice gave them the audio description the morning after. They assigned a pair of deputies to walk the Missouri banks each day to watch for the victim's missing part. And they stationed a capable man on the main streets of Bismarck and Mandan for a while to listen carefully for the *Ping-ping-ping Chang!* of the incriminated car. But mostly the police force drove daily from overlook to overlook above the river, gregariously speculating and looking off from the bluffs for inspiration.

Henry Swainson sometimes saw their car mirrors flash from his spot downstream and across the Missouri. He was painting hard this particular evening, reciting to himself a gimpy ballad he had discovered in his inner repertory and come to favor.

ONE SUMMER BY THE RIVER

Up Bunker Hill, down Okinawa—
Boys will dream when the air grows careless.
Through Gettysburg and Belleau Wood,
All day they dream the Mexican Hairless.

The Philippines and old Verdun—
Her legs were long, her beauty peerless.
Pea Ridge, Manassas, Corregidor—
Muck and mire, they dream the Mexican Hairless.

San Juan Hill and Yorktown—
Thoughts are lean and the sunshine fearless.
Shiloh, the Bulge, the Plains of Abe—
All day they dream the Mexican Hairless.

He was at the same time composing in his mind a letter to the editor of a regional newspaper that had printed a dubious review of Henry's paintings—a trifling handful of them—on exhibit in a quiet bank lobby. Something about an "irresponsible palette" and a "disturbing fungoid orange."

Henry composed his reply fastidiously. He wanted to get it right in two or three sentences and be done with it. Boot the young pup and be done with it . . .

"My dear sir. As anyone familiar in any degree with the history of the upper Missouri River in the Dakota territory would well know, there has, for some century and a half, existed in that region a unique and unmistakable shade of orange, an orange endemic to the upper Missouri, let it be said, owing its origin to the advent of ground turmeric (the well-known culinary spice) among the Mandan and Hidatsa peoples of this locale, in whose villages the Caucasian traders sold it as a potent and highly esteemed dye to be applied by native artisans to such materials as porcupine quills, feathers, or the most delicate buckskins (obtained in trade from nomadic hunters of the more westerly

ONE SUMMER BY THE RIVER

prairies), where its chanterelle hue was immediately at home beside the local clay-derived paints of the Knife River quarries. But, tiresome to say, given the all too common anomaly of a modern viewer lacking the slightest familiarity with such historical subtleties, such a proto-orange in a landscape might well pulse on unappreciated in unseeing eyes beneath prematurely raised bushy eyebrows . . ."

Boot the young whippersnapper and be done with it.

*

A few days later the phenomenon began to unravel. Just as the first ash leaves went golden in the coulees there was a tacit sense of *Enough* in the young people and the mime began to slow. Cicadas began to sing, a few at a time, in the dusty trees.

Some of the girls decided to visit Beatrice Voice before the thing was over. They needed, without saying so, to sit with an old woman in their antique garb and leach whatever iota of sarcasm had been in the mime from the start. It wasn't much, but it would be best to sit there for an hour and leach it beside an old woman who had strangled puppies in her day for the feast foods and thrown them on the fire to burn off the hair and butchered them for the big iron kettle.

Eliza was waiting in front of the post office for her friends. She wore the calico dress she washed out every night and held the bleached lavender parasol rolled up in her hand. But she had her own shoes on today. Onions came out of the post office and walked over to her. "You look nice in that dress." He told her about the Chickasaw Nightingale, an Indian girl named Daisy Underwood from Ardmore, Oklahoma. A beautiful voice. Studied music in all the good schools out east. Toured the whole U.S.A. This was back about 1920. She sang for Tetrazzini herself. "My mother heard her on the radio down in Tulsa. Oh, she had a beautiful voice. They called her the Chickasaw Nightingale. Then she ran off and married some rich oil man."

Eliza and the girls drove north on the little highway, following the

ONE SUMMER BY THE RIVER

river, and down the hill to Beatrice Voice's house. She was standing in her yard with both hands on her cane, listening. "God bless you girls!" The young sat in a row along the edge of her porch in their old print dresses and talked a little and dawdled with their shoes, asked a formal question or two.

"I was born in 1902, over there west of Mud Creek. I grew up over there and then we moved over to Bluestem. That's where I got married the first time. That was 1919."

"Who was there?"

"Who was there? In 1919? I'll tell you who was there! Ice was there. Old Ice and young Ice. The Burgoyne girls were there. The Berry sisters from McLaughlin were there, and so were some of their brothers. All those Hawks were there, and some of the Teals—Lottie Teal was there. Dirt was there. Box Elder was there. Willy Nilly and the Red Birds were there.

"Everyone was there." She began waving her cane like a baton. "Fog was there. Lungs was there. Duck Legs was there, and Froglips. Throwup was there. And old Squashballs was there, too. And Dog Droppings. Rotten Bone was there. And Ghost Pecker, junior and senior. And Flies-on-the-Arse—he was there. He was always around there somewhere."

Downstream two miles a band of boys were bathing in the Missouri. They waded in up to their hams, lathered, then lobbed the bar of soap upstream just far enough that it floated back by when it was needed. They dressed, hiked up the old suspenders and the formless pants, and drove slowly up the rough dirt road to Robert Onions's.

Onions was standing down on the riverbank. He had lived beside the Missouri his entire life. He had thrown things in and pulled things out and wondered momentarily about things coursing by too far out to reach. When he saw the boys getting out of the car and putting on their big second-hand Stetsons he hollered and walked up to greet

ONE SUMMER BY THE RIVER

them. After a while he said, "Let me show you what I found in the river this morning."

He returned from the house carrying a plastic toy rowboat a couple of feet long. Lashed carefully into it were fifteen or twenty human figures made from wooden clothespins. They looked like home-crafted Christmas tree ornaments, angels or choirboys robed in red and white ribbon, with simple beatific expressions drawn on their faces. They all reclined face-up in rows, braced, it seemed, to run a cataract or plunge over a fall. Onions poured out a half cup of brownish bilge water and showed the boat around to all the boys. Later he turned aside to Delano and said, "You look good in that hat."

*

Several days after, Delano and Onions were walking, unbeknownst to each other, the backcountry breaks along Mink River, the wide quiet valley a few miles west of the Missouri. The morning was cool and the sunflowers moist to the touch. Delano was moving slowly downriver. He was alone and looking for something, something private, you could see that from the way he walked, something beneficial and sure for the finding, small enough to fit in a shirt pocket. Maybe sweetgrass or osier bark. He was coming down the valley from the west.

Onions was walking up from the east, up the valley not far from the stream, and he had the same walk, the same way of moving and gently looking, around at the ground and up at the low honey-colored bluffs lining the valley. A person sitting on the top there would see at once that he was looking for something quiet and personal, too. Maybe Black Sampson root, maybe flag root to sweeten the breath.

The old man and the young moved toward one another, each with their easy wandering zigzag. Meadowlarks flushed before them and blackbird flocks lifted scolding from the sunflower beds. And then, from far off, the men saw each other. A simple enough recognition— anyone could be walking that Mink valley one or two at a time—that

ONE SUMMER BY THE RIVER

instantly included the privacy of the other's mission. And the approach from that point on became a kind of ballet. Neither showed a sign of having seen the other. They continued in their rhythms, but the non-chalance was studied now; they kept a furtive eye on one another—Onions could follow the boy's big white hat—subconsciously gauging the other's secretive mission without the slightest desire to know what it was.

They paused to look at a black-eyed Susan or turned to watch a hawk glide over the bluffs. In ten minutes they came together and both looked up with formal faked surprise and called hello, moved in closer and chatted of casual public things for a few moments, then moved on their respective ways. Onions stopped seconds later and turned around to holler: "I'm going to marry your sister."

*

Old Henry was painting his three-hundredth August sunset, laying on his favorite orange with loving strokes, the orange with a healthy jot of turmeric in it. He sang as he worked: "Fry me a liver, fry me a liver—I fried a liver for you." And then he saw the head come bobbing down the river, a turnip-white relic of a head with the dour expression of a much-put-upon medieval saint. Henry walked over to look as it nodded in the river grasses. "Is that you? Is it you in the bulrushes, Moses?" He wedged it securely against the riverbank with the legs of his easel and hurried up to the house.

"Margaret," he yelled to his wife, "we had better call the Department of Decapitation!"

*

The wedding feast—Eliza had driven alone up to see Beatrice Voice one evening, found her dozing on her porch: "Should I marry Robert Onions?" "Sure you should. Marry him! God bless you! He's only seventy years old. He's a good man. Just hide his car keys and tie his bal-

ONE SUMMER BY THE RIVER

locks to the bedpost every night. You'll do just fine!"—the wedding feast a week later was about the last of the young people's mime. Whatever thought it up and blew it in was sailing on.

The celebrants stood around the tables in Onions's yard on the knoll above the river. The old gathered on one side in the shade of the house, the young congregated on the other, and they all wore their nearly identical clothing one final time. The narrow Model-T shoes with buffalo burrs in their laces, the shawls and striped suspenders. Only the middle-aged guests, the generation in between, looked oddly out of order and uninformed in their polyester shirts and denims, appeared flatfooted, even inadequate in the hilltop sun.

They ate cake and ice cream and Beatrice was rolling her blind eyes, telling woolly stories of insatiable old men after dark. Late afternoon, Onions came from the house with a cluster of helium balloons and after a brief word set them loose by the river.

"We're going airborne."

Half an hour later, Henry, bent beside his easel, saw them float over high above the Missouri, cheery little specks he believed for a moment were creatures of his own playing tag across his cornea, then recognized as minor foreign bodies in the vista, transient flecks strayed in from some unknown upstream palette, and paused to blow his nose and retie his shoes until they passed from sight.

ONE SUMMER BY THE RIVER

MONTANA MOSAIC

A white-haired couple ("Snow-on-the-mountain") sit in their small travel trailer. They have stopped for a bite at a rest area above the Yellowstone River, from whose shade they observe the warming Montana morning beyond: blowsy frowsy sweet clover along the highway, parched hills to the north known locally as the Big Sheep Range. The pair conscientiously chew their thin tuna sandwiches, looking disinterestedly from tiny porthole to porthole.

The old man breaks a long silence.

"Did you ever drive over to Wapakoneta in '49 to see Bob Shenling?"

The woman turns to him as if from a dream, her mouth open— "Did I what!?"

"You heard me." He spoke in a heavily rehearsed level fashion. "Did you go over to see Bob Shenling in Wapak when I was working up in Michigan that summer?"

The stunned woman blanches in amazement, grasps the edge of the table—"*Gene!?!*"

*

Down on the Tongue River highway an elderly Cheyenne man and a teenaged Cheyenne boy are driving along, when the man spies a pronghorn lying dead in the ditch, over by the fence line, and reaches left to touch the boy's arm and tells him to stop the car.

"Back up . . . I want you to get those horns for me."

They both turn to look over at the carcass.

"Those are nice big horns. Looks like it's been lying there a good while. They should come off pretty easy."

The boy sets the brake and gets out, walks noncommittally around to the ditch-side of the car.

"They might stink though," the old man warns with a chord of glee in his tone.

The boy walks over and looks down at the animal, his hands in his Levi pockets.

"Put your foot on the head and just pull on the horn," the man calls from the car. "That's the way . . . Give it a little twist . . . Shake it back and forth."

The boy pulls and tugs, waving away flies with his free hand. When the horn breaks loose from its core, he jumps back—"Sheee! That stinks alright."

The old man laughs from the car window.

The boy circles the pronghorn and comes in from the other direction. He holds his nose with one hand this time and works off the second black horn and leaps away, tossing it onto the grass with the first.

The old man beckons him over, gives him a plastic bread bag he had pulled from his pants pocket. "Go over by the fence and pick some sage. Put the horns in there with it and tie it up good and tight."

The boy packs them up and puts them in the trunk of the car.

"All right," the old man says as they start off. "That will be good. After they air out for a while I'm going to clean them up and sand them down real shiny. Make drinking cups out of them. My granddad used to make them like that for sun dances."

The boy looked over at him as he wiped one hand on his pant leg.

"I told you they would stink," the old man chuckled, and he was chuckling for a mile down the road. "There's nothing in the world ever stinks like a antelope horn."

MONTANA MOSAIC

*

Farther upstream, two long, high-gloss cattle trucks sit shoulder to shoulder, idling in a café parking lot. High-velocity horizontal splashes of cowshit streak their slotted sides. Above the windshields their names are painted in elaborate cursive script: one the "Goodnight Irene," the other the "Enola Gay."

At a booth inside the café, a large Texan (he of the "Goodnight Irene") wearing large turquoise rings and a pheasant feather in his straw Stetson, nods confidingly to his compadre across the table, speaking in a lava-slow basso profundo around a mouthful of bacon and eggs, nodding and nodding: "I don't care what they say—I admire that in a woman."

*

And farther yet upstream, near a threadbare Indian town on one side of the river, Indian boys are idling near the narrow bridge. Three older boys lean over in midspan, watching for suckers to plink with a .22 rifle. Fifty swallows loop and dive above them. The tallest boy, the boy with the rifle, is the one who masterminded the tossing of the contra- band army-surplus teargas into the Slim Jim Bar late one night last fall after the owner had thrown his cohort out.

By the time the three wander back to the Indian side of the river— the stream marks the reservation boundary, railroad tracks run along the far side—a single canoe appears around a bend. Two white men with fishing rods are in it. The boys watch it drift along with no great interest. A canoe or two went by most summer days. When it was just downstream of them the tall boy flips a hand-size clod in its general direction. It hits the water ten feet short of the canoe, just where he wanted it—*kerplunk*. The fishermen turn to look for a formal three- count, the boys gaze poker-faced at the water, and then the current carries the craft well out of any communicative range not counting the rifle.

MONTANA MOSAIC

The older boys shuffle away toward the village, and two small lads come up from the riverside, from under the bridge, to take their places, poking at the day, winging stones at a surfacing fish or a drifting twig, waiting perhaps for a train to enter the picture.

As they reach the far end of the bridge, one of them notices a man walking along the tracks in their direction. A short, heavy man with a bedroll and a rucksack over his shoulder, plodding along the right-of-way waste, emerging from behind a stand of dirty head-high thistles and a jumble of castoff tar-blotched ties.

When he sees the boys he stops and looks them over, saunters in and pauses.

"You won't catch many fish by beaning them with a rock."

Near at hand he appears fat, fatter than a wayfaring stranger is supposed to be. A friendly enough face, lightly incriminated by the eyes of a snapping turtle above the voice of a sugary little girl.

"Is there a grocery store over in that town?"

"No."

"Well I guess I'll go hungry for a while then. Unless you boys have a nice fish you want to give me."

He watches them tossing pebbles for a few moments, then starts back toward the tracks. But he turns to them a minute later.

"You boys ever heard of Al Kaline?"

The boys shake their heads.

"Pooh!" He walks a step or two, turns again.

"How about Harvey Haddix? . . . Pooh!" And tromps off down the gravelly bed.

In a quarter hour the boys are tired of the bridge and wander home. They sit at the kitchen table sipping Kool-Aid.

"We saw a man going along the railroad tracks," one of them volunteers to his mother.

"What kind of man?"

"A white man."

MONTANA MOSAIC

"Was it a tramp?"

"I don't know. He was fat. He had a blanket. He smelled like a porcupine."

"Did he say anything to you?"

"He was looking for someone."

"Who?"

"Somebody named Harvey."

"Harvey?" The woman glances at the grandmother sitting nearby. "The only Harvey around here is Harvey Badger Hat."

"Yeah. I think that's what he said."

The woman dries her hands on a dish towel as she walks thoughtfully over to a window and pulls aside the thin curtain to peer toward the river.

"I wonder what anyone walking down the railroad would want with him."

MONTANA MOSAIC

HARD GREEN CHERRIES

Sometimes of late the Great Plains seem, when I turn to them, cast the inner eye for sounding or sustenance, a lesser thing than they were ten years ago, a region now somehow reduced as a poetical entity and captured as a human milieu, not only as a result of frequent crossings and recrossings but by recurrent mention and modeling, as if the space and fertile roll of it had contracted. But once we are out there again, well out there on a good sinewy road, it becomes obvious that the grist is still there, and the gristle; that it is still a long, long way from Iron Lightning to Powderville; that it was the mind and its astrolabe that had weakened, presumed, dozed . . .

I went to high school with the girl. She was a ranch girl, a beauty oft sung up and down the Rosebud valley of Montana, with long auburn hair and legs of the thousand-ship-launching variety. For a while there she owned an old Chevy Thriftmaster pickup with a "Cowboy Butts Drive Me Nuts" bumper sticker on it. She was also renowned, in the whisper theater of the day, as a devout demi-vierge. I wouldn't know anything about that—she consorted only with ranchers' sons, never looked twice at a town boy.

Last fall I was back in the valley and stopped to say hello at the ranch set nearly a half mile off the road, up close to the piney bluffs. We had a glass of iced tea in the shade of the lawn. Her husband, a slightly older, heavily sideburned man I barely recalled, was gone for the day.

It was a handsome place with mature trees and beehives and several years' worth of hay in the stackyard. A herd of brindle brown heifers lolled autumnally in one corner of a pasture as if they had been gently blown there. She had a proper kitchen garden, a six-foot miniature windmill with morning glories climbing up it, and a pair of tall half-breed wolf-dogs that stalked around the yard, stiff-legged, blondish, looking oddly inept and genetically ill at ease.

She asked, after a while, if I remembered Jimmy Rides Out, an Indian boy we went to school with. She and her husband had awakened one early morning to find Jimmy outside in the driveway, asleep in his old car. It turned out he was there wondering if he could catch a ride into Miles City, if anyone was going that way in the next day or two.

"That's how it was in high school when he lived down the road from my folks. He was always coming over for a ride to school or to a ball-game in town. That was fine."

But recently he began to show up once or twice a week, hoping for a lift somewhere. His old car wasn't trustworthy for any extended travel.

"I finally had to tell him things were different now. It got so we never knew when he would come by."

"Was he on the sauce?"

"No. He's got himself cleaned up. He's still a really nice guy. But I know Randy didn't like him hanging around, it made him nervous. I hated to do it, but I had to tell him not to come over anymore."

I always liked Jimmy Rides Out. He was forthright and nimble-witted, with a dark native face of timeless cut, high cheeks and strong nose, a broad mouth slightly lifted on one side in what might be mistaken for a nascent snarl, steady deep eyes with something wild as treeline in their spacing—a face of experience and tact well beyond any single life-time, even as he sat on a village park bench or rounded the final turn in a schoolboy mile relay.

HARD GREEN CHERRIES

I knew about the car. I had seen Jimmy the previous summer and we talked for a while. He told me times were a little tougher than usual. But he was helping out in a local gang-control program, and he had a new enterprise of his own: he told me to watch for his one-of-a-kind homemade "billboard" he had erected beside the road on his family land and rented by the month to announce a new café or body shop in the vicinity. And he was living in his old Mercury—not so much of necessity but from a point of eerie honor, the fact that his older brother (who died a year earlier from assorted torments) had closed out his life living in *his* car, and having been a good man and beloved brother deserved a certain sacrificial emulation.

Jimmy was twenty-five or twenty-six at the time and had acquired a reputation connected to such instinctual noblesse oblige and the power of the look on his face. The latter had become a famous thing in the Rosebud country. When he found occasion to bear it down, to settle it on a person of dallying words or watery backbone, it was something to behold.

The first time I heard of it was when a panel of advancemen for a strip-mine company came to the reservation to try to convince the people to open up their lands to the bulldozers and how happy they would be when the first checks were cut. Jimmy slowly moved into position at the back of the room, found a space to peer through, and leveled that smoking, enzymatic look at the men in the gray suits and held it on them until they couldn't help but feel and look around to find it, and their words, people attest, began to crumble and cake up in their mouths and their shoes began to squirm and slipslide around beneath their folding chairs.

From that point on, Jimmy had a knack of sensing moments that required his gift, his regard. When a regional politician set up at the fair and began the gladhand; when a Mormon squad came through looking for Indian babies to adopt; when a pair of skinheads stopped on the town square soliciting Indian support for a rifle-pure what's-so-

HARD GREEN CHERRIES

funny high-plains utopia—Jimmy would eventually wander in and lower the beam till the semistutter set in and the bolo ties began to twitch and tighten and the handkerchiefs came out of the pockets. He even had the governor snorting and hacking from mysterious causes one Fourth of July, and essentially sabotaged a team of Los Angeles dream researchers and their caissons of EEG gear.

I witnessed a lesser example last summer, at a neighborhood pow-wow the day after Jimmy and I talked. There was a group of college-age white boys passing through town on their touring bicycles and they stopped at the powwow to have a look. They were wearing their bumblebee spandex cycling suits and expensive sunglasses and were having a noisy, oblivious time of it, even at moments when they should not have, during a brief memorial or a giveaway speech. Jimmy of course materialized a few feet from their place in the shade and quietly gave them the old full-blood rawhide-and-cavern-water beam. In five minutes they were strapping on their helmets, flustered and snigger-ing, and finally pedaling away. I was glad to see he hadn't lost his touch.

As I moved on later that day I spotted his one-of-a-kind billboard on a sagey stretch near the road: big block letters on plywood. "Emile's Place: Flats Fixed. Gas and Sweetgrass."

*

Comedy traditionally employs cluttered stages; less laughable stories a spare space. And the woman down the valley hit trouble in the big-gest way, a way that also had the cavern water in it. I heard it yesterday, the 28th of June, the day of the long, long way from Iron Lightning to Powderville, when I stopped at a crossroads café.

She arrived home one day this spring and found the wolf-dogs out in the field behind the barn; they had forgotten themselves and pulled down and were eating an Easter calf, and the woman had forgotten herself and ran to take the thing away and the dogs, or rather the

HARD GREEN CHERRIES

wolves, turned on her and sliced her down and tore open her throat and found that blood to their liking as well . . .

And today I am driving back the way I came, wishing I were nearer a slow-rolling lathery sea. The winding gravel road is a terra-cotta red and the coulees and draws are full of hard green cherries.

HARD GREEN CHERRIES

ACKNOWLEDGMENTS

The brief speculation about melancholy in the story "Talk across Water" is based on a passage by philosopher Sheldon Wolin in his essay "Revolutionary Action Today." Many of these stories appeared in *Sworn before Cranes* (New York: Orion Books, 1994) and *Grasshopper Falls* (New York: Hanging Loose Press, 2000). "Hoecakes" appeared in *The Delineator* (New York, 2016), an anthology published and edited by Larry Fagin.